the fifth floor

a novel
by julie oleszek

mockingbird publishing
batavia, il

To my sisters and brothers:
Lin, Jim, Scott, Pat, Can, Mike, Greg, Liz, and Daphne.
For Liz, in Heaven.

one

The first doctor my mother drags me to is a tall, thin man. He seems to think his direct approach will intimidate me, and maybe it would if I cared, but I don't. I follow him into his office, leaving my mother staring at my back from the waiting room. He climbs behind his enormous desk piled with papers and files of patients and motions for me to sit in one of the wing-backed chairs opposite him in front of his desk. I sit and he stares.

"Stand up and turn around," he says with as little compassion as he can gather.

I turn slowly, and the motion has me feeling dizzy. Again, he stares, making me uncomfortable.

"How old are you?"

"Seventeen."

"Your mother said you haven't eaten in over three weeks. Is that true?"

I shrug.

"If you don't eat, you know, I will be forced to put you into a hospital bed with tubes running down your throat and into your stomach so we can feed you. You don't want that, do you?"

"No," I reply.

He leans back in his office chair. His clasped hands, except for his two index fingers which are pressed together pointing toward the ceiling, lean steadily against his chest, and his elbows rest on the chair's arms. "So tell me, what's on your mind?"

"Nothing."

"It's rather difficult to think of nothing, wouldn't you agree?"

I am barely breathing let alone thinking. Just being here is exhausting.

"What month is it?"

February? No. I think it's March. "March."

"Do you like high school?"

It's a crap load of bullshit. "Yes," I lie.

"Are you involved in after school activities? Sports? What about friends?

How did I get here? Which way is out? The door—it's over there. Where is the waiting room? There's a short hallway—outside this office, past two other office doors. The waiting room—at the end of the hallway—opens to the left.

"Are you going to answer my questions, Anna?"

What questions? Did he ask about my classes? Grades? Months ago I might have given him the truth. Classes—crap! Grades—crap! Today I stare at my hands, deep in thought of things I am trying desperately to ignore. "No," I whisper, slumping further into the chair.

He suppresses a sign of frustration, but I don't care. I didn't ask for this. I don't want to be here.

"Well young lady, I can see you're in no mood for conversation. Maybe next week you'll be ready to talk." He nods toward the door, then looks at me calmly. He casually pulls a folder from the top of piled papers and begins writing.

The moment I crawl into my mother's car, I fall asleep. I never see him again.

THE SAME WEEK, I find myself sitting in another doctor's office.

"Hello Anna, I am Dr. Ellison."

Dr. Ellison is a woman with purpose. She's about as tall as my twenty-five-year-old sister Marie, who is 5'7", and has an olive complexion like my younger sister Bridg. There is a desk in her office, but she doesn't sit behind it. Instead, she sits in a leather chair that hisses with puffs of air when she sits down. I sit in the same type of chair, across from Dr. Ellison, facing a large outside window.

"Tell me about yourself," she says. Her voice is real, somewhere between calming and strong. I don't say a word.

"If you're not ready to talk, and if you don't mind, then I will. I have two little boys at home, and I am grateful to talk with young adults like you who offer more of a meaningful conversation than my little ones."

I am captivated by the way she offers information about her home life as though we are conversing over lunch. Her shoulder-length hair bounces when she talks, much like her words do.

"Would you like to play Chinese checkers?" she asks. "There is no need to talk to play, but you will need strategy to win." Her manner is confident without being condescending, and though I don't feel like her equal, I know we are on the same path.

"No thanks."

"You will know when the time is right," she says. She continues talking about other things, pausing a few times to ask a question, but I offer nothing but a nod. I sense she understands me even though I don't understand myself.

Outside the big, glass window, the sun sparkles in the blue sky, but the frost growing from the corners of the window reminds me of the bitter cold outside. The clouds are puffy and a brilliant white. The treetops, although completely bare, present themselves as strong bodies of life. It all looks surreal.

An hour passes, and I have not spoken more than two words.

"You are a very sick girl, Anna, and to let you go home is to let you die. I am not willing to allow that to happen."

Reality slams against me. Panic begins to rush my chest, squeezing air quickly from my lungs. It is not the mention of death. Considering the way things have been, I have known for some time that dying was inevitable. I had gotten used to the idea. Hunger pangs had long passed, and my exhaustion had grown heavier every day. I had decided weeks ago that if I should die, it would be virtually painless, and now Dr. Ellison is refusing to let it happen.

I fear what her words mean. It will take work to keep myself alive, and I no longer have the drive or the strength to make it happen. Those days are over.

No. I can't.

I look at Dr. Ellison. Her unspoken words tell me I will do what she asks even though it might be against my will.

"You have a choice," she says, standing up, ready for whatever game has just begun, "we can go peacefully to the hospital, or I can call for assistance."

two

$\mathcal{M}$y eyes fly open. Clutched in the crook of my elbow, just as he was when I fell asleep, is Jingles, the stuffed dog I found among my pile of presents last Christmas. I stare through the darkness, searching for the other set of bunk beds. Not wanting to disturb my older sisters, I scurry across the bedroom floor and dive into Liz's bottom bunk, surprising her awake.

"I had a bad dream," I whisper. "Can I sleep with you?"

"Mm-hm," she mumbles, unraveling her sheet, inviting me under.

I lay with my back flat against Liz's back and Jingles tucked against my chest until I return to sleep.

"READY?" LIZ SAYS, rocking her body back and forth like we do when we are waiting for the perfect second to jump into a twirling jump rope. The wind pushes through the open window, blowing the green, floor-length drapes out into the open room.

"Go!" Liz shrieks. We run under one drape and plaster ourselves to the wall, holding our breath.

"Don't let it touch us," I say, sucking in my stomach so hard I can barely get the words out. The drape floats back toward us, to its hanging position. We press our heels and backs further into the wall.

"Pray for wind," Liz says, and I say a prayer, but the next

gust sucks the drape toward the open window, encasing us like a shroud. I like it when this happens because Liz can't say the drape touched me first, making me the loser.

"Girls, it's a beautiful summer day. Go play outside," my mother says.

Liz and I jump from the top step down to the foyer, ignoring the five steps in between. She opens the sliding glass door and runs across the cement patio and through our large backyard toward the swing set, leaving me to follow. I close the door behind us, slowing me down.

"Me first!" I have no chance of keeping up with Liz, who runs faster because she is eight and I am five.

"Go ahead," she says, turning a few cartwheels, waiting for me to climb to the top.

I hang upside down by my knees from the bar that stretches across the top and swing back and forth like a trapeze artist at the circus. Everyone's backyards are upside down, turning blocks of green grass into a mystical sky and the sky into an endless ocean. I focus on the overgrown willow tree up on the hill. It's a few houses away, but I can see it clearly, and every time the wind blows, its branches appear to be reaching for me, ready to catch me if I fall.

I finally have enough momentum. I spot Liz's position below with her outstretched arms and opened hands ready to tighten around mine for my dismount. One final swing up toward the sky and my bent knees straighten, letting go from the top bar. In midair, I direct my legs toward the ground as Liz and I connect hands. I land on my feet, like I have a hundred times. Liz releases our grip and is already climbing to the top when I throw my arms up like a gymnast sticking a risky landing. I turn around, my arms still lifted high, pretending to show my daredevil dismount to wowed judges and an applauding audience.

"Hurry up and move, Anna. It's my turn."

I step back, waiting for Liz to hang upside down from

the top.

"Are you ready?" she says. Her blonde curls unfold from the top of her head as she swings back and forth, gaining momentum.

"Oooooonne," she says.

Standing on my tiptoes, her fingertips touch mine before she swings back away from me, pumping her arms back and forth a few more times.

"Twooo."

Again her fingertips touch mine. "I'm ready," I say, preparing for her next move.

"Three!" we yell.

Our outstretched fingers grasp, barely taking hold until Liz releases her hooked knees from the top bar, allowing our grip to tighten. Using every muscle to hold tightly on to my big sister's hands, she rotates halfway so that she can land on her feet. When she does, Liz throws her hands into a V, sticking her landing. Jumping wildly, I throw my hands into a V too. "You did it, Sissy!" I shriek. I quickly look around, praying nobody is nearby who will remind me that calling her Sissy is baby talk.

I begin the climb up the swing set again, when our mom calls from the back window.

"Supper!"

Liz and I race to the bathroom to wash our hands. I run one finger across the bar of soap and then across the back of my hand before rinsing, giving my hands a clean smell in case my mom checks. Washing with only water is too risky because if I'm sent back, I may be left with mostly beans and pineapple chunks instead of the bite-size hot dog pieces my mom adds to her pork and beans casserole. Growing up the ninth child of ten in 1972 has definite perks, but dinnertime is not one of them.

The two ends of the table are pulled out making it bigger, but even now we don't all fit. Gabe sits at one end giving him easy access to food, which he is already reaching for; his arm stretching over the tomatoes and cucumbers, grabbing at the rolls and piling three on his plate before reaching for the casserole. Meg sits across from him at the other end because she's left-handed. She too gets first dibs before the rest of us squeeze into our usual spots, but since my mom says she eats like a bird, I don't worry about her scooping up too many hot dog chunks.

I sit against the wall in the trayless highchair I outgrew three years ago. As long as I don't get teased for sitting in a baby's chair, I like it because I'm as tall as Marie, who is sitting between Liz and me. Behind Liz's chair, in the center of the wall, is a two-plug outlet.

"Don't let your hair touch it," my mom says every time Liz leans back in her chair, "or you'll get electrocuted." Liz's head bobs forward as she pushes a hot dog chunk into her mouth. "Lizzy, bring your food to your mouth, not your mouth to your food," my mom says. Liz jerks her head back, her hair touching the outlet.

"Your hair!" I yell, horrified Liz will explode into sparks at any second.

"For Heaven's sake, eat your dinner," my mother says.

Timmy and Kyle sit across from Liz and me, and Bridg is pushed against the far wall. She looks small sitting in her highchair, especially matched up against my older siblings, but my mom says Bridgett's going to be tall someday. She's picking at pieces of pineapple that are so itty-bitty, I can't understand how she's able to get them from her tray to her mouth.

Finally taking the spoon that has been passed around too many times—once, right past me—I scoop up three hot dog chunks and plop them on my plate before stirring the casserole looking for more. "Crap, they're all gone."

"Ooooh, Anna said crap," comes from someone around the table.

"Don't say crap, Anna," my mother says.

I take a roll and begin to eat as Gabe is going in for seconds. He finds a hot dog and places it on my plate. I smile, but as fast as a rabbit, Marie jabs it with her fork and pops it into her mouth. "More for me, less for you," she says, smirking. Kyle and Timmy laugh, but I don't.

Mom is leaning against the stove, holding her dinner plate in one hand and fork in the other, eating. Jim is too, but he's standing tall, up against the refrigerator. I guess he was destined to eat standing up the second he was born, because as the oldest boy of ten kids, I have never seen him take a place at the dinner table.

My dad will eat much later, after he's home from work and has had time to view his stamp collection. Then he hides away eating alone in my parents' bedroom watching *Walter Cronkite*. I figure my mother doesn't want me to hear about Vietnam or Watergate because she closes the bedroom door whenever either comes on. I don't mind though because with my dad in his bedroom and the door closed, there's a better chance he'll get his peace and quiet after a long day.

"WHERE YOU GOING?" I ask Jim when I see him pick up his jacket and head for the front door.

"Where *are* you going?" my mom repeats, eyeing me to correct myself.

"Bill's. Want to come?"

"Yep." I run for my coat and head up the street with Jim, walking hand in hand to his friend's house.

Jim is reserved, like my mother, so I don't expect him to toss me about on our walk like Gabe does. My mother says Gabe has more of my father's Irish nature than her English ways. Instead, I count the houses as we pass each one. Every fourth house is just like ours, including the driveway and garage. *Two. Ten more to go. Seven. Five more to go. Twelve.* We turn into Bill's driveway, ring the bell, and walk into a house exactly like ours. We head downstairs from the foyer. I want to jump from the top step down to the bottom, but I hold back, taking one step at a time. I sit on the basement floor quietly listening to Jim and Bill talk about army stuff and traveling to faraway lands.

"I'm getting out of here, Bill. Good-bye Chicago, hello world."

"Thirty miles west of Chicago," I say proudly, remembering Mom's answer when I had asked how far Chicago is from Downers Grove. Surprised, Jim and Bill stop talking for a split second, look at me, and laugh before continuing their conversation. I don't ask, but I wonder why Jim wants to leave so badly.

ON SEPTEMBER 17, a month before his eighteenth birthday, Jim appears from his downstairs bedroom dressed and ready to leave for the Air Force. My mother positions her camera, ready to take a picture. I bounce in next to Jim, not wanting to miss the opportunity to be smack dab in the middle of the snapshot.

"Anna, move away. I want to get a picture of your brother."

I slink away slowly. My mom snaps a shot and waves the picture around as soon as it comes from her camera. I am in the background looking down, my face sagging, and my brown braids loosely hanging forward.

"Jim, watch me tie my shoes," I say, feeling a sense of urgency. Marie taught me how to tie last night, and if I don't show him this minute he will never know how smart I am.

"Fantastic," he says and leaves before I have my second shoe tied.

"He's going to Greece and then England," my mother tells me, but I know about the Vietnam War because I listen when nobody thinks I'm around. Creeping around corners and hiding under beds work. My mom finally strung bells through my shoelaces when I was two, so she could hear where I was hiding.

The house seems different after Jim leaves, until after dinner, then chaos continues like normal. Trying to get someone to watch long enough while I tie my shoelaces is hit or miss. Wanting to be anywhere but alone, I give up my practice and go searching for excitement elsewhere. When I find Liz climbing the walls, I forget about missing Jim and untied shoelaces.

"I'll make a bridge with my legs and you pretend to be a boat going under," Liz says, climbing the kitchen doorway, scooting her hands and feet inch by inch up the doorframe separating the kitchen from the living room.

Liz's palms lay flat against the wall as high as the door's frame. Her bare feet grip the sides just below her palms making her look like a wooden puppet; the kind with a pull string, and when the string is pulled, its legs and arms jut out like a jumping jack.

"Hurry and go under!" Liz says.

I point my prayer-like hands outward and sway from side to side underneath Liz's legs pretending to be a boat moving across the water. My shoulder bumps her left foot, bringing her tumbling to the floor. Liz stands holding her arm. It looks strange the way it twists in two directions, the lower half hanging crooked below her elbow. My mouth opens ready to scream at the ghastly sight, but before a single sound escapes, my mother scoops Liz into her arms, running for the garage door. I am at my mother's heels so I am not forgotten; like I was two years ago at the mall, when I decided it would be better to watch my mom go down the escalator instead of hopping on. She shoves us both into the blue station wagon and rushes to the hospital.

The doctor studies my sister's arm as I sit quietly in the corner chair. With a quick twist, he snaps Liz's arm back into place. I cringe with my eyes tightly shut, realizing too late that I should have plugged my ears. Slowly, I open my eyes. Liz's face is white.

It seems like an eternity passes before her color returns. A layer of gauze is wrapped around Liz's broken arm, and then some kind of cement paste is slathered on top. She is given a sling to wrap around her neck, letting her casted arm hang loosely from her shoulder. I quietly sit in the back of the station wagon on our way home because I know Liz's arm hurts. I cradle my hand into her good hand, and Liz holds on.

"You won't have to practice the piano," I whisper. A smile, much like the Grinch's when he thinks he can stop Christmas from coming, appears on Liz's face.

three

"*T*en children?" my teacher says. She's astonished after I tell her my sister Frances is coming for me after school today. She asks how old my sister is and when I tell her nineteen, it leads to more questions.

It's the end of March, and until now, Mrs. Kinney hasn't been interested in finding out anything about me. She likes me; it's just she likes the kids who sleep during nap time better. I never sleep during nap time, and I feel sorry for the kids who do because they miss out on imagining things like flying kites and swinging and climbing trees.

"How many girls and how many boys in your family?"

"Six girls and four boys."

"Now, let's see," she says, holding up five fingers on one hand and her thumb on the other. "Six plus four more..."

Ten. Ten. I hear my mother's voice inside my head, *"Patience is a virtue,"* but I can't help myself. "Ten," I say, thinking Mrs. Kinney should know by now that six plus four equals ten.

"Can you name them all?"

"What a dumb question," some of my siblings would have said, but I act like it's not dumb so I don't hurt my teacher's feelings. "Yes," I say instead. "Frances, Jim, Gabe, Meg, Marie, Kyle, Timmy, Liz, me, and Bridg."

"Bridge?" Mrs. Kinney questions, scrunching her nose showing me she's confused.

"Her real name is Bridgett, but we call her Bridg."

The two-and-a-half hours it takes for kindergarten to end is like watching molasses drip, but eventually, I'm packing up my reader and heading out the door to look for Frances. I feel like a big shot waving to my classmates as they step onto the bus without me. I see Frances pull up in my mother's blue station wagon. I run to it, happy to hop into the front seat with all the kids looking out the bus windows, probably wondering how I got so lucky to have an older sister who can drive.

"How about McDonald's for lunch?" Frances asks.

"Yeah!" I had been to McDonald's once before and dreaming of eating french fries again is just too much. And french fries are all I want by the time we get to the counter.

"That's all, no hamburger?" Frances says.

I shake my head indicating I want only fries. It may be never until I eat McDonald's again. My mom believes in vegetables and fruits and making her own bread, not french fries.

"How's kindergarten?"

"Good," I say, pulling a long fry from its bag.

"Nice teacher?"

"Um-hm." Frances left for college last August, before I started kindergarten, so she doesn't know much about it.

By the time Frances and I arrive home, my mother has already started cooking dinner. I run up the front steps, through the living room, and into the kitchen. Mom is skinning apples. I take hold of one peel from the huge pile in front of her, and because my mom can skin an apple without breaking the peel, I know it's going to be extra long. I lift it high above my mouth and lower it in, chewing as it enters. Frances hangs the car keys on the hook that's screwed into the side of one of the cabinets and turns down the hallway to her room, probably to try on her wedding dress again. She's getting married in June, and she's tried it on a hundred times since she got home from school two days ago.

Bridg is in her duck rocker. She is two and really cute, when she's happy. She has brown wispy curls at the end of each straight strand of hair that bounce when she runs. Ever since she learned how to run less than a month ago, it's the only thing she wants to do. Even now she's squirming, wanting to get out from underneath the strap holding her to the seat.

"Rock her, Anna," my mother says, coring the apples and cutting the pieces into quarters.

Bridg's rocker has a large plastic duck on each side of a wooden seat. The duck's feet make up the runners. I sit on my butt, lean back, and prop myself up on my hands. Placing my feet on the wooden bar that stretches from one duck foot to the other, I rock the duck in short quick bursts, making Bridg laugh until she's had enough.

"Mom, she wants to get out," I yell, trying to pull her out myself. My mom takes over, and I follow Frances into the bathroom and stand on the commode lid and watch her brush her long blonde hair. She pulls it back, lifts it up, and then lets it fall, brushing it again before she places her veil on her head.

"How are you going to wear it?"

"I'm not sure yet," she replies, taking mascara from her makeup bag. She pumps the tiny brush back and forth to load it up with blackness. She stares into the mirror, raising her eyebrows and opening her mouth as she applies coat after coat. Her eyes are so pretty. They are see-through blue, like the stained glass windows in church. I look in the mirror at my brown eyes.

"I wish I had blue eyes."

Frances picks up a straight pin and begins separating each eyelash so they are not clumped together. "You have the only brown eyes in the family. That's kind of cool."

I smile because Frances is right.

The front door opens, then shuts with a loud slam.

Opens, shuts. Opens, shuts. My older brothers and sisters are arriving home from school, and the slamming of the front door is always the first sign of the commotion about to begin.

As soon as Liz gets home, she takes my place in the bathroom because Liz has as much fun with Frances as I do with Gabe.

"When can I visit you in Maine? Remember...Mom said I could." Liz says to Frances.

"In a couple of years, I promise," Frances says, looking at Liz through the mirror and adjusting her veil.

Liz giggles with excitement, "I can't wait."

The doorbell rings, and I run to see who's here. Four girls are standing outside the door wanting to know if Gabe is home.

"No," I say. As soon as I close the door, I run upstairs to my parents' bedroom window to watch their next move. They walk down the driveway looking disappointed, and then gather on the sidewalk pretending to be minding their own business, but I know they are waiting for Gabe's return. If he sees them, he'll spend time with them instead of me. It's okay to be the center of attention around Gabe's buddies, but when it comes to girls, I follow a different set of unspoken rules. Gabe makes girls laugh by doing nothing but opening his mouth. He'll laugh and then they'll laugh. And then he'll push his dirt bike from the garage so the girls can gather closer. He'll race up and down the street, each girl getting a ride and a turn to tightly squeeze their arms around Gabe's strong middle.

"It's all a bit dramatic," I mumble, watching the girls stand around waiting for my brother to come home. I like it better when Gabe hangs with boys because pretty girls have a way of making me go unnoticed.

When they finally leave, I head outside, hoping Gabe will be home soon and that he hasn't stopped at a friend's house first. Gabe is seventeen and because I am six, he is able to toss me about like a baseball. When he chases me through the house, I scream with excitement, trying to stay one step ahead of him. And when he catches me, he grabs me by my ankles. "C'mon, Anna," he says, "stand as straight as a board." With a strong grip around my ankles, he flips me upside down, my head hanging inches above the floor. There's the occasional bump or bruise causing me to hold my head or grasp my leg, hopping in circles from pain, but I rarely cry. Crying is for weaklings, and older siblings find names for criers, ones like faker or chicken, both of which I hate.

Gabe and three of his friends round the corner, all holding sandwiches. He is taller than the others and the only one in the group with dark brown, wavy hair, so he's easy to pick out even from five houses away. I wait patiently on the sidewalk until he's close enough to notice me.

"Hey Big Rat, run and get us mustard," Gabe says. And off I run, happy for the attention. When I return, Gabe lifts me from underneath my arms. Swinging me about causes my legs to dart out, hitting his friends. They try to catch my legs to avoid impact, but I move just in time so they miss. "Way to go, Big Rat."

Gabe puts me down and picks up his sandwich from the hood of our mother's car. He smears a pile of mustard on his baloney using the top piece of bread like a knife, takes one gigantic bite, and starts talking with his mouth full; something our mother would not appreciate if she were here. All four start in about cars, but I know they'll eventually talk about other things, like girls. If I'm quiet, I can stay and listen.

SHARING A BEDROOM with three older sisters is one of those ninth-child-out-of-ten perks. We have two sets of bunk beds in our room, and mine is under Meg's. Marie and Liz sleep in the other set of bunk beds near the window, and Bridg's crib sits in the corner by the closet. Meg and I are against the wall next to the door to the hallway and across from my parents' bedroom. It's the best spot because I can see the hall light under the crack of our bedroom door. I listen for footsteps and look for shadows, so I know exactly when to pretend to be sleeping.

If I'm still awake when Meg and Marie settle into their beds for the night, I listen to their conversations about boys or plans to buy the Eagles' *Desperado* album. Meg puts a few of her favorite 45s on her stereo and turns the volume way down. As each one drops, I'm secretly hoping for my favorites too, like "The Lion Sleeps Tonight" and "American Pie." It's comforting hearing my sisters' whispers over the music, but I pray to fall asleep before they do because I don't want to be the only one awake in the house.

But then Meg and Marie go and spoil it all when Frances leaves for her honeymoon. They separate our bunk beds and move to her bedroom, leaving Liz, Bridg, and I with only each other. Liz's bed stays in the same corner, but mine is moved next to hers, jutting out from the wall under the window. Bridg's crib is moved to where Meg and I used to sleep. I like having my bed closer to Liz's, but it doesn't make up for Meg and Marie moving to their own room.

"It is something you'll have to accept," my mother informs me, "because it's just the way it is. Besides, every cloud has a silver lining."

I soon find the silver lining. With my sisters in their new room, Liz and I can do things we never could before. We stay up, after our bedroom door is closed for the night, looking out our window at the stars. Liz points to the brightest one. "That's Heaven."

"Are you sure?" I sometimes ask, staring at its brightness and wondering if Heaven is as pretty as it sounds.

"I'm sure," Liz tells me.

Other nights we watch bugs flying around the streetlamp or listen to our neighbors talking on their back patios, anything but sleep. And on nights when I'm scared of the dark, Liz snuggles under my sheets and tells me secrets, gently rubbing the inside of my hand until I fall asleep.

BY MID-SUMMER, Liz and I are like our own separate clan. Instead of treating me like a little kid, Liz and I are equals, even though I'm six and she's nine. On rainy days, we sneak around the house, tearing sheets and blankets from beds to use for building forts. We fling blankets over and around, creating cave-like dungeons between our two beds. Inside we scheme and plan our escape into the wild with wolves following close behind. We imagine making it to safety, but outside our cave, danger lurks around every corner.

When we finally grow tired of our fort, we leave the blankets behind and head for the living room. Liz does this thing she calls the walk-a-bird walk. She walks across the room, crisscrossing her skinny legs and twisting one foot in front of the other, making each step a bit wobblier than the one before. Her blonde curls bounce wildly, and my laughter eagerly keeps her walking around, stumbling about like a drunken sailor. My older sisters roll their eyes, horrified to be related to us.

On sunny days, we pack picnic lunches to eat in the backyard. Liz likes mayonnaise sandwiches, but I don't, so she packs me a baggie full of pickles. We run to our swing set, baggies in hand, and climb onto the glider to eat our lunch. Standing across from each other, we pump with all our might, lifting the glider higher and higher so the swing set teeters on the edge of tipping over as one of the legs rises out of the shallow hole in the ground meant to keep the set steady. We quickly sit and eat, gliding for a few seconds before taking hold of our food with our teeth and pumping again.

The glider slows almost to a stop as Liz and I finish our lunches. We stare at the gigantic willow tree that occupies almost the entire yard catty-corner to ours. We consider our adventure up into its branches before we march, like war heroes on a mission, to climb it. Once we are as high as we can climb, we scare ourselves with army talk. "One false move, soldier, and you'll be as dead as the daisy you fall on," we say to each other.

We spend hours in the tree, moving from branch to branch like sloths, taking hold of one branch before letting go of the other. Finished with our climb, Liz and I descend from the tree's top and return to our swing set. We perform circus acts of twirling and flipping, using the glider as our trapeze.

By the end of summer, Liz and I are inseparable. We play rough and fear nothing. We don't just run—we sprint. We can tag every boy in the neighborhood in a mean game of Ghost in the Graveyard, jump in and out of a twirling jump rope better than most of the girls, and race our bikes down our street, pedaling at top speeds. "No guts, no glory." That's what my brothers say anyway.

four

I will soon enter first grade, and Liz will be in fourth. Preparing for school means, "Early to bed and early to rise, makes a man healthy, wealthy, and wise." That's what my mom says. I like it better when she says, "All work and no play makes Johnny a dull boy."

As fast as summers go, school years drag, and first grade is no different from kindergarten except for two things. One, this year I don't believe Kyle and Timmy when they tell me my teacher will chase me down the hall and scratch out my eyes, and two, I love my teacher.

"Anna, my heart," Miss Caroline says, hugging my shoulder into her hip. I smile, happy to hear such nice things. I don't tell her my family wouldn't be caught dead saying such things at home, afraid if she knows, she'll stop too.

One day, I overhear Miss Caroline and my mother.

"She's a very good student, especially good at math," Miss Caroline says.

"Oh yes. She counted before she recited her alphabet."

Never before hearing my mother say something important like this tempts me to jump from the hallway and into the classroom to reveal my cover, but I stay hidden and listen.

My mom meets me at the end of the school hallway—where I was supposed to be when she conferenced with my teacher.

"Miss Caroline says you have a lot of friends at school,

and that you may enjoy joining a Brownie troop for afterschool friendships."

I do have friends, but I really don't have much use for them outside of school when I have Liz who builds forts and climbs trees, and brothers who build kites and launch rockets.

"You know too much for your own good, Anna," my mother says, referring to all the things a girl of six should not know, like girlfriends and boyfriends and tough talk I learn from my older siblings. "I agree with your teacher. Brownies will be good for you."

"LIZZY," MY MOTHER calls from her bedroom window. It's a perfect October day to be outside, and we both know it's about to be ruined.

We pretend we don't hear her, but by the fourth and fifth call, we know there is no getting around it. We head inside, acting like we are heading toward doom. Liz bends forward, her arms loosely swinging in front of her like an ape, head down, taking heavy steps. I copy her, following behind into the house and up the stairs until she is face to face with the piano bench. Last year when the piano teacher moved into our neighborhood, Liz was excited to take lessons, but now we both know it was a bad decision.

I sit behind her playing jacks. I look under the piano bench. Watching her skinny legs dangling from the other side cracks me up. She looks over at me, crosses her eyes, and puckers her lips together while she pings away on the black and white keys. I laugh and Liz giggles until my mother spoils our fun by sending me to my room. Liz continues her drills, one ping at a time. I'm on my bedroom floor, playing jacks, smiling from ear to ear.

ON WEEKENDS WHEN Liz is gone at a sleepover, Meg says I can sleep in her bed. Excited, I can barely sit still while Meg does her nightly bedtime ritual. She rolls her wet hair around empty frozen orange juice containers she uses as large curlers because otherwise, she says, her ringlets will frizz, making her hair spring from her head in all directions. I sit on the counter top in the bathroom, holding hairclips out in front of her until she needs one. She looks funny when she's done with three big cardboard cans down the center of her head and one big can on each side.

"Go get your bag," Meg says.

Twirling in circles like a ballerina, I spin to my room and grab my pillow and the brown lunch bag crammed with my pajamas and meet Meg in her room. I jump back and forth from Meg's bed to Marie's bed as Meg looks through her 45s.

"What do you want to listen to?" Meg asks.

"The..." I jump to Marie's bed. "Lion..." I jump to Meg's bed. "Sleeps..." I jump to Marie's bed. "Tonight." I jump to Meg's bed, this time bouncing on my knees.

Meg pushes the yellow, round, plastic piece into the hole of "The Lion Sleeps Tonight" and slides it down the skinny, metal spindle onto the turntable. We sing together, bobbing our heads to the beat. I know all the words by heart because Meg plays it for me every time I ask.

I stay up way past my bedtime since I am sleeping with Meg. After I change into my pajamas, we climb under the covers. Meg lays her head strategically on her pillow so her curlers don't move. She looks uncomfortable staring at the opposite wall instead of the ceiling like I do when I lay my head on my pillow. I sing songs to Meg after the lights are out, but not for long because I'm afraid she'll fall asleep before me.

"Hey, Meg," Marie whispers from her bed. "Good night, good morning, good afternoon. Pick one."

I have heard this game played many times, listening from my bed when I should have been sleeping.

"Marie, I'm not picking one," Meg says, knowing what she's in for.

"C'mon, just this once, and then I won't ask again."

"Good morning," Meg says. Silence lasts only seconds.

"Good night, good morning, good afternoon. Pick one," Marie says again.

"Nope. I'm not doing it," Meg says.

"C'mon, just this once, and then I won't ask again."

"Good afternoon," Meg says.

"Good night, good morning, good afternoon. Pick one," Marie says again.

I know Meg will continue until Marie tires of the game.

RUMMAGING THROUGH THE paper bags after Saturday morning grocery shopping, Liz and I are on a mission to find the one bag of cookies my mother buys every week. When we do, we eat a few, avoiding the coconut ones. Liz pulls her favorites from the bag—the ones with the plastic looking cherry stuck in their centers. I fish around for my favorites— the plain white ones. We each stuff two in our pockets for later because Meg and Marie and the others will soon creep from their rooms knowing food has arrived, and they too will seek out the only treat we get all week. If we take too many, they will become suspicious; besides, I want to avoid being called a slob. Hiding cookies is as scary as asking for more food at dinnertime because there's a chance I could be teased. I'd rather go hungry than be teased, but cookies are so irresistible. I run from the kitchen to hide the cookies in my dresser drawer for tomorrow.

On Sunday morning, Liz and I tiptoe to the kitchen before the others get up.

"Get the glasses," Liz says, pulling on the milk carton's blue handle. It almost hits the floor when she pulls it from the refrigerator shelf. I quietly drag a chair to the counter and take two glasses from the cupboard, careful to keep them from clinking together. I hop down off the chair and put the glasses on the table.

"Pull it back and squeeze forward," I say, reminding Liz how Mom does it when we struggle to open a new carton of milk.

The milk gushes from the heavy carton into the glass and overflows, spilling milk onto the table and down to the floor. We unroll miles of paper towels to clean it up. We mop milk around in circles, wring the towels over the sink, and get back on our hands and knees, repeating this until we get it cleaned. We place the much lighter milk carton back in the refrigerator, shove the paper towels to the bottom of the garbage can, and quickly drink the milk that made it into the glasses. We wipe the glasses dry, place them back in the cupboard, and hurry back to bed. We hide under our covers to eat our hidden cookies. Liz and I pretend to be asleep until we cannot resist the growing commotion in the house. We find Mom on her hands and knees washing the kitchen floor. We turn away.

THANKSGIVING COMES AND goes, and the season of Christmas is upon us. Christmas Eve is the most exciting night of the year because we exchange gifts between us kids. Bridgett, Liz, and I, being the youngest three, get the most presents. We receive gifts like Hula-Hoops and Barbie dolls. Gabe spoils us with Big Wheels and other riding toys. Jim sends gifts from overseas, and Frances mails handmade dresses for tomorrow morning, soaps, brushes, and perfumes that make Liz and I feel as though we are much older. Meg and Marie make us dolls and sew bedding and pillows for the dolls' beds.

The evening doesn't end with gifts. We stuff ourselves with bite-size hot dogs or ham slices spread with cream cheese and rolled around pickles then cut into bite-size pieces. The table is flowing with cupcakes and cookies, nuts and tangerines. I eat the cutout cookies of Santa and Christmas trees topped with white icing and sprinkled with red and green sugar. The rest of the year we're stuck eating dinners with no desserts. Saturdays being the worst—liver and onions—but not tonight because tonight is Christmas Eve, and we eat everything we possibly can.

When we gather in the living room, Marie writes our names on small pieces of paper and places them in the old biscuit basket my mom uses every night for her burnt dinner rolls. My dad holds the basket above his head, shaking it. It's rare that my dad wants to be near the commotion of a full house, but Christmastime is one of the few occasions he's happy to include himself in our big family.

"Whose name will be first?" he says.

My heart jumps with anticipation. *Please, please, please call me first.* The oldest always pulls the first name, but because Frances and Jim don't live here anymore, and Gabe and Meg left after opening gifts, Marie picks the first name.

"Timmy," she calls, and I sink with disappointment. Timmy Scotch tapes his name to the right side of the couch so my parents know where to put his Christmas presents. Kyle chooses the next name. It's Gabe, but since he left to be with his girlfriend, he'll be stuck with a spot nobody wants.

Timmy chooses a name. "Anna."

I laugh, jumping wildly with excitement. I skip to the green and yellow striped chair that's set between the piano and long drape that hangs by the side of the large living room window and tape my name on it. Liz gets the other striped chair near the drape on the opposite side of the window. Kyle tapes his name on the left side of the couch, and Marie chooses the piano bench. The names are placed in the same place as last year and the year before. I wonder if they will be placed the same way next year. *I believe they will.*

Trying to sleep on Christmas Eve is like trying to put a bat to bed after dark. My dad's loud snores make me nervous thinking he and my mom will forget to put the presents out. I don't believe in Santa, but I pretend to around Bridg. I tell her stories of how Santa slides down the chimney, and we sing songs about sugarplums, even though I don't know what a sugarplum is. I wish I believed in Santa, but growing up the ninth child of ten meant the impossibility of keeping these kinds of secrets hidden, so my mother gave up trying to pretend the whole red suit and reindeer thing. Bridg is lucky because now my siblings are older, and they don't care to spill the beans about Santa and his reindeer being a farce, so Bridg gets to believe.

Somehow I fall asleep, and my parents remember to put the gifts in our special places. Liz and I wake early and creep down the hallway, stopping to stare at the mountains of gifts filling every inch of the living room. Boxes wrapped in paper and ribbons are placed perfectly in each of our assigned spots. My parents must have been up all night to get the packages just right. Things like bikes and dollhouses are left unwrapped, already assembled to be put to use right away. It is just a matter of time before my parents hear us and venture from their room. And then my brothers come from their downstairs bedroom. Liz and I run to wake Meg and Marie, who enjoy sleep more than anything, even on Christmas morning. Bridg toddles down the hallway knowing the commotion she hears means fun, and wanting to be part of it, she claps her hands in excitement.

Timmy grabs a dining room chair and moves it to the living room for my father, because it's only when my father is seated and smoking a cigarette and my mother is back from the kitchen that we can open our gifts. I've already counted my gifts three times before my father gets situated. Liz sits on a stool belonging to her brand new vanity, waiting patiently.

I sit in front of my chair, rocking back and forth on my legs, lifting to my knees, clasping my fingers. "C'mon Mom," I call into the kitchen.

"Patience is a virtue," she calls back, trying to get everything prepared for afterward. She comes from the kitchen. I can't hold it any longer. Liz and I beg to open gifts.

"Ok, go at it." My father barely gets the words from his mouth before paper is flying in all directions.

"Don't lose instructions," my father says periodically through all the chaos.

And within minutes it's over, and my father is fanning the big black garbage bag, filling it with air, making room for boxes, paper, and ribbon.

Liz takes the large Barbie head from her pile of opened gifts and places it on her vanity, combing the doll's hair as Bridg watches. I set my very own table with my new china dishes and tea set. Meg and Marie snuggle into their new fuzzy slippers and robes. Timmy inspects his camera, and Kyle is wobbling on his unicycle down the hallway, hanging onto the walls for balance.

Liz and I eat breakfast at my new dining table and pour milk from my teapot. Everyone else pours themselves a glass of milk and takes two or three pieces of warm, apricot coffee cake and heads back to their pile to protect what's theirs. Then it's time to get ready for church, leaving our gifts behind.

How could a perfectly perfect day be ruined by church?

five

Kyle and Timmy are my closest brothers in age and are more about sophisticated play, different from my adventures with Liz and my thrill-seeking fun with Gabe.

Kyle is tall and skinny, so skinny that he's nicknamed Boney. He wears his belt tightly buckled into the last hole so he can keep his pants from falling off, leaving the leftover strap hanging almost down to his knees. He has one giant blonde curl of hair that he sweeps to the right side of his forehead, over and over when he's working at his science table.

Kyle's science experiments pique my interest more than Liz's curiosity, but we both like to be around when he has one of his experiments ready. His science table sits in the basement loaded with screws and nails, foil, rags, stinky liquids, and plenty of parts from machines he has dismantled. Sometimes when Kyle works on a project, I stand back and watch. He doesn't let me touch his stuff, but I don't mind because when he's not around, I do.

Ready to launch his rocket one spring afternoon, Timmy, Liz and I venture outdoors following Kyle to an inconspicuous spot at the end of the street. I know we're up to no good when Kyle pulls matches from his pants pocket.

"Can I light it?" Timmy asks.

"Nope. Mom says only me."

I know better. My mother does not allow Kyle to use matches. Kyle strikes match after match, attempting to ignite the wick hanging from the bottom of the rocket. It finally sparks, and surprisingly, the rocket launches high into the sky. When it tumbles down to Earth, Liz and I scramble to catch it.

"That's it?" Liz says, as we make our way home. "One launch?"

"Yeah. One launch, that's it?" I say.

We both laugh. Kyle ignores us.

Timmy is as short as Kyle is tall, like Batman and Robin, and he likes magic more than science. Liz and I gladly watch his performances, wanting to believe the impossible.

"This is a magic glass," he says in his best magician's voice as he fills a glass with water. "By using this magic wand," he waves it above the glass, "and saying the magic word, Abracadabra, the water will not empty from the glass." Timmy tips the glass and nothing comes out. I throw my arms up, my hands in tight fists. "Yippee!" I howl. I know it can't really happen this way, but I'm amazed Timmy made it work.

"Abracadabra," he says again, waving the wand above the glass. "I will pour the water back into the pitcher." And he does.

The first time he performed this trick, he tipped the glass over my head, and the water poured out. After that, I never again volunteered as his assistant. I plan on figuring out how the trick works as soon as I find where he keeps his magic case.

On rare occasions, Kyle and Timmy let Liz and I do more than just watch. Kite making is one of these rare occasions. Timmy and I gather sticks from outside, while Kyle finds string usually somewhere in the drawer of his science table, and Liz raids my mother's sewing basket for left over material. Kyle and Timmy choose two sticks of just the right size and string them together. Using sheets of brown paper bags from the grocery store, Kyle cuts a kite shape from the paper, large enough to tightly wrap around the frame made from the crisscrossed sticks.

Liz and I are allowed to work on the tail. "The longer it is the better chance it has of staying up," Kyle instructs, as he shows us how to do it perfectly. We tear pieces of cloth and tie them together, making it extra long.

Kyle holds the kite, and while running down the street, he tosses it into the wind as Timmy holds the roll of string. Once the kite catches the wind, it flips around like a fish out of water, and when it crash lands, Liz and I run after it, bringing it back to our brothers. They repair what needs repairing and try again, switching roles of who should hold the string and who should run down the street. After ten or more crash landings, Liz sends me to retrieve it alone.

FIRST GRADE ENDS and summer begins. Kyle and Timmy, shovels in tow, take a running leap, flying over the creek to get to the open field across the street from our house. Liz and I cross, using large rocks as a footbridge. My brothers pick a spot and start digging; dirt flying in all directions. They want to get the hole deep enough so they can use it as a hideout. To hide from what, I'm not really sure, but since I don't want to be a bother, I don't ask. Occasionally Liz and I are allowed to help, but mostly we watch.

On days when we all become bored with the hole, we head back to the creek, which winds around the field and through several neighborhoods by way of drain tunnels. Liz and I jump from rock to rock, careful not to let the rippling water soak our sandals. Kyle and Timmy venture far into the drain tunnels. Liz and I follow, but only far enough to where we can still see the light at the tunnel's entrance before we turn around and head back out again. I like it this way because I'd rather be among the reeds and rocks than in the depths of the tunnels.

One Saturday, as my brothers explore the tunnels, I make my way to the small puddles to search for minnows or a toad making its way from the creek's bank into the water.

"I'm going home," Liz says.

It surprises me at first that Liz doesn't want to play, but once I am back to my search, I don't mind being alone as long as I hear my brothers laughing and screaming from inside the tunnels. They walk far into the pipes and stand below the nearest above ground grate where curb water drains during storms. Kyle and Timmy scream from underground, scaring the unsuspecting walkers up above. I like pretending my brothers become lost in the tunnels as the day draws to a close. I become a brave knight in shining armor and trot home to inform my mother that her sons have been lost forever in the underground sewer drains. Somehow, they always make it out alive and ruin my moment of fame.

I love my imagination. I pretend my mom and dad say things like, "You're beautiful, Anna," or "How smart you are, Anna," or "I love you, Anna." I imagine Jim staying home just to be with me, or Kyle saying, "Sit at my science table any time you want."

On weekends, my father's International Harvester Scout sits in the driveway, becoming a jungle gym of fun. Usually, Liz and I climb all over it, jumping from the hood or the roof and tumbling down onto the grass, but today it's only me jumping. Liz stands below counting to three before I leap over the quicksand below. When Liz's friends come over from up the street, I stop my silly play because Liz doesn't play with me as much when her friends come around. The four of us sit on the hood of the Scout, our legs dangling.

"Let's go to the creek," Sherry says. Missy and Liz agree. All three slide off the hood and so do I, ready to follow.

"Does she always have to tag along?" Sherry says.

"Anna, we're going alone. Go play with Bridg."

I watch Liz walking away, farther and farther down the street. She doesn't bother to look back to see that I haven't moved. I take off running past the bushes where I know Liz can't see me even if she decides to look back. I walk into the house like nothing is wrong. My mom is reading a stupid baby book to Bridgett, and Kyle is hammering something in the basement, probably making a mess, and Marie is on the phone. For a mere second, I consider waiting for her to finish talking to her dumb friend so I can be with her, but she doesn't want the likes of me hanging around. Her sole mission is to be somewhere other than home, out with her friends and having a good time. She doesn't have any qualms telling me to get lost, that she doesn't want a kid sister tagging along.

I walk down the hall to my bedroom and into my closet and slide the doors closed. I imagine Liz and her friends jumping from rock to rock and going deep into the tunnels like Kyle and Timmy. *They'll probably catch a toad and keep it for a pet.* I force back tears. Even if someone finds me here, they will not see me cry. Fat chance because the tears come.

six

I don't like being called Big Rat anymore. Gabe and Jim nicknamed Frances Henrietta Hippo, a nickname they thought was hysterical, even though Frances still gets upset by it when they refer to her in this way. Frances is thin, so I don't get the joke. I wonder if this is why Meg is always on a diet; maybe she's afraid of being rebranded with a nickname like Hippo instead of Pit. I never thought about it back then, but I do now.

Soon after the start of second grade, my mother signed me up for Brownies and dance. I like both, but since my dance classes are at the same studio as Meg's, I like dancing better.

"Grab my toe shoes, will you?" Meg says. "They're in my closet." I run to get them, digging through piles of clothes and other junk before I find them hanging from a hook as high as the clothes rod.

"What are you doing?" my mother calls when I run down the hallway and past the kitchen as fast as I can.

"Getting Meg's toe shoes for her," I call back.

"Anna, what am I going to do with you?" I hear my mother say before the door slams closed. She thinks everyone should do for themselves, but I like it this way.

I run out to the car with Meg's toe shoes dangling from my neck and jump into the front seat. I seldom get a chance to sit up front with everyone calling "front" before me, so I look forward to Tuesdays, when I know it's just Meg and me in the car.

Meg's class is first, so I wait in the viewing area while she practices dancing on her toes. I watch the girls in Meg's class looking in the mirrors, secretly comparing their bodies to one another.

My friends don't worry about weight, but I do. I begin to compare myself to the girls in my class. I am small, much smaller than the other girls, and yet I am teased at home. Sometimes I'm called a slob for taking seconds during dinner or called fat when trying to fit into hand me downs, so I've taken to avoiding both. I act like I don't care because if I bring attention to it and someone picks up on it, their teasing will be worse. *I wish my nickname was Boney, like Kyle, instead of Big Rat.*

At school, I start to eat from my lunch bag, pulling food, bit by bit, concealing it in my hand from the bag to my mouth so nobody will think I'm taking too much food. And then one day, I forget my lunch at home. Mrs. Irmangard tells the class to share part of their lunch with me. Doritos, Hostess Cupcakes and halved jelly sandwiches, too much to eat, sit in front of me on my desk. Having all this bad food embarrasses me. My mother packs fruit and tuna sandwiches, not chips and desserts. I want to eat a cupcake, but I am afraid someone will notice. I cautiously take a small bite. Charlie, the boy I kissed last year at recess, leans toward me and whispers, "You look like a pig." I stop mid-chew, staring forward and trying to ignore Charlie's remark. My saliva softens what's in my mouth, and I force it down. I'm hungry and I want to eat more. Tears start to flood my eyes. *Don't cry, don't cry.* I can't hold back any longer. Tears streak down my cheeks. *I will never talk to you again, Charlie Parks*

FALL IN CHICAGO is cold. Neighborhoods are deserted the day after Halloween, and days are long and boring as we wait for the first heavy snow that will allow us to sled. Bridgett is three and a half and able to keep up with Liz and me. We are more like a separate family of three than the three youngest of ten. Kyle and Timmy simply have different interests, and Marie and Meg are young adults now. Gabe has a serious girlfriend, and it seems like eternity since I've seen Frances and Jim. I am bothered that our chaotic household seems to be settling down. I don't like how the constant flow of traffic coming through the front door—that used to open and close more than any other front door in the neighborhood—has stopped. I don't remember change being this difficult. I want Gabe to swing me around, and Meg to play her records for me, and Kyle to fly kites. Change, apparently, is a part of life because that's what my mother told me.

I'm happy when Liz asks if I want to play on our swing set. It's only a few days after Halloween, but since trick-or-treating Liz seems to be choosing to do things other than playing with me.

"Hats," my mother reminds us, but we soon forget.

Liz opens the sliding glass door and waits, closing the door behind me when I'm finally outside. We run for the swing set.

"Can I go first?" I say, excited to be playing.

"Yeah, go ahead."

I climb to the top of the swing set and hang from the top bar, clasping my knees as tightly as possible around it. My pants are slippery, making it harder for my bent legs to hang on like they do when I'm wearing shorts. I gain momentum, swinging back and forth. Liz is waiting below until I'm ready. "Okay," I say, and at the count of three, I unbend my knees while Liz grabs for my hands and pulls me toward her.

I throw my arms into the air. "Perfect stick, Anna."

Liz climbs to the top.

"C'mon. Hurry up," I say.

Liz is finally hanging from the top bar, swinging back and forth.

"Get ready, Anna," she says, stretching her hands toward

me with every back swing, our fingers touching each time, preparing to grasp tightly at the count of three. "One...two... three."

Faster than I can blink, Liz is on the ground. A thud rips through my ears and then through my heart before I am able to move.

"Are you okay?" I gasp, and when she doesn't move, I fall to my knees next to her.

"Get up, Sissy! Please, get up!" I yell, pushing at her limp body.

Liz slowly rolls from her front to her back, a noise coming from her throat, "Agkh."

"I thought you were dead!" My chest feels weird, like my coat is open to the cold air, but when I look down, it's still zipped. "Are you okay?"

"Let's go in," she says, getting up slowly. "Agkh."

BECAUSE IT'S A Saturday and a cold November morning, the house is still asleep. A glimmer of dawn comes through my window, settling onto my face as I lie in my bed. I'm not sure what makes me turn and look over to Liz's bed, but I do. I wonder where she is when I find it empty. Alone with all the quiet that surrounds me, I lie still, listening to my breathing and any sounds the house might offer. My ears target in on noises coming from the living room. It sounds like crying. It takes every ounce of courage my body can muster to step from my bed and creep down our hallway to the living room.

Liz is on the couch. She is stretched out on her back with tears trickling down her cheeks. I stare at her in confusion. I grab the afghan that drapes our couch to cover her. I climb under at the opposite end so that my head rests at Liz's feet. She hasn't called for my mom, I guess, because she fears being called a faker if our siblings come from their rooms and see she's crying. Liz and I don't like to be called fakers. I go to school with earaches because it's better than waiting for my older siblings to come home from school and tease me. I figure Liz thinks the same way.

I try to figure out what's wrong, and then I remember. *She fell.* Liz fell on her head yesterday, or maybe it happened last week. I don't understand why I can't remember. My body chills and my breathing changes. I listen to my breathing as I lie at Liz's feet tucked under the afghan—sucks of long, choppy gasps, and then a short, harsh puff of air is released.

When Liz calms, I calm. She's feeling better, I think, because she tells me she's going back to bed. We walk together down the hall, turning into our bedroom and climbing into our separate beds. Liz is sleeping now, but I lie awake.

Suddenly I remember. *I didn't catch her.*

I DON'T RECALL exactly when the headaches began for Liz. Actually, I don't even recall her ever complaining of headaches or fussing over them. Instead, I notice our play is different. Instead of running we walk, and when I climb the big willow tree, Liz rests at the bottom. I notice she wants to play hide-and-seek more than tag. Bedtime becomes quiet. When I sneak over to Liz's bed, we don't lift the sheets high into the air with our feet, holding secret conversations underneath like we used to; instead she snuggles next to me holding my hand, lying quietly. Tonight like most nights, I slip back into my own bed after I realize Liz has fallen asleep. I'm confused, but I remember my mother's words about change and accepting it.

I wake early one morning to see my mother and father in our bedroom dressing Liz. My father places Liz's shoes on her feet as my mother directs Liz's arms through her coat. She lies limp as the commotion silently happens. I watch from my bed, sitting as straight as an arrow, in utter confusion. Without taking her eyes away from dressing Liz, my mother explains that Liz needs to be brought to the hospital because of her headaches.

"Can I go?"

"Go jump into bed with Meg," my mom says.

I am terrified. My father lifts Liz into his arms, walks down the hallway, through the garage door, and to the car. I summon strength to run to the window in my parents' room that looks out onto the driveway. The car lights swiftly move down the driveway, into the street, and then Liz is gone.

Liz's stay in the hospital is short, and yet it's the longest and most grueling time of my life. Christmas break from school makes the days seem even longer. In the past they seemed shorter with all the craziness of a house full of kids baking cookies, making gifts for one another, and staying up late to watch holiday movies, eating popcorn and cuddling in warm, fuzzy blankets like last year. Each day is the same as the one before. My parents spend their days and evenings at the hospital with Liz, and I spend hours staring out their bedroom window waiting for the car to pull into the driveway, hoping Liz will be in the backseat. An eerie silence surrounds me. I hear nothing, not a single voice, nor a single footstep. I blow my breath, fogging one of the nine windowpanes. I rub out two holes for my eyes and look through. *This time the car will bring her home.* It doesn't.

Frances flies home from Maine to manage the house but mostly to care for Bridg and me. I fall asleep alone and wake alone, and everything in between morning and night teeters on unrest.

Liz's Christmas presents are wrapped and placed on the chair just like the year before and the year before that, but this year we have not picked names from the basket. We open our gifts, but the stillness that surrounds the commotion is uncanny. Wrappers are quietly peeled from the boxes instead of ripped in every direction, and breakfast is quick. Everyone avoids looking at Liz's presents sitting in the chair, but I stare.

"Are you going to bring Liz her presents?" My voice is

barely heard.

"Santa visited Liz in the hospital and brought gifts to her there," my mother says.

By evening, Liz's wrapped presents are placed into a large black garbage bag. Gabe carries the bag from the living room to the basement, and I follow him. He places it on the old table in the far back, near an old rusty filing cabinet. The next day and the days after that, I sneak to the basement to see Liz's bag sitting on the table. Dust has already settled on it. I pull a wrapped gift from the bag, holding it close to my chest, hoping it will entice Liz to come home. The bag doesn't move, not even an inch, nor does Liz ever reappear in our home.

Frances's movements are slow as she climbs our stairs after arriving home from visiting Liz at the hospital. Three of my siblings trail behind her. I smile and giggle and hold my arms out to greet her, but Frances pleads with me to stop. I don't care what Frances begs of me because she is nearly at the top step, and I am so happy to finally have her home.

"Liz is..." Frances's deafening yell gushes through my ears, breaking my focus. My mind stops, and Frances's words are lost to my memory and stored away.

Being a girl of almost eight, I am too young to realize the ramifications of what Frances has just said. I can't identify with her words so I smile, and it sticks. I don't know if I should remove it or even how. Everyone except for Bridg looks hopeless. Their expressions confuse me. Something explodes inside my head. My eyes are dizzy, and my legs tingle like they have fallen asleep. I fight to stay standing.

FROM SOMEWHERE IN the distance I hear an echo of giggling. My breathing falls silent. As I watch Frances stagger to the couch and let her body go limp, a breeze from the closed window blows the drape out from the wall, and it gently settles back into place. And in that split second, my brain rewinds, erasing fragments of memory, protecting my mind and body from shutting down completely. Now time leaps ahead just enough to keep me breathing. I go to the couch, lay my head on Frances's lap, and cry.

The days following Liz's death are worse than unbearable. They are unspeakable. I hear unfamiliar words like gravesite and coffin. Bridgett and I are in the way, and if not for Bridg's cries of wanting to be held, we might have been forgotten in the confusion. I try to comfort Bridg by holding her hand, but she pulls away, wanting Mom. I don't blame her, because I do too. I want to be around the others too, although they don't even look familiar. Their faces are distorted and look frozen in time. I look around. Everything is wrong, terribly wrong. Everyone is here, but nobody has a place. There is no protection, no laughter, and no walk-a-bird walk.

My mother thinks it's best if Bridgett and I don't see Liz in a coffin and later laid to rest. *Whatever that means.* We are carted off to a neighbor's house, away from our siblings, away from our parents, away from everyone we trust.

I am aware of being in a strange house with strange people. Keeping my little sister safe is now my job. I play Barbies with her, but my mind focuses on my surroundings. I listen for every noise. I think of escape routes. Ideas pour into my head of how to best protect Bridgett in a quick moment. Day passes quietly into night. It seems to be hours before someone comes for us. I am plunked into bed. Exhaustion lures me to sleep until I am awakened by wetness around me. I lie still, so frightened I can't move, until I hear a familiar voice. It's Gabe's. Indescribable relief rushes through me. I must hurry and yell for him before he leaves.

"Gabe," I call. He immediately comes into the room.

"I wet the bed," I say, embarrassed.

He gently reaches for my hand and leads me to the bathroom, giving me clean underwear and pajamas. When I finish in the bathroom, Gabe holds my hand and leads me back to bed, which has been changed with clean sheets and blankets. He tucks me in and makes sure Bridg is covered too before he slips through the bedroom door and into the dark hallway. A moment later, the hallway light switches on.

"Leave the light on for the little girls." I hear Gabe say.

seven

I start back to school a week or so later, I guess. Things are fuzzy, and the world seems like a different place. Day reaches into night with no dawn or dusk to speak of. The nights are cold and lifeless, as are the days. I can't seem to get a grip on my surroundings. My classroom seems to have doubled in size. My desk and chair are cold, unlike before. Mrs. Irmangard seems withdrawn. Miles of space seem to separate me from my classmates. I want to touch them to make sure they're here, but I don't because I will get into trouble. Everyone's voices are deep, like when I talk through a long cardboard tube left over from Christmas wrapping paper.

I can't place my learning. I can't remember if it's time for reading or math, time for lunch, or time for recess. I follow the other kids to the gym, the music classroom, or art room, but once I arrive I can't figure out how I got here.

Mrs. Lynch, the meanest teacher in the school, holds up one large sheet of red construction paper. "Boys and girrr…" *Her mouth moves slower than before, and then it stops.* She holds up a paper valentine heart with a folded paper box in front of it.

Kids leave their seats to pick up a sheet of red paper, paper lace, glue, and scissors. I gather the same material by watching the others. Ivan sits next to me tracing a cardboard heart onto the red paper, so I do too. He picks up his scissors and begins cutting, and I do too. I watch his every move.

"Mrs. Lynch," he says, thrusting his hand into the air,

"Anna is copying me."

I freeze. Mrs. Lynch the Grinch, a name my brothers had given her, discovers I have little accomplished. She stands over me with her large fists on her large hips, frowning. She scares me and I want to cry, but I don't.

"Where is your lace?" she asks, shaking her head in disgust.

I don't utter a word. She points to it on the floor, signaling me to pick it up. I do, but art class is over, and instead of gluing it onto the heart, I hurry to make sure I don't get separated from the others.

Most teachers are disapproving of me, and I don't understand why. I want to make it right, fix everything from going wrong, but I can't identify the problem. Like never before, I realize there are smart kids and dumb kids, and I am being pegged as dumb.

Gravely confused, my senses begin to surge into overtime. I feel deaf, and yet I hear every sound around me. Moving chairs irritate my ears as they scrape across the floor with a surrounding echo. Placing my chin in the heels of my hands and my hands on my cheeks, I sneak my fingers into my ears. Standing for the Pledge of Allegiance is unbearable. Chairs pushing out, pushing in, pulling out, scooting in sound like trains roaring by, shaking our classroom.

Footsteps are distinctly louder than normal. I am acutely aware of every movement in the hallway. The classroom door opens to a visiting teacher, and I propel into high alert—my heart pounding and my head tingling with pins and needles, rushing adrenaline through my body. I long to be home near my mother, but I cannot recall where home is.

TODAY MY BROWNIE troop is to sing for the congregation of a local church. I used to run into Brownie meetings with my friends—happy to be part of the group, singing our Brownie pledge about Brownie smiles tucked inside our Brownie pockets. But today I don't want to sing or sit with my friends, who don't really seem like friends anymore. I go because I have to go.

Crowds of people surround me. I lose sight of my mother and begin to panic. The troop leader tries to comfort me, "Anna, your mom will be here soon." But I will have none of her nonsense. Scanning the neighboring pews with radar-like eyes, I pull away from her grip. Faces distort and colors blend into one giant mass, becoming darker with each blink of my eyes. I hear peoples' whispers clearly. My silent sobs grow violently out of control. My body convulses in terror. My mother hurries over and pulls me toward her, but I retract from her embrace as though being enclosed in her arms will stop me from remaining alert.

Concentrating on my surroundings, I sit rigid at my mother's side. My blood pumps through my veins. My heart thumps loudly. A burning sensation grows deep inside my chest, and with no other way to lessen my anxiety, I begin to hum, drowning out the world around me. The cries of babies fade and so do the recited prayers of priests and the singing of parishioners, but sounding loud and clear is a deep buzzing filling my ears, synchronizing with my humming. Something gnaws at me. Something is terribly wrong.

I AM AT my sister's gravesite. How I get here, my dream doesn't show; I am just here. Her headstone appears through my blurred vision. Sitting in the middle of Liz's grave is a large, black garbage bag. I hear my voice tell me not to touch it, but my hands reach for it, ignoring my own plea. As I open the bag, Liz's bones spill out at my feet, and then she appears, facing me. We stare at one another briefly before she lunges at me, holding the butcher knife from my mother's kitchen above her head. Surrounded by terror, seconds pass before I launch into a frantic escape as Liz follows closely behind, knife in hand. I step away from myself and view my nightmare as a bystander. I scream to Anna, "Wake up! Wake up!"

My eyes fly open.

I wake lying in urine, trying to keep from panting too loudly, fearing I am still living my nightmare as it emerges from under my sheets and around my bed. I want to stay under my covers with my eyes closed, but my hot breath suffocates me. It is all too much.

"Mohhhm," I softly call, but a moment later I scream for her.

She hurries into my room. I pray that my sisters in the next room don't wake. My sheets are changed, and I climb back into bed. My mother sits by my side, stroking my hair. "Tell me what happened," she says. But I won't talk. I can't talk. I shouldn't talk. I don't understand my nightmares, but I am sure they are evil.

Please, God. Bring Liz back and take me instead. Turns out God doesn't want me.

May arrives. I climb into blue tights and a blue ballerina's costume covered in sequins and feathers. I slide on my blue tutu and slip on my blue ballet slippers.

"This is the last one, Anna, and then you will be done," my mother reminds me. Her rule of finishing what you start has me dancing tonight at my ballet recital.

Once my mother leaves me backstage, I panic. My dance teacher shoves me in the cardboard rocket ship because I am to be the first one to run from it and out onto the stage. The music starts. Since there is a trail of ballerinas behind me, I go—not because I want to, but because the girl behind me pushes me through the cut-out cardboard door. Right away I catch sight of Bridg with my mother in the audience, allowing me to relax. I dance through the routine, sliding to the left, sliding to the right, forward and back. I omit the twirls, fearing I might lose sight of them both.

There is no need for my mother to come and find me; I go to her right off the stage.

"Am I good, Mom?" I ask.

"You were very good, Anna," she says.

"No," I complain, "Am I good?"

My mother looks at me closely, pausing and squinting her eyes. "Yes, Anna you are very good."

AT HOME I can be away from Bridgett and not worry, but in crowds I hold her hand. During Saturday morning grocery shopping, I watch her like a hawk, running up and down the aisles alongside her. When Bridg sets her eyes on the toy section, it allows me to settle a bit, knowing the toys will keep her occupied until it's time to leave. I keep track of my mother's whereabouts by memory. *She is in the fruits section, bread aisle, beans aisle, cookie aisle...*

"C'mon, Bridg, Mom's buying cookies," I say, pressuring her away from the toys and toward our mother.

I watch her at the checkout line, out the store's doors, and to the car. Then my father drives down the street to the meat market, which is so small there is no chance of Bridg and me getting separated. My father pulls onto the gravel lot, and Bridg and I climb out from the backseat, while my mother waits in the car. We follow our father into the market for one reason and one reason only—we are hoping he'll buy us each a candy bar. He stands in line waiting for his number to be called as Bridg and I drool with the assortment of chocolates laid out in front of us near the cash register.

My father sees us, I know he does, but he says nothing. He has more important things to think about than us. I like to imagine it differently. "Go ahead girls, pick anything you want." But it never happens this way. He puts us through the torture of asking.

"I asked last time," I say to Bridgett, "so you have to ask him."

"No you didn't," Bridg says, reminding me she asked last. It's true, she did ask last week, like she does most weeks, but

Bridg has more courage than I do; besides, my father doesn't seem as bothered by her as he is by me.

Bridg takes four or five steps closer to our dad. She looks puny next to him, especially when he stands with his legs spread a foot apart leaning slightly backward like he is now. His crossed arms resting on his belly make him look bigger than he is and scarier too. Bridg waits for just the right moment to interrupt, as I listen to Dad and the butcher talking about the meat industry. There's a slight pause. Bridget gets ready.

"Liver this week?"

"Yes, sir. Pick out a good one."

The butcher selects a brownish piece of meat. My nose instinctively wrinkles. It will be fried tonight with onions.

"Can we get a candy bar?"

"Sure," Dad says, looking quickly to Bridgett and then back at the butcher.

Bridg bounces back to me at the candy counter. She chooses a Marathon bar. I choose a Charleston Chew because it is the longest and thickest candy bar on the shelf. If I get it eaten before we get home, nobody can say I was greedy for choosing the biggest one. As soon as Dad pays for the meat and our chocolate, we run to the car and climb into the backseat and start in on our candy.

Mom and Dad bring grocery bag after grocery bag into the house as Bridg and I unload each one, looking for the cookies. When we get them open, Bridg takes the chocolate ones and I take the vanilla ones. My brothers and sisters dig in for their share. By lunch time, only a handful of cookies will be left—the white ones with a cherry pushed into their centers—and by dinner even those will be gone. I wonder if anyone remembers that those were Liz's favorites. If they do, they don't say so.

eight

I tell my mom I can't go to third grade because I am too dumb and that I don't understand anything. She schedules a conference with Mrs. Irmangard who tells my mother it's plain nonsense for me to say such things. So I find myself sitting in Mrs. Brookfield's third grade class.

I am petrified each morning walking into school. When I am in the building, I am petrified I am late. When I get to my classroom, I am petrified to move from my desk. When school lets out in the afternoon, I'm petrified I won't find my mother's car. I search for it in a panic, relieved only when I spot it and see Bridg waiting in the backseat.

The best thing about Mrs. Brookfield is that she doesn't bother me. The worst thing about Mrs. Brookfield is that she doesn't bother *with* me. She often avoids asking me to read aloud in group or answer questions in class, and it confuses me. During reading time she places me with the black birds instead of the cardinals like last year. Everyone in my group is reading slowly, and I want to hurry them along; instead, I focus on the classroom door and windows, pretending to follow along in my reader. *Can I fit through that window? What if I'm left at school? Where can I hide...in the bushes near the fifth grade door? I hope Bridg is safe.*

"Anna," Mrs. Brookfield says, looking at me like she's called my name more than once. "It's your turn to read."

I look at the page and stare at blurred words, my heart racing. Mrs. Brookfield reaches over another kid and turns a

49

NAPERVILLE NORTH HIGH SCHOOL

couple pages in my reader. "Right here," she says, pointing to where I should begin. "You need to follow along, Anna, or you won't learn how to read."

I do know how to read.

When I return to school in January, Mrs. Brookfield gives us a blank sheet of lined paper. We are to write our letters in cursive so she can see who practiced over Christmas break.

"There's more," she says. "Those of you who have perfected your cursive will be allowed to visit the office for a special prize."

Later in the day, Linda and Susan are allowed to go down to the office. I stare at the classroom door in anticipation to see their prize. They each return with a blue ink pen, ringing the tiny bell that is attached to the end of it.

"They are to stay at school," Mrs. Brookfield says, "and you have my permission to use them when we copy sentences from the board." By the end of the week five more kids receive their pens, and by the next week almost the whole classroom is ringing during sentence writing.

It's my birthday tomorrow, and I know I am going to make Mrs. Brookfield proud. After dinner, I sit at the dining room table and practice, just like always, but tonight I don't practice letters; I practice by writing a poem.

First I write the title, Sissy. I stop and erase the letters. I begin again. My Sister. Slowly up and down with loops and hooks. My poem tells about my sister and how much I miss her. When I finish, I reread my poem, admiring my cursive. Then, I run to my bedroom and stuff it in between my two mattresses before anyone can see it.

By the end of third grade, I tell my mother I should not go to fourth grade because I am too dumb.

"That's nonsense," she says. So on to fourth grade I go, followed by fifth like everyone else.

Bridgett and I are in the same school this year, and I walk her to her first grade classroom every day before I head upstairs to fifth grade. I like helping others ever since my fourth grade teacher noted several times what a kind girl I was. I liked that she thought so.

I notice Bridg likes school. She's a good reader, good at math and writing, and has lots of friends. It reminds me of how I felt in first grade—I liked it, too.

"She counted before she recited her alphabet." I had told my mom I was too dumb for third and fourth grade, but maybe I'm not dumb.

My fifth grade teacher proves me wrong. She calls on me, but when I hesitate to eliminate all possible wrong answers, she breathes a long, drawn out sigh and moves on to someone who's quick to answer.

I am not quite ten, but I will be after Christmas break. I wonder what it's like to die when you're ten. I want to ask my mom, but I don't because I think she's forgotten about Liz. Nobody ever talks about her, but I do, in bed after Bridg is asleep. I tell Liz I'm sorry, but she doesn't answer me. I don't think she wants to forgive me because in my nightmares she frightens me.

Going from fifth grade to sixth grade isn't a huge difference since it's the same school, just in a smaller building that sits next to the elementary building—out the door, walk a few yards, and step through the doors of the other building. My classmates are the same. We still see Mrs. Lynch once a week for art and Mr. Nelson, the gym teacher, who teaches all eight grades too. We are assigned teachers at the beginning of the year just like last year. We switch rooms for different subjects but as a whole class. So really nothing is different, except I wonder if my teachers know about Liz since Liz never made it to sixth grade.

I have learned that quiet is good, so I stay quiet most of the time, following my classmates from one room to the next. Mr. Freska teaches social studies. He tells jokes I don't understand. I laugh along with the other kids, but I look away in case someone asks me what he means. He also pokes fun at kids, and I have been his target more than once. He likes to ask me questions he thinks I don't know.

"Okay, buoys and gulls, I want everyone to subtract 1865 from 1978..." *I quickly estimate in my head. 65 to 75 is 10, add a hundred years. About 110.* "and Anna," Mr. Freska says, smirking, "will show us up on the board."

My lungs swell, and I hold my breath. I walk to the board and pick up the chalk. I nervously write 1865 first because it's the first number Mr. Freska said, and underneath I write today's year, lining up the numbers perfectly beneath 1865. I stare at the two numbers. *Five minus eight.* I place a one next to the five and subtract, cross out the six, write a five, put a one, subtract, and keep going. I struggle and Mr. Freska knows it. He begins to chuckle.

Why isn't it working? I know this stuff. I feel eyes on my back. My hands turn ice cold, making it difficult to hold the chalk.

"Looks like Anna will need to go back to math class. Who agrees?"

I turn to see hands in the air. My face burns with embarrassment. Between classes I barely make it to the bathroom stall before tears trickle down my face.

"Faker!" I yell ruthlessly under my breath. *Stop crying like a baby.*

This is no worse than when Mr. Gommet turned a shade of purple a couple of months ago when he misheard the verb I identified in the sentence he had written on the board. The more he yelled, the worse my guesses and the more enraged he became. I named every last word until only one remained—the word I said when he first asked. Apparently he hadn't heard me.

"Don't mind him," my mother would have said if she had heard him yell the way he did. She has no patience for screaming maniacs.

Today is no worse. I wipe my eyes and stop my crying. When I make my way to my next class, no one would have guessed I'd been crying.

MY SEVENTH GRADE teacher, Mrs. Collins, gives the class an assignment. We are to choose a part of nature and write about it. I decide to write about the Redwood Forest since I spent almost every afternoon last summer in the branches of an old oak tree eating my lunch.

"Its beauty," I write, "is so inspiring that even forest animals stop and admire it." I describe the spectacular strength of the trees and how their branches soar like angels, reaching for the sky.

I think back to the old oak. My lunch sack often sat on a large branch, tucked in a crevice, unopened because I busied myself looking at the world below me. It didn't matter that I was only a few yards up in the branches, being off the ground made the world seem different. Chaos disappeared from below. I imagined climbing high into the redwoods would be far better than my old oak tree.

Then something I don't expect happens later in the week. Mrs. Collins pulls my story from a pile of papers on her desk and reads it aloud. Her voice sounds heavenly the way she reads the words I have written. She ends, "Mountains have great heights and oceans have great depths, but there is no greater beauty than a redwood forest."

My classmates clap and stare with admiration. My smile starts small, as if I am not sure I should smile at all, but there is no holding back. My smile stretches so wide it hurts. I am glorified for only a few minutes, but the feeling of being on top of the world stays with me when I leave the classroom. And when Mr. Freska passes me in the hallway, I don't even care because Mrs. Collins called me a talented writer.

nine

I wake ready for Gabe's wedding.

"Get up, girls. It's a beautiful March day for a wedding," my mother says, opening our window blinds.

Last year, in February, Meg was married. It had been a blustery cold day, and we spent the day running from place to place so our toes didn't freeze. My mother, I can tell, is happy for today, but I hate that Gabe is leaving, just like I hated it when Meg left.

By mid-morning Gabe is dressed in his tux. The photographer uses our large living room window for lighting, positioning everyone perfectly, as he snaps pictures every few seconds. We're waiting for Frances to arrive before taking group pictures. She moved back from Maine a couple years ago. Now busy with her family, Frances is usually last to arrive. When the front door opens, I look to the stairs leading down to the foyer. Frances makes her way up the steps. Kyle and Timmy come from the basement and follow her upstairs. Something quickly flashes in my head, or maybe in front of me, like a picture, but one that's not really there. For a second I feel like I can't breathe, and then it's gone.

The photographer positions my family so we're either sitting on the gold colored couch or standing behind it. Frances and I are standing next to each other. The camera flashes every few seconds causing the furniture in the living room to go in and out of focus. First it's the piano, then the striped chairs, and then the window. My breakfast gurgles in the pit of my stomach. I think I am going to vomit, but I can't leave my spot from behind the couch. Nobody can know I am sick. My fake smile fades because I can't hold it any longer. The photographer is first to notice, ending our group picture session. I make my way to my parents' bathroom, where no one will look for me, and sit on the floor behind the locked door. My thoughts focus on the stairs leading up into the living room.

Frances, Kyle, Timmy.

ten

I attend high school where no one knows me. No one knows of my sister's death either, and I am thankful. I am like every other kid in the school, but again I find myself unable to focus on schoolwork. Thoughts of death and being lost and trapped begin to surface at school, at home, and out with friends. My heart races during most of my day, and even small sounds are distinctly profound.

I forget how I arrive places. My stomach churns when the bus pulls into the school parking lot. The school's entrance seems miles away from the bus drop. Inside, things look distorted. I make my way into the narrow hallways, surrounded by huge kids, being pushed in every direction, sometimes forgetting where I am going. I look to break away, trying to escape my thumping heart. A battle rages through my head.

Where is my locker? What if I can't find it? What is the combination? Left 37, right one full turn, stop at 25, left 2...37, 25, 2...37, 25, 2.

Waiting for the last bell of the day, I pray to make it to the right bus, and only after I recognize a familiar rider do I relax, but even then the route looks different than the day before. Though I seldom remember daily events, I am calmed when I step off the bus and walk up the driveway knowing Oreo will be in the foyer to greet me. Bridg picked her dog out a few months ago from the Hinsdale Humane Society and named her Oreo because of her black and white fur.

As soon as I open the door Oreo is wagging her tail so violently her whole body is shaking. "Hi pup," I say, scratching behind her ears. She follows me upstairs and down the hallway into my bedroom. She hops onto my bed and curls up in the same spot just like she has every night since we brought her home.

Unfamiliar memories begin to emerge. They appear in flashes, the silent kind, like lightning when a storm is in the distance. Flashes of Liz and I holding hands, swinging and laughing, and climbing trees surge through my head.

I have a difficult time separating my vivid nightmares from reality. I close my eyes and imagine ideal story lines from television shows and place myself in scenes surrounded by love, wanting these families to become my reality. Deep down I recognize I am living a fantasy, but only fantasy keeps my thoughts away from my reoccurring nightmares while I lie in bed awake. But when I finally succumb to sleep, demons fill my dreams with evil beyond my comprehension.

I'm trapped like a caged animal; unending fences block any chance of escape. Evil figures with no faces and blurred bodies, wanting to harm me, reach into holes where I am curled into a ball hiding behind tree roots. I dig violently through the dirt, and then climbing out into an open field, I run. Evil chases me, coming closer and closer.

"Make it to my bed," I beg.

My eyes fly open, but my bed remains my prison.

THE DEMANDS OF high school are becoming more and more agonizing. Teachers and counselors falsely perceive my failing grades as laziness.

"You need to try harder, Anna."

"What do you expect if you don't work at it?"

"Maybe basic classes will be a better fit for you next year."

Report card day is a big event for the teachers and

the smart kids, but for everyone else it is nothing more than another reason to end the day early and get the hell away from school. I make my way to my homeroom, Mrs. Myerson's classroom, like forty other students.

I settle into my assigned seat and wait to be called, not like I am expecting anything good to come of the next twenty minutes. I imagine for a moment what a report card with straight A's might feel like. I probably study harder than half the kids here, but they reap the benefits of success instead of me. I feel defeated most of the time, working endless hours on assignments and studying to have my countless efforts go unnoticed. *What the hell does it matter, anyway?*

I look at Mrs. Myerson sitting behind her desk. Besides the fact that she is fat and has the ability to eat a chocolate long john donut every morning in less than four bites, she has other distasteful weaknesses. She never smiles. She teaches English from the depths of her chair, which is tightly crammed between her desk and the chalkboard. I figure her legs are quite large in order to hold her body in an upright position; although I admit, I have never seen her outside the perimeter of her desk nor waddling through the hallways.

Mrs. Myerson calls students, one at a time, making comments after she takes a sneak preview of their report card. Most students turn with a smile; some don't care either way. My anger festers as I sit in front of this one-person firing squad.

She calls my name. I am desperately trying to hide my perspiration as I lock my arms closely to my sides. By the time I reach her desk, my face swells with heat; I am so nervous I want to vomit, but I hold it together. My throat closes as I reach for the small worthless paper that means so little and so much at the same time.

Mrs. Myerson's voice booms with every one of her critical remarks. "These are less than studious efforts on your part, wouldn't you agree?"

I arch my eyebrows and slightly tilt my head, reflecting my teacher's expression disrespectfully.

"You better shape up," she adds as I return to my desk.

Shape up? I smile at the irony. *Look who's talking!*

I desperately seek escape as stares pierce my heart like a dagger. It isn't her words that bother me so much as it is the feeling of defeat. I am no longer happy with the mere effort of trying.

I begin to separate myself from my friends, and they notice. They attempt to find out what is wrong, but their efforts are useless. My only true friend is dead, and to tell others that I speak with her will raise red flags. Hopelessness overcomes my thoughts. My grades suffer greatly, but I no longer care. I don't try. I don't want to. I simply see school as a worthless job. Again, voices seem miles away. Again, I concentrate on my surroundings.

eleven

In June, after Marie's wedding, I move into her old room. It feels weird not sharing a bedroom for the first time ever. Summers are not the same as years ago. Commotion has all but disappeared. By the time Kyle leaves in July for a school in Fort Worth, and Timmy leaves in early August for Southern Illinois University, Bridg and I are left with too much quiet.

I seldom call Meg or Frances or Gabe, who are all too busy with their kids to notice me. I barely know Jim; he's been gone so long. And by the start of my junior year in high school, I am more alone than ever before. If not for Oreo's constant presence, I would think it was me who was dead.

This year is no different from the last two. The more I try to halt memories from surfacing, the more forcefully they emerge. Frequent flashes of images become overwhelming. Reoccurring dreams of being lost in my high school hallways, looking for certain classrooms and exits, are unrelenting. Being trapped in boxes and closets with no escape is especially scary, causing me to jolt awake in the middle of the night, often with crusted eyes and a wet pillow.

I try to rejuvenate myself by going to football games, but crowds are overwhelming. The bleachers give me a feeling of confinement like my dreams. Making room for someone squeezing in worries me. I strategically watch my friends reacting to similar situations and act as they do, hoping they can't read my mind, but eventually this too becomes difficult. I focus on exits and plans of escape for every situation. My heart pumps frantically in fear of losing sight of something I cannot explain.

IN LATE DECEMBER, the first noticeable sign that something is terribly wrong occurs. I am sitting on the couch for many hours into the night. My mother gets out of bed for some unapparent reason and notices me sitting in complete darkness.

Frightened by my unexpected appearance, she stops abruptly. Her voice rupturing through the thick quiet, "What are you doing, Anna?"

Slowly I turn toward her, my face tingling as though it is crumbling into pieces. An unfamiliar whisper slips over my lips, "I'm waiting."

"Waiting for what?"

"For Liz to come home. I've waited so long, and she still hasn't come." It is the first time I have ever uttered these words, and as they slip past my lips, I know my wait is over.

Death wraps itself around me, triggering a certainty that my sister is never coming home. She will never again sleep in the bed next to mine that is down the hall, to the left, and under the window where we looked at stars when our mother thought we were tucked in bed asleep. Liz will never walk like a drunken sailor in her version of the walk-a-bird walk. We will never again climb trees or picnic in the backyard or swing on the swings. She will never again smile at me, she will not say my name, she will never hold my hand, nor will I ever hold hers.

My mind begins unraveling painful events, and I am fully aware there is no stopping its power. I can no longer separate present and past with unexpected events around every corner. With two simple words, "I'm waiting," thoughts pour through my head. Bright bursts of light flash before my eyes. My mouth opens, wanting to scream, but nothing happens. A power from deep within my soul rages with anguish. My gut contracts with such force that every muscle is frozen to my inner core. I attempt to release its rigid hold, but the strength of my body is too intense. My surroundings blur, and a moment before blacking out, it comes.

Piercing, deafening screams are heaving from deep within. My body thrashes on the same couch where I once covered my sister with an afghan many years before. The same couch where she lie crying from painful headaches that had started only weeks before her death. I cannot control my body or my mind. I want the memories to stop, but they keep surging forward.

Lifting myself onto the back part of the couch, I push against the wall trying to force it down, but its strength matches mine. It is solid and powerful, and the certainty that it will remain comforts me. And although the wall is forcefully holding me, I choose when to let go. I drop down onto the couch. I lay my head in the same spot where Liz's head rested on that dreadful day when I was seven and trying to comfort my dying sister. It had not been enough. The flashes of light become constant, forming one bright light. My eyes close as blackness surrounds me.

Night turns into day and maybe the next day into night again. I'm not sure how long I lay on my bed, but my mom doesn't bother to disturb my sleep. I hear her creep down the hall and into my room. It's not hard to fake sleep with my body in the exact position as the last time she checked on me. I have little explanation for what happened, so I stay here pretending to be unaware of her presence. If I stir, she will want to be here with me, sitting on the side of my bed.

How could I ever possibly tell my mother that I am living my nightmares?

Why? Why didn't you take me in her place?-

New Year's Eve is surreal. Some family comes around, unlike last year or the year before. I am in bed early, but Marie and Frances remain. The mumbled conversation coming from the kitchen is odd. They should be laughing tonight, but they're not. Their voices are serious, rarely heard this way around this house. I figure they are talking about me and I want to hate them for it, but I don't. I simply don't care.

"Anna," Marie says, knocking on my bedroom door. "Anna, are you awake?"

Oreo hops onto my bed and immediately lies down close to my head. Marie stretches out on one side of my bed, props on her elbow with her head resting on her hand. "I miss her too."

My ears target in on her words, but I appear undisturbed.

"Do you remember that weird walk she did? The walk-a-bird walk. You guys used to walk around the house singing, 'a walk-a-bird walk'." Marie sings the words just like we used to.

Marie comforts me, and I am glad she is here. She continues to talk about everyday things in her life, and I listen. Only when my eyes begin to close does she quietly get up to leave, tiptoeing toward my bedroom door.

"Marie," I say.

She looks over her shoulder. "Yeah."

"I do remember."

"I figured you did."

Oreo has no intention of leaving with Marie. I reach ever so slightly until my two fingertips can gently stroke her muzzle. "Good pup," I whisper.

SCHOOL RESUMES IN January after Christmas break. Memories of when I returned to second grade after Liz's death flood my thoughts. My friends and family seem distant and lifeless. Voices are distorted. I am consumed with loss.

I can't go through this. They are right, every one of them. I am a faker and lazy and a nothing.

On the bus I stare out the window. Trees look more barren than I remember. I see a tire swing in the front yard of someone's house. I think about Liz and the picnic lunches we ate swinging on the glider, holding sandwiches and pickles tight in our teeth, as we pumped as hard as we could.

"What's up with you?" my best friend says. I had not felt her nudging me. "Are you going or not?"

"Going where?" I ask.

"The Father-Daughter Dance."

"My dad's on a business trip next week," I lie. I don't bother telling her the truth because she won't understand my father. Janet knows he travels for work, but she doesn't know that on nights when my father is home, he goes straight to his bedroom to study his stamp collection. She'd question why he eats dinner so late by himself and drinks beer in front of the TV before bed. He doesn't want to be bothered with a daughter or a dance. Janet won't understand that my father is not a take-your-daughter-to-the-dance kind of guy.

"Who am I supposed to go with then?" she asks. I don't give it another thought because Janet's popular, and she'll have a friend to go with by the time we're off the bus.

Studying for midterms is more difficult than before. I sit at my desk night after night reading my textbooks, except I don't turn the pages. I stare at the same page reading the same paragraph again and again, each time shaking my head, trying to clear unrelated thoughts before starting over. I lean back in my chair and stare at the calendar above my desk.

"Five. I have to get through only five exams this week," I say aloud.

The calendar blends together with the wall behind it. An image of a swing set flashes on it. My head twitches and my eyes flutter, bringing the calendar back into clear view. I close my geometry textbook and head to bed.

I make it through geometry and English exams on Tuesday and health and social studies exams on Wednesday. Thursday I make my way to evolution class, ready to be done. I walk in with other students and make my way to my seat. There are two very long science counters, each separating two rows of nine desks. My desk is just to the right of Mr. Loften's desk which sits on an elevated platform, giving him a slightly higher view of the classroom. We settle in as Mr. Loften takes attendance. He discusses time, bathroom procedures, talking, and other rules and regulations I have heard too many times this week. As soon as the test packets are handed to each student, silence fills the room. The typical multiple-choice questions, fill in the blank, and true or false fills the seven page packet.

I look at the clock when I turn to the final page of questions. Fifteen minutes remain before the bell will ring.

I look at question sixty-one, "_____ developed the theory of evolution." *Charles Darwin.* Sixty-two. The words blur, like they have several times already. My thoughts sidetrack and instead of refocusing on my final, I look to my right. Most everyone is hurried, trying to finish. A few are leaning back in their chairs with their eyes closed, waiting for the bell to ring. Others are calmly reviewing their answers. From the corner of my eye, I notice Mike and Jenny secretly sharing answers. I smile.

To my left, I focus on Mr. Loften's crisscrossed legs under his desk. He's a nice guy, I figure. He gave me a B in biology my freshman year when I probably earned a C. Unlike fat Mrs. Myerson or Mr. Surrick whose raging hormones drive him to notice only pretty girls, I think Mr. Loften would recognize me outside his classroom.

He's unaware of my stare and of my thoughts. *Stupid... this test...this class. Who in hell cares if I evolved from a single-celled organism or from Adam and Eve?*

I look back to the clock, a few minutes left. The bell rings and everyone makes their way to Mr. Loften's desk, leaving him with a pile of tests. I remain seated. I smile at the obvious differences in my classmates. Those needing everything to be perfect view their test while walking to Mr. Loften's desk. "Thank you," they say, placing their packet neatly in the pile.

Those who care more about what their peers think plop their test on the pile without looking, chatting as they leave the classroom. And those who likely circled C for every multiple-choice answer toss their test on Mr. Loften's desk, disregarding the already formed pile. *I fit nowhere.*

"Time is up," Mr. Loften says, looking over at me.

I ponder his choice of words. They mean nothing more than hand the test in, I suppose, but I think about it differently. *What if time is up?*

"Hand it in, Anna," Mr. Loften says. "If you don't know the answers by now, you won't in the next thirty seconds."

I do know the answers, most of them, but I don't care if Mr. Loften knows it or not. I get up from my seat. I walk the three steps to his desk. I look to Mr. Loften and then to my test. I rip it in two, toss it into the garbage can, and walk out the door.

"Anna," Mr. Loften calls after me.

I keep on walking. *My time is up.*

I HAVE GONE more than a week without food. Water is my only relief, but even drinking is a chore. It is difficult to think and nearly impossible to function. I want to sleep, but when I crawl into bed, I force myself to lie awake, afraid of what sleep might bring.

I am exhausted. I crawl out of bed and slowly make it to the bathroom. Showers take so much effort that I go days without washing my hair. School days are unbearable. Seconds tick by slowly. One class after another is one disappointment after another.

Make it to lunch period, I convince myself.

I sit with my friends, listening; glad I don't have to say much with all the talkers in the group.

Janet is the first to notice. "Where's your lunch, Anna?"

"I ate a big breakfast," I lie.

"You said that the other day, along with, 'I forgot it,'

and, 'I'm eating later.' Are you eating at all? 'Cause you look skinny."

I want to tell her that I don't deserve to eat or have picnics or have lunch in old oak trees or live or even die, but I don't.

Make it to two, two thirty, three. Each time I look at the clock, I repeat my thoughts as the day nears to an end. When the bell rings, I am swallowed up by hordes of students entering the hallways and pushing toward an exit. Finally at home, I lie on my bed. I don't move to do homework or study. I don't call friends or make plans for the weekend. I just lie on my mattress, and it too seems to swallow me up. Sleep comes early tonight, much like last night and the night before.

Getting ready for school today is no different than yesterday, except today I decide I just can't go on like this any longer. In the closed bathroom, I sit on the edge of the tub trying to pull my pajama shirt up and over my head, but I can't. Exhausted by the mere effort of trying, I lower it back around me. I think of what today will bring. Working against disappointments and failures will take strength. It's all too much to think about. Placing my head in my hands and knowing I have nothing to offer, I simply give in to my weakness.

"Anna," my mom calls from outside the bathroom door, and when I don't answer, she lets herself in. She finds me drooped on the side of the tub.

I look up at her. "I can't do it anymore," I whisper.

Pulling myself up from the tub's side, I slowly slink down the hallway and into my room where I lie down. Hanging half off the bed, I sleep. I don't go to school today or tomorrow or the day after, simply because I can't. I haven't eaten in over twenty days, not a single bite.

twelve

That's how I ended up in Dr. Ellison's office on a cold March day with a choice of going peacefully to the hospital or taking a stand against this bullshit. She didn't give me a choice to go home and die. Maybe because I am drained or maybe I sense this is my last shred of hope. Whatever the reason, I go quietly without a fight.

Dr. Ellison and I sit in the back seat of my mother's car as she drives us to the hospital. My anxiety is rising. The unknown puts me on guard. Before I had the choice to live or die, and now Dr. Ellison is calling the shots. My heart races, and shallow breath escapes through my nose in small bursts of vapor into the surrounding cold air. Panic takes ahold of me. The roads blur, intersecting in unusual bends and turns. The clarity I gathered less than an hour ago is gone. Now my mother's car makes me feel as though I have boarded a moving train. I regret my decision.

We arrive at the hospital, walk into the lobby, and then take the elevator up to the fifth floor. The elevator walls trap me, and by the time the door opens, I am lightheaded and my knees are weak. I am helped to a couch in the waiting area. I put my head forward in my hands. I attempt to lean my head back, but I fall down sideways across the couch.

I am aware of voices around me, but I see nothing, smell nothing, and feel nothing.

A quick spark flashes inside my head, or maybe it's on the wall. I close my eyes, wanting everything to disappear, but another flash appears, triggering a memory of long ago.

I stare at the opened gate. "Continue on." My voice echoes, but instead of fading into the distance, my voice grows louder until my ears fill with loud telephone wire-like buzzing.

My heart tightens as the only pine tree on the grounds comes into view. Twenty-one steps past the pine tree and eight steps to the left and I will be at Liz's gravesite. I have counted it many times on our weekly visits here after church, Bridg and me and my parents. My head begins to hurt. The tightness in my chest is so severe I stop at step twelve and allow myself to breathe.

I look around the grounds. Bridg pulls at my hand coaxing me to play. She doesn't understand. So we skip about turning cartwheels and somersaults in the grass. We run to and from the statue of Jesus and race each other to the water pump where our father fills water jugs for Liz's flowers. Just steps away, a glint of sunlight shining off the polished granite stone catches my eye. I fall to my hands and knees and gently run my hand over its smooth surface. I sit back on the grass, hugging my knees to my chest. The stone fades, then the water pump. I look to the statue. The sun shines brightly behind it, and then it too fades into the distance.

Muffled voices of what sounds like an army of people in a panic surround me. Their voices grow louder, my ears hum, my chest and head release their pain, and I am engulfed in complete blackness.

thirteen

I wake to a white room. The walls are white without a single picture hanging from them. The beds are framed in a dull gray steel and covered with white sheets and white blankets. The pillows and their cases are white too. The gown I find myself in is white with faded blue stars. I am disgusted to think someone has seen my grotesquely pale and naked body when they undressed me and put me in this awful thing. Had I been awake, I would have jumped against the wall to blend right in, disappearing from their view.

I am in one of the two twin beds in the room. A dingy, brown nightstand stands next to each bed and opposite the bed's footboards stands two dingy desks. A giant window, the only welcoming object in the room, stretches across the wall alongside the other bed. It is unoccupied at the moment, but since I am pushed against the plain white wall, I figure there must be a roommate somewhere who got first dibs on the prime spot. I am in no hurry to meet her, ever, if I can help it. I wonder what's down below the window's view but figure now is not the time to check it out since I'm a bit disoriented and completely out of my comfort zone. I cannot see the bedroom door from where I lie, but I listen carefully to the distant voices coming from around the corner.

I move my hands upward toward my face and look at them. No IVs. Only a medical bracelet labeled with my name and ID number; a good sign that I'll be able to move about the room. I scan the room for a closet, wondering where my clothes might be, but no luck. I assume they have been stored in either the nightstand or desk that is on this side of the room. *If they have done away with my favorite shoes, I will throw a fit.* Again I look around, this time noticing oddities. This is no ordinary hospital room. There is no call button, no machines attached to the wall, no monitors, not a single outlet is visible. I lie back, staring up at the ceiling. The surrounding walls close in on me as my eyes close.

I force myself to get up and find a bathroom or else I am going to wet the bed. A wave of dizziness forces me down sideways onto my pillow. I lie still, waiting for the dizziness to fade. I try again, first moving to my forearm, then pushing myself slowly with my hand up into a sitting position. The light-headedness tries to take control, but I will myself to focus. I sit at a ninety-degree angle with my legs hanging off the bed. I press my hands firmly on the mattress on each side of my body to steady myself. I slide my left hip toward the edge, then my right, until my feet touch the floor. I position my feet and push my hands slowly against the mattress, lifting myself upward and forward until I am standing

My belly gurgles, but with nothing in it, there's no chance of anything making its way to my mouth. Turning toward faint voices, I walk slowly, using the bed as a safety net, keeping my right hand in constant contact with the mattress until I reach the footboard. Around the corner from the end of my bed is the bedroom door, and sitting to the left of the door is a small closet area where my clothes are hanging and my shoes are placed neatly on the bottom shelf. To the right is a single bathroom to be used by me and a roommate, which I now acknowledge as fact since the bathroom looks used.

Pushing the door open, I creep inside. To the immediate left, two cabinet doors that I don't bother to open sit below a small sink and countertop. Above the sink, a mirror made from some type of metal instead of glass is plastered to the wall. The commode appears clean but used since the lid is in its upright position.

A small dish-like pan sits to one side of the commode, similar to what a toddler uses during potty training. *It looks clean;* an assumption I think good enough to avoid inspecting it any further. A narrow shower stall crowds the wall just inches from the commode. *My skinny body will be in my favor.*

I close the door and find there is no lock. I lift my gown. My legs are squeezed so tightly my thighs tingle. Unaware anyone is near, the door opens and I quickly cover myself.

"What the hell!" I push the door against the intruder. "I'm in here!"

"Anna, I'm Virginia, your nurse for today. I need you to use the bowl near the toilet," she says. *Shit! That thing is for me! There is no way in hell I'm peeing into a toddler's potty-chair.* "Let me show you how to use it."

"No thanks," I say, opening the door. "I don't need to go."

"Hi, Anna. I hope I didn't scare you." Virginia quickly steps in and stoops down to pick up the dish. "Turn it upside down and it looks like an old fashioned nurse's hat, don't you think? Just lift the toilet seat, place the bowl underneath, pull down the seat, and voila! Sit and pee without missing a drip."

Virginia is about one hundred years old and as lively and quick spirited as a teenager. Her gray and tightly curled hair smells freshly permed. Her wrinkled forehead shows her age, but her warm eyes and her endless energy lead me to believe she may be younger than I think. She holds my arm to help me to my bed and guides me onto my back. She tugs at the stethoscope that hangs around her neck and whips it into her ears. She moves the flat piece to different spots around my belly, stopping to listen for a few seconds before she moves it again.

"I can't hear a thing, Sweetheart, with your bladder so full," Virginia says. Her sympathy showing through her smile.

"Let me help you. I promise, the bowl thing isn't that bad."

I'm on the verge of going right here, but I don't want Virginia thinking she's right.

"C'mon, here we go." Virginia hoists me up too quickly, throwing me off balance. I can feel her strength behind her gentle grip. "Lean against me," she says, as we walk to the bathroom.

Nice thought, but I don't need you. "I got it," I sneer so she lets go, barely. "Really, I got this. I've been using the bathroom on my own since I turned two, and I don't need your help."

I hope somewhere in a report my mother hasn't spilled her guts about my childhood bed-wetting issues. I lift my gown and start peeing before I am completely seated. It pings loudly against the plastic thing, and I redden from embarrassment. I finish and just sit. *Now what? Throw the toilet paper where? In the plastic thing? How sickening is that?*

Virginia must assume I am finished because by the time I am deliberating on what to do with the toilet paper, she barges in. There is no keeping her out, so I don't try. I am too weak and tired and humiliated beyond words.

"Step aside young lady, and I'll help you out." She takes the bowl with her gloved hands and holding it up toward the light, she reads the numbers on the side as I quickly throw the paper in the commode.

"Twenty-nine cc's," she says, flushing my pee down the commode. She rinses the bowl in the sink and places it back in its original spot on the floor. "That's all that's to it."

Taking her clipboard from the sink's countertop, she charts what I guess to be twenty-nine cc's, whatever that means.

"Each day your nurse or MHT will chart your urine output."

Virginia walks beside me as I head for the bed. I want

to ask what she means by MHT, but past experiences keep me quiet. Virginia listens to my belly again. I have no idea for what until she asks how long it's been since my last bowel movement. This time I ask because I have no idea what she means.

"Poop. How long since you've pooped?"

Just when I thought this nightmare couldn't get any worse, it does. My family never discussed these matters. We never talked about illnesses or bathroom issues or anything showing weakness, but I assume Virginia doesn't care about any of that, the way she is staring at me waiting for an answer. I look away, heat radiating from my face.

Virginia quickly smiles after noticing my embarrassment. "Ah, everyone does it."

"I don't know," I whisper, unable to share something so humiliating.

"It's okay, Darlin'. I'll take another listen later. Well then, anything I can get for you?"

"My clothes, please," I answer.

"Not yet, Honey. After we run a few tests then you can get dressed. Okay?"

I look at the white wall, tired beyond words. Today seems surreal. I am certain there is more to come, but these first hours on the fifth floor deeply engrave into my thoughts. I want to delete today and yesterday and the last ten years, but I can't. I lay my head on the pillow and look around one last time. The surrounding white suddenly brightens before creating a narrow-like tunnel coming toward me as I drift off to sleep.

fourteen

$\mathcal{A}$ man wakes me and helps me to a bed on wheels. I am horrified from embarrassment as he wheels me into elevators and down corridors, past people who stare like I am some invalid. Voices sound off in my head. *Weakling... faker...* I concentrate on where I am being taken, but with so many turns and in and out of elevators, I finally give up in frustration. I close my eyes, hoping to go unnoticed. We come to a stop where I am left alone in a cold hallway, laid out for all to see. Freezing, I try warming myself in this awful place, huddling under the one thin sheet covering me.

There are several doors leading into rooms. I pray to be wheeled into one sooner than later to get away from the nurses and doctors walking by me. My only godsend is that they pay no attention to the fact that I am half-naked lying flat on my back in the middle of the hallway. I could be dying, choking on my own drool, or going into cardiac arrest and die before even one nurse unwillingly looked my way. *If some sick stiff wanted to die, this hallway would be the perfect spot.*

A woman dressed in white from head-to-toe pushes me into a room with gigantic machines hanging from the ceiling and walls. She tells me I'm here for x-rays and an ultrasound of my stomach. Then she hands over a plastic, see-through cup with some white-looking paste inside. She explains that I'll need to drink it in order to show a better picture of my abdomen. I taste it and immediately gag. *No way am I getting this crap down without puking,* but I do. For the next hour, sip by sip, I gag and choke my way through six ounces of barium.

I FIND MYSELF back where I started on the fifth floor, in the same room and alone. I want everyone to leave me alone. I don't want anyone listening to my heart or belly or taking pictures of my gut. I want out, but beyond this bedroom is a locked exit. A knock startles me, and before I have a chance to prepare for yet another intruder, a man pushing a cart on wheels enters my room.

"You must be Anna. My name is Chad, and I will be helping you while you are here."

My heart skips a beat. He stands upright, and I see that he is tall. He finger-combs his short, blonde hair over to the right and away from his face, but it bounces back immediately. He looks at me with the most beautiful blue eyes I have ever seen, ocean blue with little glimmering specks of white.

He rolls the cart closer to my bed and uncovers a plate of food. "I've brought your dinner." His words release my gaze. Instantly I am aware of my nakedness underneath my thin gown and quickly pull the sheet up to my chin. He pulls a chair from the opposite corner of the room next to my bed and sits down. Pinned to his shirt, a name tag reveals his name and printed underneath his name in small letters reads his title, Mental Health Technician. *MHT*, I assume.

"It's going to be difficult eating lying down, wouldn't you agree?"

What? If he thinks I am eating this crap load of food, he's wrong. I look away, unwilling to express my thoughts.

"Eventually, I want you to be able to sit in the dining area with everyone else, but first you will need to keep something down."

"I don't need you here watching my every move while I eat," I say, with no intention of eating. I pull my covers closer to my chin. Chad empathizes with my embarrassment and leaves the room for a moment, but even with him gone, his aftershave leaves behind an enticing smell. He returns with another gown of the same color and a funky, faded design.

"Here, put this over the one you have on. I'll be outside your door, so let me know when you've finished."

I try to figure out the best way to manipulate the gown to cover every possible body part, but I soon give up, realizing it's impossible. I sit on my bed and lean against the wall. I leave Chad lingering in the hall, refusing to let him think he is needed here. *He can stand outside my room all day and night for all I care*. Although his company is comforting, I don't allow myself to let him in on this secret.

Obviously Chad isn't easily fooled because he reappears moments after I am situated. "Glad to see you sitting up. Let's see...you've got Jell-O, toast, and a chocolate Ensure," he says in a way that tells me to choose one.

"No thanks, I'm not hungry." It's true that I'm not hungry. The first couple of days without food, intense growling came from my stomach. Then a few days later, the hunger pangs were awful, painful most of the time. Then they stopped. I couldn't feel them any longer.

"Do you know why you are here?"

I assume Chad knows why I am here, but if he isn't mentioning the food thing then I'm not about to bring attention to it. "Nope," I reply, giving Chad the head's up that I'm in no mood for a lecture.

"How old are you?"

"Seventeen."

"Where do you go to school?"

Thinking I can deter this back and forth banter, I sarcastically remark, "Right now, nowhere."

"Well let's say before you got here then. Do you have a favorite subject?"

"Not really."

"Is there anything about school you enjoy?"

"Hmm...give me a sec. Nope."

"How about outside of school? What do you like to do?"

What is this...the fucking third degree? Anger fuels a fire inside of me. I want to refuse to continue this absurd inquiry, but if I stop, Chad might leave. I don't want him here, and yet I do. None of this makes sense. All I really want is to shake my head and have the last twenty-four hours disappear.

Chad gets up to leave. "The toast is cold and I've never been a Jell-O fan myself, so I don't blame you if you don't eat either, but you'll need to drink the Ensure within the next hour." His words are kind, but like Dr. Ellison, I can tell he means what he says. "If you use the bathroom, let me know so I can chart your output."

I am more comfortable after Chad leaves. I have no intention of swallowing one sip of this nasty drink or telling him when I pee or anything else he might ask me to do.

I am exhausted. The sun sits lower in the sky as dusk creeps in from around the corner. I figure it is around half-past six as I look around the room for a clock. No luck. I wonder where my mother is. I haven't seen her since I found myself alone in here, nor have I seen any trace of a roommate, for which I am grateful. I hear a knock on the door as Dr. Ellison enters my room. *My God! Does anyone believe in leaving me alone?*

"How do you like your room?"

Is she kidding me? "It's very colorful."

She smiles, looking around at each wall. "Well hopefully, some posters will make it your own."

Posters? Why the hell would I hang posters? How long is she planning on keeping me locked up in here?

"I see you haven't started your Ensure. You have about twenty minutes to finish it, so you'll need to get started."

"I'm not hungry."

"Nevertheless, you'll drink it."

"Actually, no I won't."

"I would rather see you eat on your own, Anna, but if

I see a need to help you with this, I won't hesitate to order a feeding tube to be placed through your nose and down to your stomach."

I huff, rolling my eyes in disgust, trying to mask my embarrassment of being looked upon as weak. I am annoyed by the way she remains calm when I show her how irritated I am at what she has said. *I don't need to worry about this now. I need my mother here. She needs to see what's happening in this awful place.*

"Is my mother here?"

"Yes."

"When can I see her?"

"In about thirty minutes. By then, you will have finished the Ensure and hopefully have a bit more energy. As of now your kidneys are still functioning, but they need to be strengthened. You are a very sick young lady. We are all here to help you get better, and there are things you must do to help yourself too. My first goal is to get your body functioning the way it is meant to. I'll need you to eat and gain weight."

I turn away.

"I will see you tomorrow. Chad will be here into the evening if you have any questions."

"I do have a question." I flare with contempt. "And when did you say I get outta here?"

"I didn't say, but when I know you are ready, you will go home."

"Super!" I say sarcastically.

When Dr. Ellison leaves the room, I feel bad having spoken to her so rudely. *This isn't like me, or wasn't like me.* I don't like the way I've become so hostile toward others, but I can't seem to control it from happening. I think of the shocked looks coming from the faces of those who thought of me as quiet and kind, sorry I have disappointed them. I quickly push my guilty thoughts aside.

I look at the can of Ensure and a Styrofoam cup sitting

on the rolling cart. I pick up the can, noticing it has already been opened. I pour the chocolaty mixture into the cup to have a better view. I take a sip. "Chocolate, my ass," I snort. *This tastes more like the white crap I had earlier today*. I get a couple sips down.

I could dump it, I nervously think. It's unlike me to lie, but I cannot drink this stuff. Chad will be here any minute. I know it's now or never. A new energy rises from my gut. I dart into the bathroom and pour most of the contents down the drain but leave a small amount inside the cup. I turn on the water to rinse away the remains and hurry back to my bed. I keep a hold of the cup, so when Chad returns I can drink the last sip, acting as if I have just downed the whole thing.

What am I doing? This isn't me. I have always been an honest person, and now I sit here thinking of lies to tell Chad. I concentrate on slowing my breath, but I can't. My vision blurs and buzzing overtakes my hearing. *Oh my God! I am going to puke. Hold it together.*

Enough time passes before Chad knocks on my door and enters, so much so that my breathing has returned to normal, but inside I'm shaking to death. I'm convinced my face is radiating heat, revealing my lie.

"Not too bad, I hope," Chad says.

"No," I whisper, locking my eyes on the window, refusing to look at him

He holds out his hand. I take the last sip and hand over the cup.

"Nice," he says, charting something. "Did you use the bathroom yet?

My body temperature rises a couple of degrees. *Stay calm.* "Not yet."

"Your mom is waiting to see you. Should I show her in?"

"I want to get dressed first."

"Not yet, Anna. You'll have blood work and a physical tomorrow. Once you..."

"Fuck this! I don't need to be here...and I'll put on clothes when I want!" I scream, hurdling off my bed toward the closet. My clothes are gone. I stare at the closet with my back toward Chad. *What is happening?*

A few seconds pass. It occurs to me that this is serious. I need to play my cards right, or I will be here forever. Screaming will spoil my chances of ever leaving. I need to fight smart in order to survive. Strategy takes brains, and I will not be a pawn in this game. I will not be defeated. I am going to win. I turn to face Chad. "Can I see my mother, please?"

When my mother enters the room, I see she has been crying; something I have never seen her do. It worsens the already awkward feel in the room. She looks at me. I am embarrassed to be in this gown in front of her. She doesn't hug me because she doesn't know how, nor do I. Hugging seldom occurs in our house, if ever, and surely this hasn't changed simply because I am here.

"How are you?" she sighs.

"Fine, I guess."

An hour ago, I had planned to convince my mother to take me home, that being on the fifth floor would not help me, but now I realize this visit is just a formality. No parent in their right mind leaves their child alone with strangers without first knowing they are safe. The doctors and staff know this. My mother is here because she needs to be here, not because I've asked to see her. There will be no convincing her I need to be at home. She had seen me wither away there. *No, she isn't here to take me home. She is here to leave me.*

"Chad seems nice," my mother says.

I shrug my shoulders. "I guess."

Our conversation is dry, like one we might have over choosing a paint color. I feel my mother's pain, and I feel sorry for her. I act as if nothing is wrong, not because I'm angry, but because this is just the way it is. When Chad comes in to say visiting hours are over, we say our good-byes with a quick wave and a quiet, "See you later." Both of us know it will be longer than a day before we see each other again, yet neither of us mentions it. Chad shows her to the locked door right outside my bedroom. I follow at a short distance. It is the first time I step into the hallway since I arrived earlier today. My mother walks through the door, and by the way her shoulders heave, I know she is crying. *She may not be here to take me home today, but she will be my way out. She will be the one who will see my position.* It is difficult for me to admit, but I am convinced I will need her.

Chad walks with me back into the room. "It's time to settle in for the night. You've had a busy day. I want you to try to use the bathroom before you get ready for bed."

I walk into the bathroom and place the bowl loudly on the commode so Chad thinks it's being used. I don't sit because I have nothing to pee. I wait just long enough before I take the bowl from the commode and place it back on the floor. When I exit the bathroom, I tell him I can't go.

I look over and notice a girl pacing the room like she has to go badly.

"Anna, this is Lottie. Lottie, this is Anna."

"Hi," I say, looking to her for a reply, but she says nothing. She doesn't even look at me. She is tall and thin and crazy looking by the way she has her short, curly hair pulled back in a ponytail. Only a small clump stays tied in the rubber band as the rest bounces about wildly, making me wonder if she and Harpo Marx have the same beautician. She makes her way into the bathroom, looking at neither Chad nor me. *Weird.*

Chad looks at me with his eyebrows raised. "Did you drink your Ensure?" he asks.

My breath slows. I feel a band tighten around my chest. *Oh my God! How could I be so stupid? The chart. What goes in must come out.* My face warms. If I continue this lie I will lose ground and Chad's trust, but I don't want to admit my deceit either. Caught red-handed, there is no way out. I try to act confident, but when I look at Chad, I lose my nerve and begin to hyperventilate. "It was so gross. I couldn't force it down."

"Get ready for bed, Anna. Lights out at ten," he says and leaves the room.

I am embarrassed, more because I failed miserably at a simple lie than Chad's disappointment in me.

I wake up in the middle of the night to the dark, scared, and confused. After a few seconds, I remember where I am. The quiet is unsettling. I look over trying to see Lottie through the pitch black but no such luck. I sit up, swing my legs around, and reach for the floor. I fumble around using my memory as a guide to the bathroom. I turn on the bathroom light to use as a night-light and then quickly dart back to bed and jump in, making sure my feet aren't too close to the underneath part in case someone is hiding there, waiting to grab my legs.

Lottie stirs. She sits straight up and mumbles something I cannot understand. I watch her get out of bed and lumber to the bathroom. I lie still as though I am dead asleep. Her arms are long and skinny and move back and forth faster than her legs, making her oddly unbalanced. She switches off the bathroom light. Complete darkness again and my fear takes over. I cannot see or hear Lottie, making me nervous, until I hear her climb into bed. I wait patiently, pretending I haven't heard or seen a thing. When her breathing grows heavier with every passing minute, I make my way to the bathroom again to turn on the light and quickly jump back into bed.

Lottie heaves herself from her bed, and within two or three horrifying jumps, she is hovering over me screaming names at me.

"You bitch!" she screams as she reaches over me, clawing at the wall on the other side of my bed. She begins pounding my mattress, barely missing my head with each punch. She is a raving maniac. Realizing I cannot fight her rage or strength, I manage to escape from her flailing arms by scooting on my back farther down the bed, using my heels to pull myself toward the footboard, and then springing over it in one quick movement. I run for the door, fleeing right into someone's hold. I thrash about trying to escape from their grip, screaming for my release.

"Anna! It's Chad."

I wouldn't have cared much who it was; nobody could make me stay anywhere near a crazy lunatic.

"Calm down, Anna," Chad says, trying to reassure me that everything is okay.

Lottie continues screaming obscenities as two men run past to secure a hold on her. Trying to break free of Chad's grip, I begin to thrash more violently. "Leave me the hell alone!"

He tightens his hold around my arms and buckles my knees from underneath me. I'm on the floor in seconds. Faster than I can think straight, my arms are crisscrossed across my body, and Chad's legs cover mine, securing me tightly so I can't move. My anger gets the best of me, but barely able to breathe, I try to relax and then wriggle away, but it's impossible. With no one in the room but Chad and me, I calm down and realize how ridiculous I must look.

"I'll release you, but you will need to remain calm," he says, enunciating every word. "Is that a deal?"

I nod, giving him the okay. He releases slowly, and I assure him I am not going to make the same mistake twice. When I am able, I scoot away and fly into my bed.

Chad stands, straightening his shirt. "We will keep Lottie in a different room for the night. You'll be okay. Try to get some sleep." He turns toward the door.

"Chad," I ask, "will you switch on the bathroom light?"

He smiles. "Sure."

He closes the bedroom door behind him. I concentrate

on the ceiling, forcing back tears until there is no chance of crying. *I will not lose.*

fifteen

I wake to a hint of dawn coming through the windows from across the room. Lottie's bed is still unmade and unoccupied. I hear little commotion in the hallway. My room is at the far end of the unit near the exit door; *a good place to be*. I had gathered as much information about my surroundings as possible after I said good-bye to my mother. There was little to see from where I stood, but I noticed four more bedroom doors stretching down the long hallway to a large area encased in windows where I saw several nurses.

I lie in bed staring out the window, and from nowhere, a frail woman nears my bed, startling me. I try to act undisturbed, but my insides gush blood into my veins. She's Indian and looks like she has been buried twice over. Her skin is so wrinkled, I look again to make sure it's not a shrunken head placed on a living body. She has tubes and gloves and all sorts of things in a small tub-like basket. If not for remembering Chad mentioning something about blood tests, I might have thought she was here for some weird science experiment using me for her specimen. Entertained by my imagination, I half smile.

The woman comes to my bedside without saying more than, "Good morning." She reaches for my wrist, comparing my ID bracelet with her notes, and then reaches for my arm, looking for a good vein. The rubber band she ties to my upper arm catches some loose skin and it pinches like the dickens, but I decide to stay quiet since I am more worried about what's to come. It's unnatural to watch a thin, sharp needle pierce through skin, but somehow it brings less pain knowing the exact time I'll be pricked, so I watch the needle enter. The Indian woman sucks out four tubes of blood before I wonder if she plans on keeping a few tubes for her breakfast. My arm begins to register the pain with the fifth tube of blood.

"Have enough?" I ask with such sarcasm that she neither looks at me nor answers.

"That's it," she says and gathers her things and is gone.

I tuck my arm underneath the covers, wondering if I feel drained because my blood has been siphoned or because of the last eighteen hours of my life. A shower turns on near the far wall. *Guess there is life in this hellhole after all.*

I wonder who's in the room next to mine. The door to this room and the next room's door are only inches apart— something I had noted last night. I hope it's not another lunatic because being surrounded by two loonies will put me over the top. If I had my way it would be Houdini rooming next door.

The place livens up with a few knocks on doors and "Good mornings" coming from down the hall. Although commotion has always been a comfort to me, I am nervous about today. I sit up and crawl to the end of my bed to look in the closet—still no clothes. My door is cracked open but only enough for me to see a sliver of the hallway. I hear the big exit door open, so I quickly sit back against the wall at the bottom of my bed. I listen for a knock on my door but hear nothing. I sit motionless staring out the window.

The exit door is opening and closing more frequently, and commotion is growing with every passing minute. I contemplate who's entering or exiting. I imagine if it were me, I would be exiting and running for my life. The door opens again and I feel a sense of release, but then the sound of it latching makes me feel ill. I shake my head trying to rid these thoughts from my mind.

I have got to think clearly. "There's only one way out of this stinking place, and it is through that door," I whisper.

I think about Dr. Ellison's comment, "When I know you are ready, then you will go home." This is going to take some strategizing on my part because I have no idea what she means.

Dr. Ellison knocks once before walking into my room, giving me only a second to clear my thoughts and straighten up. I get an eerie feeling because she's here at the exact moment I am contemplating our last conversation, and it has me wondering if she can read my thoughts. *Just my luck.* She is holding a long tube and a clear bag filled with some sort of liquid. I tense without letting on that my blood pressure has just jumped to an unsafe level.

"Good morning." She smiles, and instantly I feel a bit better but still cautious of why she is here carrying tubes and stuff.

"Could you lie down on your back, please?" she asks, and I obey.

I sense she means business, and I have no intention of stirring things up because I figure it's better to be on her good side. She sits on the edge of my bed, making herself comfortable. She opens my gown, causing my face to redden from embarrassment.

I can barely look at myself in the mirror and here I am open for the world to see. She listens to my belly and my heart as I stare at the boring white wall. After what seems like eternity, she closes my gown. I quickly close it tighter and reposition my arms down by my sides.

"How are you feeling?" she asks.

"Fine." I turn toward her but keep my eyes lowered.

"I heard you had a rough night."

"Whatever."

"Lottie is a bit eccentric, but she won't hurt you."

Shit, she almost killed me.

I am reminded of the things Dr. Ellison carried into the room when she picks up the tubing. "I ordered this for you..." she says, pointing to the bag of liquid.

She has my attention. My eyes are now on hers.

"I hear you are unwilling to eat on your own, giving me no choice but to have this feeding tube inserted through your nose and down your throat. Dr. Hammond is awaiting my page. He will explain the procedure."

She pauses, probably giving me time to process, but I don't need time—I need a way out.

"It will be unpleasant. I would rather see you up and about, joining the others here, but if restraining your activities and feeding you through a tube keeps you alive, then it must be done."

I am more humiliated than horrified at what she is telling me, but if I look away she might send for the other doctor.

"Why?" I ask, pretending I don't know.

I hadn't drunk that crap last night, and now I am up to my eyeballs in trouble. There is no time to let her answer my question or finish her explanation of this ludicrous torture. This feeding tube thing could be a scare tactic, but I'm afraid to risk that it's not. I have known Dr. Ellison for less than twenty-four hours, and it doesn't take brains to know she isn't the threatening type. Taking this any less than serious could be, and probably would be, a mistake.

"I'll eat," I plead. "I'm sorry I lied about the Ensure, but I told Chad the truth when he asked." I am now spilling my guts. It's obvious the two communicated what had happened, so why not? I look at her with confessing eyes, trying to persuade her to give me a second chance.

A fat woman walks into my room.

"Give us just a few moments, Carol," Dr. Ellison says, and the fat woman walks away. My heart skips a beat. *Have I just beaten my odds?*

"This will be your only opportunity to make this right.

You are starving yourself, and I will not stand around and let it happen. Do you understand?"

I nod.

"Carol will be your nurse during the day. She and I and Chad will work closely together to help you. When they are not on duty, other staff members will be given your information as well. There are no secrets between us. What you tell one of us will be charted and discussed amongst us all so we can learn how to best help you."

Yeah, right!

"We work closely as a team which means our conversations will be based on what you tell us. Your honesty is essential to your progress. Other patients will know only what you decide to tell them. I want you to know this up front." Dr. Ellison pauses, eyeing me to give her a sign that her message has been heard. I give her a slight nod and then look away.

"Carol will be in to get you in a moment. She will get your weight and take your blood pressure first thing every morning. Your meals will be brought to you until you are strong enough to eat with the other patients."

I stop listening, irritated that she thinks I'm weak.

She pats my arm and gets up to leave. "I will check in on you later this afternoon."

I sit tight-faced with my eyes narrowed. *Help me? Yeah, right. Manipulate is more like it.* Trying to remember the last time someone offered help seems so out of reach that Dr. Ellison's comments make me angry. Accepting help is a false hope and I do not intend to fall into this trap. I think about the teachers who criticized and ignored me. Their lessons of rejection had taught me firsthand not to trust those who claim to want to help. I chuckle to myself. *Looks like my education is a benefit after all.*

Carol returns. She walks into the bathroom and then out again. *Probably checking on my bathroom business,* I think, and it angers me.

"Hello, Anna. My name is Carol."

She doesn't wait for me to reply to her hello which is fine by me.

"Come with me and we'll take your weight."

"You'll, not we'll," I correct under my breath.

She leads me across the hall from my bedroom, walking faster than a typical person carrying extra weight. Though her hair looks as if it was slathered with mousse and left to air-dry, making her long curls look waxy, she is nicely dressed in slacks and a blouse, both of which fit her body perfectly.

I get a better view of the unit than I did last night. Past the fourth bedroom door is a lounge area, I assume, because I can see the back of a long couch and hear the morning news. What I assume to be the nurse's station sits directly behind the lounge area. A connecting hallway, across from the third bedroom door, leads somewhere I can't see from where I am standing, but a recessed water fountain is visible where the two corridors meet. A greasy food smell lingers, so I guess the eating area Chad mentioned last night must be nearby.

Carol walks into a small laundry room that accommodates a washer and dryer and an official doctor's scale. Along the back wall are three shelves of clean sheets, blankets, and hospital gowns. The running dryer makes the room warm and snug. She slides the three weights to 0, points to the platform, and tells me to hop on, so I do. I notice the top bar represents pounds in increments of fifty, and the middle bar represents pounds in increments of one, from zero to fifty. A third bar shows numbers one through sixteen. I assume these represent ounces. *Holy crap! They are serious.*

Carol carefully moves the top weight across the bar to 100. It's going to be too heavy, but I let her figure it out by herself, as I say nothing. When the balance drops to the other side, she slides the weight to 50. She moves the middle weight swiftly across the bar to about 30 and then slowly until the balance begins to teeter at 40. She nudges the weight in small increments with her finger until the balance hovers halfway between too heavy and too light. She doesn't touch the third weight. I feel as though I'm being weighed more like a sack of potatoes than a person by the way Carol looks closely at each number like she's figuring out how much I'll cost at the register.

"Ninety-three pounds," she says, charting my weight. "Now we have a starting number as a reference."

When Carol looks at me, I notice she isn't wearing any makeup. I wonder if she woke up late this morning or if she always lets her hair and face go untouched. Although makeup, I believe, might ruin the good color that comes from her already flushed cheeks. Her eyes are soft and caring, but she looks sad as though she is brokenhearted. Something stirs inside of me; I force it to stop.

We walk back to my room, just footsteps away. Carol grabs the blood pressure equipment from the hallway, rolling it alongside her. She sits in the chair next to my bed and takes my blood pressure.

"Eighty-seven over fifty-eight," she says, charting yet another stupid detail. She takes my temperature and my pulse and charts both.

"Is this going to be an everyday thing?" I huff.

"Yes," she confirms, ignoring my frustration.

She puts her clipboard down and pulls the chair from Lottie the Loony's side of the room over to my side.

"Is she still my roommate?" I ask, pointing nonchalantly to the other side of the room.

"Yes, she is. You'll see that she is fine to room with once you get to know her."

"I don't plan on getting to know her."

"Why?"

"Because she's a freak, that's why."

"Well, regardless, she is your roommate."

We both sit in silence for a moment. *What is she still doing here?* My eyes begin to wander everywhere but to her.

"Your mom told us you haven't been eating at home," Carol begins. "Is there a reason you've made this choice?"

I don't know—maybe because I'm a fat slob. I truly feel this way most of the time. But because of Carol's bulky size I am embarrassed to talk about my weight, so I stick with a simple, "I don't know."

A tall, frumpy man pushes the same cart on wheels from last night into my room.

"You must be Anna. I'm Isaac," he says as he pushes the cart toward me.

He and Carol exchange smiles and a few quick reminders, most of which I don't understand, then he leaves. The plate of food is covered with a lid. I don't want to imagine what's under it. To the side sits an opened can of chocolate flavored Ensure and a Styrofoam cup. Just seeing it makes me mad.

How can they force me to eat? It should be up to me what and when I decide to eat, not them. Not being able to fester about it any longer, I speak up, "I want to eat alone. I don't need you watching me eat like I'm two."

"During meals someone will be with you. This won't change for a while, so it's better if you understand now that this is nonnegotiable."

She lifts the lid, and a piece of toast stares me in the face. Mini plastic cups of jam and butter are on the side.

"You'll have thirty minutes to finish your breakfast." Carol looks at me with kindness, but I know she is serious about her instructions.

"What is it with you guys and all the time restraints and my eating habits—an hour to drink this, thirty minutes to eat that. You're all obsessive," I criticize.

"Let's talk about something other than food while you eat."

I'm angry, but Carol's composure tells me she will not

engage in my frustration.

"Do you have brothers and sisters?"

I want to give her the silent treatment, but something compels me to answer. "Yes."

"How many?"

"Eight." Something stirs from deep within my gut.

"Wow! How many of each?"

I take a big breath, filling my lungs. "I'm not putting any crap on my toast even if you say I have to." I angrily pick up the toast and take a small bite, ignoring her last question. I chew and chew and chew. My stomach is in knots, and I want to explode.

"Why are you so frustrated?"

I twist my body, turning away from Carol as far as possible, which is no more than six inches considering the position of our chairs. I take another bite of my toast. Carol gets the message and picks up her chart and begins writing. *I don't care. She can write whatever she wants in her chart. It makes no difference to me.* I keep my eyes on the wall taking small bites. The toast is completely cold and crumbly. Halfway through, I put it back on the plate. I reach for the Ensure and the cup. I bring it close to my body and pour the contents in.

I can't believe they are forcing me to do this. I want to cry, but I refuse to let anyone see such weakness. I am not going to give them the upper hand. I take a sip and then another. I am disgusted at the thought of losing ground.

"You have about ten minutes to finish up."

Thinking of an idea, I look over at Carol and use my calmest possible voice, "Carol, how can everyone expect me to know what time it is if I don't have a clock in my room?"

"I'll see that you get one today." She smiles.

I take a chance as I carefully chose my words, "After I finish this...," pointing to the cup in my hand, "can we consider that I have eaten enough for now?"

"And the rest of the toast," she says.

That didn't go anywhere but downhill. I pick up the stone-cold toast and begin to take bites. I want to throw it against the wall along with the crap that I'm drinking, but I must play my cards right. I'll have a clock soon, but for now I need to concentrate on getting this food down my throat.

I finish my breakfast without a second to spare. I feel bloated and ill. I get up to use the bathroom.

Carol looks up. "Keep the door open."

"What? Why?"

"I want your food to stay down," she replies.

"Oh my God! I'm not going to throw it up. I swear. I've never done that."

"If you're going to pee, make sure to use the measuring bowl."

I walk into the bathroom and slam the door.

Oh God, what a stupid move. What am I going to do, push against the door when she tries to opens it?

I quickly open the door as Carol is reaching for the handle. I feel my heart bursting through my chest. I am embarrassed by my reaction and fearful of what she might do, but Carol doesn't even come close to commenting on what just happened. She takes a few steps back away from the door, giving me privacy. I sense she stays nearby to stop me from throwing my pee down the commode. I take the bowl, place it under the ring, and sit down. I rest my forearms on my thighs and my head in my hands. I'm completely self-conscious as I wait. It won't come. I feel it, but I can't go with someone standing right outside the bathroom door.

"Turn on the water. It will help," Carol says.

I hold my gown in place, and with my underwear still wrapped around my knees, I get up and slide over to the sink and turn on the faucet. I take a few steps back to the commode and sit down and concentrate on the water. It comes, but only enough to barely cover the bottom of the bowl. I throw the paper into the commode through a small opening behind the bowl thing. I wash my hands before turning the water off.

"I'm done," I say, furious I have to comply.

Carol picks up the bowl with her gloved hands and shows me how to read the measurement. "Thirty-three cc's," she says and flushes my pee down the commode.

"Can I do this on my own next time?"

"When we're able to get a good match of your output compared to your input, we'll talk about it, but for now, I'll chart and empty."

"Why can't I just tell you the numbers?" I ask.

Given Carol's expression, I know the conversation is over.

"I need to see other patients, but group is at ten. I will be back to get you, and...," she smiles, "I'll work on getting you that clock."

I walk back into the bathroom and look into the mirror. The so-called glass distorts my features so that my head looks lopsided and my neck elongated. I ponder what Carol said about keeping my food down. I had never tried to vomit what I had eaten, but now curiosity is getting the better of me. Girls in my high school were doing it to stay thin, but the thought of vomiting in the high school bathrooms was disgusting. I drop my head over the sink and stick my finger down my throat. *They can force me eat, but they can't make me keep it down.* I gag and shudder. The control feels good. My face wrenches with every move of my finger inching closer down my throat. Nothing happens, so I finally give up.

I look into the mirror again. I notice my small gold hoops hanging from my ears, surprised that whoever undressed me hadn't stripped me of my earrings, too. I take them out and massage my ears. Behind me are two small shelves. One has toothpaste and a toothbrush, both I assume belong to Lottie the Looney. I place my earrings on the lower, empty shelf and look around hoping to find an extra toothbrush, but there isn't one, so I steal some of Lottie's toothpaste and finger-brush my teeth.

Group? I mull it over. *Sounds like I'm going to meet a group of weirdos.*

I think of the clock I've been promised and wonder what time it would show. I guess around nine thirty, but when I lie on my bed for what seems to be forever, I assume I miscalculated the time. Something stirs again in the pit of my stomach when I think back through Carol's questions regarding my brothers and sisters. Bridgett comes to mind. I wonder what she is doing and if she realizes I wasn't in my bedroom last night. Surely she did. She is thirteen and old enough to be told that I'm on "The Fifth Floor." I worry about her. I haven't done a great job protecting her in the past months, and it saddens me to think that she is losing her older sister. I wonder if she misses me. I wonder if she is praying to God to bring me home quickly. I hope not, because I know she will be disappointed to learn that God doesn't listen. It is all a farce planted in our brains by our mother. "Ask and you shall receive. Baloney!" I mutter.

sixteen

Carol retrieves me from my room for group. We turn right, heading into the hallway with the water fountain. It is only about twelve feet long and leads to another hallway that has four bedrooms. We turn left toward a set of double doors, and beyond the double doors, the hallway continues with another three or four bedrooms. I see the lounge from a different angle now. It sits smack dab in the middle of the unit and behind it is the nurse's station. Around the opposite corner is the hallway that leads to my room. The unit is shaped like a huge H.

Tucked to the left of the nurse's station is a large room with a glass door and windows where a group of adults are sitting in a circle. Carol heads toward wooden double doors on the right and I follow. We enter. I immediately become self-conscience of my gown when I see everyone else wearing street clothes. It hadn't occurred to me before now that everyone would be dressed in something other than an awful hospital gown. I want to turn and run, but the embarrassment of being dragged back is too much for me to think about.

Everyone stares at me. *This nightmare is relentless.* Carol points to a chair. I take a seat without looking at anyone. I smell the remnants of breakfast and gather this room becomes the dining area at mealtime. Carol speaks to the group about today's schedule and the focus of today's discussion. I look up, hoping to go unnoticed.

Ten chairs are arranged in a circle. The ages of everyone in this group are much younger than the adult group, where I imagine Lottie the Looney to be at this moment. Everyone looks to be teenaged except for the three adults. Isaac and another woman, who is very pregnant, are focusing on Carol, who now I assume is the head honcho. *Oh great! How lucky am I to get the nurse who knows the most about what takes place in this prison?*

The girl sitting next to me slouches in her chair, looking as though she'd rather not be here like me, but by the fact that she is dressed in jeans and a T-shirt, I figure she is closer to getting the hell out than I am.

A kid speaks up, "Hi, I'm Ben." He speaks softly. His voice is kind, something I hadn't expected after looking into his dark eyes. When he glances to the girl sitting next to him, I take a closer look. He looks Japanese or at least Asian. There's something different about him, almost like he seems out of place here, much like the orange compared to three apples on Sesame Street's game of which-one-doesn't-belong.

"My name is Gretchen," continues the girl to the left of Ben. Her voice is playful, making her sound more like a child than a teenager, especially when she shrugs one of her shoulders and tilts her head to the same side. She slowly looks to her left, keeping everyone's attention longer than she should. She has one leg tucked under her butt and the other hanging from her chair, swinging it back and forth. I catch a full glimpse of a sore in the middle of her shin every time her leg swings forward. It looks like it's been picked more than once and having a hard time healing. *A Band-Aid would be a real plus,* I think, looking away grossed out.

Next is the very pregnant lady who looks very uncomfortable sitting in her chair. "Hello, Anna. My name is Holly. I am one of the nurses here."

I hadn't heard Carol's earlier instructions, but it doesn't take a rocket scientist to follow the pattern of introductions.

NAPERVILLE NORTH HIGH SCHOOL

Holly's voice is as sweet as her disposition. She is also beautiful. Even though she looks as though she could go into labor at any moment, her body is tall and slender. She has long blonde hair, and her facial features are perfect. Her flawless skin is nice to look at given most of the teens have acne.

A boy, who looks slightly older than me, doesn't say a word, so Holly introduces him as Robert. Robert is staring at his hands and has not lifted his head once since group started. I wonder what he is thinking. He looks incredibly sad. I can't take my eyes off of him. He is tall and very thin, like he has been underfed. He looks so alone. Something in the pit of my stomach bubbles. For some reason I want to cry for him, but I concentrate diligently, shifting my eyes to the floor and ignoring the squeezing around my chest.

The boy next to Robert chimes in, "I'm Jonny, Jonny Love. My last name is Love so please call me Jonny Love."

How about I call you nothing? I quickly regret my thought. He actually looks like a nice boy but completely out of touch with reality by the way he's grinning senselessly. *Next! Let's get this over with already.*

"Hopefully, you remember me from this morning. I'm Isaac. I will be working with you most weekends, and I look forward to getting to know you better."

Not if I can help it, you won't. Isaac has a nice smile and innocent look, like a guy I can convince of most anything. I softly smile back at him.

The girl sitting next to me turns toward me. "I'm Addy."

She seems uninterested in why I'm here, and I like this about her right away. Even her introduction was telling. She hadn't said anything more than what was required. She seems more like me than the others and someone who I can possibly foresee as an ally.

Stares are now focusing on me. I try to muster up a strong voice. "I'm Anna," I say, quickly moving my eyes to the left, setting them on the fat kid who has been blowing his nose into a hanky during the introductions. *What a nerd. Who uses a hanky anymore? And I swear if you pass your germs on to me, I'll slaughter you.*

"I'm Ethan." He smiles and then blows. He's left with something hanging from his nose, so I look away. Jonny Love clears his throat to grab Ethan's attention about the last blow, and without missing a beat, Ethan blows again cleaning up the earlier mess.

We circle back to Carol, and she reminds the group of today's discussion. "Let's discuss issues you may have encountered in the past week that were difficult to resolve."

For the love of God, is she kidding? I have to sit here listening to problems. There is no way in hell I am spilling my guts for anyone. Nobody here is getting that kind of satisfaction from me. No way in hell.

I don't open my mouth, not even once, but Jonny Love does. And so do Gretchen and Ethan. Ben stays quiet most of the time, but when he does speak, he shares his thoughts on what others have said instead of speaking about himself. Robert continues to stare at his hands, never moving a muscle. I keep my eyes at a distance from him in hopes not to get too wrapped up in his thinking. Addy and I pretend to be listening, but we aren't. We both say nothing.

Ninety minutes later group finally ends. I immediately head toward my room, but Carol intersects my path and has me follow her across the lounge toward the big room where the adults are still meeting. We turn right and go through a locked door that is buzzed opened by a nurse in the station. Inside there is a bathroom, two empty rooms, and two rooms with doctor's equipment, so I guess I am here for a physical. Carol takes me into one of the rooms and introduces me to Dr. Pins. I chuckle to myself. *What a shitty name for a doctor.*

He smiles with his lips pressed together. "How are you, young lady?" He pats the examining table, instructing me to hop up. I have a feeling Dr. Pins has been a doctor for a long time by the looks of his wrinkled forehead and nearly bald head. The only hair he has is around the sides and back, and it's pretty much gray. He reminds me of Alfred Hitchcock but without the double chin and with a friendlier mood. I like the way he gently moves my hair away from my ears when he checks them. He checks my nose and throat before he asks Carol for my chart. He flips through a couple of pages. I assume to read my weight and blood pressure from this morning.

His eyebrows rise. "Ninety-three pounds isn't enough for a developing young lady."

I look down. He is matter of fact, and I have no intention of conversing with him. He asks me to lower my gown. I redden from embarrassment. He listens to my heart and lungs before asking me to lie back. He presses his stethoscope to my belly and listens intently. He presses hard on my abdomen. I wince, grabbing for his hand.

"Does that hurt?"

I nod. "Yes."

"You need to get your bowels moving, and once they do, you'll feel much better."

I am completely mortified at this point and want to disappear. *Is there no such thing as privacy?* Dr. Pins helps me place my arms back into my two gowns.

"Do you have any questions for me?" he asks.

I shake my head no.

"Okay, young lady, work on getting some meat on your bones."

Carol and I walk back toward my room while other patients follow the scent of food through the double doors where our group session was held, confirming my guess that the room is also the dining area. A large brown bag is on my desk. I automatically think my clothes have been returned, but I feel reluctant to ask about its contents. The cart on wheels is here too with a tray and a covered plate. A can of Ensure is placed next to the plate, this time vanilla flavored.

Carol pulls up a chair for herself from across the room. I sit in the chair near the cart.

"We can talk while you eat." Carol smiles and points to the windup clock on my nightstand. "You'll have thirty minutes."

How didn't I notice it first thing? "Awesome. Thanks."

"You're welcome."

I uncover my plate. There is a fresh cup of strawberries and purple grapes, a strawberry yogurt, and a small cup of prunes soaking in prune juice. *They can't be serious. I'm not eating those rancid things.*

I resist throwing a fuss about eating because no one cares to listen to my complaints. Carol, Chad, and Dr. Ellison are serious about the consequences of me trying to starve myself, so I give in for now with Carol's eagle eye on me.

"How did you feel in group this morning?" Carol asks.

I pick up each grape one at a time and push them into my mouth unwillingly and slowly. Then I pick through the strawberries. I can't handle the prunes, so I leave them on my plate as I open the yogurt.

"It's just the two of us now, so I'm thinking you might be more comfortable talking about what's on your mind. Or do you have questions I can answer?" *Nope.* I finish the strawberries and pick up the can of Ensure. The vanilla tastes just as bad as the chocolate, but I force it down. Finally, I consume everything except for the three slimy prunes.

"I hate prunes. And...they smell like dirt," I hiss.

"Today you'll eat them, but you can easily avoid them tomorrow by ordering for yourself." Carol pulls a half-sheet menu from underneath my plate. She hands me a pencil. I look at it. I have several choices for tomorrow's lunch. Prunes are listed.

"I'll make sure those aren't checked," I remark,

blackening over it with the pencil.

I begin to fester about eating the prunes. Five minutes to go and my anger grows with every passing minute. I want to yell and scream, but I hold strong to my composure. I slip a prune into my mouth and begin to gag. The next two are just as horrible. Seven minutes pass, and I'm glad I stand my ground and don't finish on time. I push the tray away from me. "Disgusting," I fume.

Carol finally mentions the bag on my desk. "Your mother dropped off a few things for you to make your stay more comfortable." *Hmmm...must be a key or a coiled rope inside.* I want to know if she's brought clothes, but I don't ask.

"Is she still here? Can I see her?" I ask hurriedly.

"No, she's not here at the moment, but you will get many opportunities to see her, Anna."

My hopes sink with desperation.

"I will be back later," Carol says, pushing the cart out of the room as she leaves.

I quickly move to the desk and open the bag. No clothes are inside, and immediately I'm disappointed. There is however a new tube of toothpaste, my toothbrush, and deodorant. I pull out pads and tampons, and I'm grossly horrified that my mother has packed these things. It doesn't look like my private stash from underneath my bathroom sink at home, and I redden thinking she has recently bought the items. *Oh God! The humiliation.*

Female issues were never discussed at home. I thought I was crapping in my pants for a week before I finally gathered enough courage to tell my mother something was wrong. She cornered me in my bedroom later the same day to explain what was happening. I was horrified. She explained how to use pads, which were about six inches thick with ties to be strung through a sanitary belt. Then, just because I wasn't horrified enough, I heard snickering coming from the hallway right outside my bedroom door. When I turned sixteen and began driving, I fended for myself, but before then, I found a new box of pads in the cabinet underneath the bathroom sink almost every month. I figured it was my mother's doing but dreaded asking.

I feel ill with the memory as I continue to pull things from the bag. Soap, a brush, gum, a couple Payday candy bars, and a deck of cards. I blush again when I pull four pair of underwear from the bag but happy to see that someone is thinking clearly about my needs. The last item I pull from the bag is a pair of white snuggies for my feet, the kind with little pom-pom balls attached to the backs.

Well aware of the probability of someone entering my room at any given second, I quickly put my socks and underwear in my nightstand drawer and hurry to the bathroom to stash my private things underneath the sink. I find nothing but small bath towels stored in the cabinet, assuring me that Loony Lottie hasn't claimed the space for herself. I'm out of breath from the mad dash and feeling dizzy, so I grab hold of the sink for a moment to regain my steadiness. I put the rest of the items in the lower drawer of my nightstand and walk over to my bed to lie down. I feel a difference in the pillow. Last night it felt stiff, but now it feels soft. I look closely and then smile. It's mine from home but covered in a hospital pillowcase. I reposition it under my head only once before I snuggle into its softness. I direct my eyes toward the clock. The time is twenty minutes after one. The ticktock absorbs the quietness. I close my eyes.

Slowly walking to her gravesite, I see a large bag which is tied at the top. Knowing the horror that lies inside does not stop me from reaching for the tie and undoing the knot. Inside are bones. "Oh God! Please, help me, somebody." I begin to run. Liz appears, close at my heels, chasing me. "Don't! Please don't kill me," I scream. In her hand, held high above her head, is the butcher knife that belongs behind the stove in my mother's kitchen. Out of breath, I continue to run toward the water pump. This is my safe place. I need to make it there before Liz catches me. Stretching my hands to reach for it...

I wake with a jerk and in a sweat. My two gowns are soaked through to my bed sheets. My breath is heavy but slows as I become familiar with my surroundings. The daylight coming in from the window has made my recovery quicker than normal. I look over to see the time and notice Lottie is lying on her bed staring at the ceiling. She gives me the creeps. Not wanting to distract her, I shift my eyes slowly to the clock. Three fifteen. I shift back to my original position and feel vulnerable lying on my back knowing at any moment Lottie, just steps away, could be over me, scratching at the walls like a caged rat. The image is horrifying yet comical, in some kind of sick way.

The hallways are very quiet, and it makes me a bit nervous. I consider sneaking across to the laundry room to fetch new sheets and gowns. I slowly crawl out of bed and move toward the bedroom door, trying not to disturb Lottie whose eyes are now closed. This brings me some comfort, hoping she has fallen asleep. I peek out past my door and neither see nor hear anyone.

Good God! The place is dead silent. Kind of spooky. Pushing myself a little farther out, I notice the nurse's station crowded with double the nurses than earlier and at least three or four doctors. *Changing of the guards*, I assume.

They appear to be deep in discussion, so I take my chances and dart across the hall to the laundry room. I stop and listen once I'm in. Nothing. I excitedly grab sheets and several gowns and get ready for my return. I dart out and back into my bedroom and nervously close the door and lean against it feeling light-headed. My shallow breathing is making it difficult to focus. "Hold it together," I murmur, looking over at Lottie to make sure she's not on the prowl.

I walk quietly to my nightstand drawer to fetch my

underwear and snuggies, opening it slowly, trying to avoid any quick movements. I reach the bathroom and close the door, twisting the handle, silencing any contact. *Damn, I wish this thing locked!* Placing my elbows on the sink and lowering my head into my hands for a short time seems to make my dizziness more manageable. I take two towels from underneath the sink, turn on the shower, undress, and hop in underneath the hot water. The hot water feels heavenly. I lean against the shower wall and let it run over my entire body. I reach for my soap and cover myself in a thick layer of suds, using it for my hair too when I realize I have no shampoo. It takes quite some time to rinse out, and even then my hair feels stringy like it does when I've been swimming. I turn off the water and listen. Not a sound. I dress in two fresh gowns and snuggies. I am grateful to have deodorant and a brush. I turn to retrieve my earrings, but they're gone.

"What the hell?" I whisper, looking around.

Carol must have discovered them while I was sleeping, and I get the creeps thinking she was in my room while I slept. I stash my used gowns and towels in the closet and place my dirty underwear in a drawer so that it doesn't touch any of the other contents. I strip my bed and add the dirty sheets to my laundry pile.

"Shit!" I scowl, having forgotten to grab a clean pillowcase.

I quietly make my bed, and it feels more like my own. Tired of lying around, I scoot to the head of my bed, positioning myself against the headboard so I can see Lottie from the corner of one eye. I begin to think of my task, which is to get out of here. *I've got to be calm and willing to do what I'm asked. Sit and listen to others spill their guts. How hard can this be?* I make a mental list.

Clothes.

Gain weight. *This will take strategy.* I don't plan on gaining weight for their purposes, and besides, I like my slender look and plan on keeping it this way.

Tell anyone who probes for information what they need to hear.

Build alliances.

My hearing instantly heightens when I hear stirring from the other bedrooms. Others are beginning to move about, and I'm thankful it's not just Looney Tunes and me left behind in this prison.

"Sleep, crazy one," I speak softly toward Lottie, waving my fingers as if I'm placing a spell on her. I giggle.

Unfortunately, she rises from her bed like a mummy and makes her way across the room. I catch a glimpse of her distressed face and unbrushed hair and my earrings hanging from her ears. *What's going on here? She's a klepto too!*

"Hey! Those are my earrings!" I shout.

She mumbles incoherently as she enters the bathroom. She flushes, but I don't hear her wash her hands. *Gross!* The bathroom door opens, and I am right there to greet her— ready to rip the earrings from her ears. As she pushes past me, I notice the earrings are gone. I dodge into the bathroom and find them where I put them last. I grab toilet paper to pick them up, moving them to one of my nightstand drawers, being careful not to touch their contamination.

Chad's sudden knock on the door startles me. He is carrying my chart and a few other loose papers.

"How's it going?" he asks.

"I really need my clothes."

"I agree!" He pulls up Lottie's chair as I take a seat in my chair. "I want to go over this with you," he says, handing me a chart with a schedule for each day. A signature line appears next to every movement I am supposed to make. Even more humiliating, rewards for good behavior are listed on the bottom of the paper.

What is this? Elementary school? I intend to scream my thoughts, but decide I will be better off if I keep my feelings to myself. I anticipate playing their game for a while until I can make it my own.

"After you accomplish each task," he continues, "one of us will sign it. Once you earn so many signatures, you can choose something you might like to do." *Leave.*

Phone call home is listed as a reward—*for the lovely price of only fifteen signatures.* Leave isn't listed.

"Each week, depending on your progress and needs, your schedule will change and so will your rewards." He smiles. "It seems overwhelming at first, but you'll get the hang of it by the end of the day."

I'm angry at the idea of having someone sign my chart every time I sneeze, but Chad's smile somehow brings me down off the edge. His eyes appear genuine and empathetic even though he knows nothing about me. He sits tall, unintentionally showing off his confidence and brilliance that seems to be wrapped up in a whole lot of seriousness.

"When your mom left last night, it surprised me to see that neither of you hugged," Chad says, trying to gain insight to my family life.

"We don't hug."

"Why not?" he continues.

I shrug my shoulders. "I don't know. Never have."

"Your mom has never hugged you?"

"Probably when I was a baby."

"Do you want to be hugged?"

"No." *Where is he going with this?* I'm puzzled by why he is showing concern about something so insignificant.

"Why not?"

"I don't know...I'd feel stupid if I hugged her. We don't do that in my family."

"Never?"

"Nope, never. Seriously, it's not an issue. I don't think about it because it's not about hugs and kisses and all that crap."

"What is it about?" he says, putting emphasis on "is."

Oh my God! When is this going to stop? What does he need to hear? Think, Anna, think...play his game. "My mother likes me. She doesn't need to hug me for me to know that," I say.

"How does she show her love for you?" *Likes, I said likes.*

"She brought me here, didn't she?" I respond harshly, hoping he gets my sarcasm.

"Yes, she did, Anna," he replies, ignoring my sarcastic remark. "How about at home?"

"She lets me use her car pretty much whenever I want."

"Anything else?"

"She gets up in the middle of night, no matter what time I call for her."

"Why do you call her for?"

"After a nightmare, she..." I stop. I realize I have just made a terrible mistake.

"Tell me about your nightmares."

Easy...stay calm. "I wouldn't call them nightmares really. They're just dreams I have sometimes. Honestly, I can't remember the last time I dreamed."

Except for the one I had an hour ago and yesterday and the night before that and all the years before that. "Tell me what happened," my mother would say, but I couldn't. I could not let it resurface. It was so frightening, bringing it to the forefront was not an option I could bear.

Chad disrupts my deep thought. "Do you like to write?"

"Yes."

"Would you consider journaling about your dreams so they're easier to remember?"

Play his game. "Sure." *Yeah right! Fat chance I'm telling anyone about the crazy nightmares I possess.*

"I'll make sure you get a journal." Chad stirs in his chair, giving me hope that this Q & A has finally come to an end. He takes my chart and signs next to One-on-One Session. "I'll bring your dinner at five."

I look over toward the clock. That's in twenty minutes.

"Tomorrow you will eat breakfast in the dining room with the other patients. I'll make sure you have your clothes before you go to bed tonight." He's pleased with my smile.

I study my chart. Monday through Friday have the exact same schedule. There are ten possible signatures per day: one for weight gain, three for the breakfast, lunch, and dinner, one for group session, another two for one-on-one sessions, one for arts and crafts, and two for Ensure which is listed next to two and seven o'clock. *With meals too? How many are they going to force me to drink?*

I think back to today's group session. Surely I can get the fat kid to indulge in some of my food during mealtime. As for weight gain, I need to drink a lot of water before Carol comes for me in the morning. I reach over to my clock and turn it over to see if it has an alarm. It does. I set it for six thirty and place it back on the nightstand. *Easy enough.*

Chad arrives with my dinner at five o'clock on the dot.

"Lucky me," I sneer. I lift the cover off the plate, deciding not to complain. I begin eating the chicken noodle soup that is grossly lukewarm. I crumble the crackers on top so I am not told later I must finish everything. My lack of control is driving me mad. I don't need to be told to eat or dress or go there and come here.

"Is your family planning on taking a vacation this summer?" Chad asks.

"Maybe to Texas."

"Where in Texas?"

I tell him we might drive to Fort Worth to visit my sister Meg. I finish my soup and start in on the salad that is nothing more than iceberg lettuce and two grape tomatoes. I drizzle on a small amount of Italian dressing to help it slide down, hoping I am safe from being asked to drink the rest of it later.

"Are you going anywhere?" I ask, showing Chad my civil

side.

"My wife and I are going to the Warren Dunes in Michigan. We camp there. Have you ever been?"

"No." He doesn't mention any kids, so I assume he's just married or doesn't want them. *I can't blame him for that.*

We continue our chitchat as I pick up my chocolate Ensure, deciding to drink it right from the can. He doesn't mention a time limit which has me thinking it's because I'm playing by his rules.

"Did you get a chance to look at your schedule for the week?" Chad asks.

"Uh-huh."

"Any questions?"

"How many Ensures do I have to drink every day?"

"Just two. They won't come with your meals after today."

I show no emotion. I finish my drink, wanting to vomit from the taste. I place the can on the tray. Chad reminds me to fill out my menu for tomorrow, which I do. I mark cottage cheese with pears and an apple. I figure the kitchen will send more food, considering the sticker on the bottom of my menu has written in big bold letters, "2200 calorie diet," but I can't bear to order any other offered choices. I give my menu and chart to Chad. He signs next to Dinner.

"Two signatures, whoop de doo." I roll my eyes out of Chad's line of sight.

"Gretchen and Addy and some of the others are watching TV. Why don't you join them?" Chad says.

"I don't want to."

"Well if you change your mind, I think it's *Cosby* night."

I don't change my mind. *Two signatures.* I look at my chart again and then tuck it away in my nightstand drawer. I lie on my bed, forcing my eyes open each time they close, worried someone will see me sleeping so early. But when I can't force myself awake any longer, I climb under my covers, glad the day is over.

seventeen

We sit in the same chairs as yesterday except for Jonny Love and Ben, who have switched places. And Holly, who I suspect got out of coming today because a man is sitting in her place. I notice two things about him right away: his gold, stud earring—his mullet makes it easy to notice—and his easygoing way. He and Jonny Love are talking about lakes and good sailing, like a conversation best friends from college might have. He eyes me and then smiles, showing his perfectly straight and white teeth. "Hi, Anna. I'm Daniel, another MHT. Welcome."

"Thanks."

"We are discussing family memories today," Carol says, "favorite and least favorite. Who would like to go first?"

Gretchen and Jonny Love raise their hands at the same time. *Not surprising.* I look at Robert. He's staring at his hands like yesterday.

"How about ladies first?" Isaac says.

Gretchen adjusts herself in her chair as though being called first means she's more important than everyone else. She pulls her hair into a ponytail and then lets it drop to her shoulders. She seems to be enjoying the attention because she stares at the ceiling for way too long, thinking of what to say. "I guess...hangin' with my friends is my favorite thing to do."

She totally misses the point, so Daniel redirects her back to family memories. Gretchen giggles and returns her eyes toward the ceiling. She comes up with a memory of some vacation to Idaho. Or maybe it was Iowa. Her worst memory, she says, is getting in trouble when she "hangs with her friends." She acts like she is twelve, but I figure she is around fifteen. She's immature and somebody I don't want as a friend. I guess we're supposed to give our two cents of advice because the others comment and ask questions, which apparently Gretchen finds amusing. I choose not to participate.

Jonny Love gently sways his hands in rhythm to his gentle voice as he speaks, kind of like he is on drugs. His stringy hair hangs in his eyes. His head looks too heavy for him by the way it juts forward. Both knees in his jeans have holes, and his belt is buckled in the last possible hole, making him look skinnier than he probably is. "I love being at my father's cabin," he says.

Perfect. To the point. Let's move on. Daniel obviously doesn't like this shortened version, so he asks Jonny what he enjoys the most about his father's cabin.

"The trees, I guess. The way they swish when the wind blows. Sometimes it's the only sound around, and it's kind of nice."

He talks about how there's no fighting at the cabin, so I figure his parents are going through a divorce. He's really quirky but genuine, and I like him. I can't imagine we'd have much of a connection, but I think if I needed a favor, he'd honor it, no questions asked.

Ethan volunteers next. I feel sorry for this kid in a pitiful kind of why. He looks as though he's easy pickins, and I can bet he is teased at school and friendless. He describes his memories as joyous, not a typical word for a kid his age. He doesn't have a least favorite family memory, so Isaac encourages him to think outside of family. He mentions school...and *Bingo*, I am right. It saddens me to hear how he is bullied. Ethan's heart is big and soft and kind. I feel bad thinking that I too am planning on using him to eat some of my food, but his extra weight has me guessing he'll be easier to convince than the others in the group.

Addy, who I didn't think was listening, speaks up, "You're a big guy. Beat 'em up, why don't cha!"

A few snickers let loose around the circle. I am disappointed in Addy, not because of her comment, but by the way she said it, arrogantly taunting Ethan.

"That's not good advice, Addy," Daniel comments.

I look over to Ethan as a teardrop runs down his right cheek. He wipes it away with his hanky.

"Hey man, I didn't mean to make you cry. I just wouldn't stand for that. You gotta show 'em you got balls." At least she isn't making fun of him. Maybe she's not so bad.

Ben moves slightly in his chair so he's facing Ethan. He looks ready to say something but hesitates. The adults seem ready to listen as though Ben acts this way every single time he's about to speak. "They uncover your weakness so theirs can stay hidden, but for every weakness they uncover in you, remember theirs are far greater." *What the hell was that?*

There's more discussion on how to help Ethan, but I find myself focusing on Ben. He has a look of confidence and poise. His comments are obviously well thought out, making his point difficult to argue. I'm attracted to him, not because of his looks, but because he's a mystery. He gives just enough information in order for others to think they know him well, but I guess they probably don't know him at all. I question why he is here on the fifth floor.

When Ben tells us his memories, he doesn't say much. I wait for someone to question him further, but no one does, and it frustrates me. I have always had a way of figuring out what makes people tick, but Ben is different. He is using the same tactic I have used most of my life—avoid the past. I wonder if he is studying me at this very moment, confused and puzzled as well. My desire to know him grows with every passing moment, not to uncover his secrets, but because across the room, I am looking into a human mirror—staring at the same eyes, same expressions, same character as me—and Ben is looking back.

I come to attention when Carol asks me to share my memories. After Ben, I had stopped listening. Now I feel cursed for not allowing myself time to think up some kind of story—real or not—I don't really care. *Wait a minute. Did Robert speak and I missed it?* I quickly glance over. He hasn't moved an inch, so I figure Carol isn't counting him.

I begin with a lie, sort of. "I like to travel with my family." I had only been on one vacation where it wasn't just Bridg and me. It was to Texas with Marie and Frances, and I think Timmy or Kyle, but I don't exactly remember.

"As for my least favorite memory," I add, "it would have to be..." Christmas comes to mind immediately, "sharing a room with so many sisters."

I can't think straight. I don't share a room; it's just Bridg and me living at home now. And when I shared a room with my four sisters, I loved it—every minute of it. It was Marie who hated sharing our tiny room with her little sisters. I stop my nerves from giving away my anxiety. I glance around the circle trying desperately to muster up a smile. I decide it's better not to contribute anything else.

When group ends, I watch Robert get up from his chair and walk slowly toward the double doors. I follow but act like I'm not. His head is down as he walks so slowly that his arms dangle limp from his shoulders. His pants barely hang on to his hips, so he holds on with one hand before they slip down completely. He turns right and disappears into the first bedroom across from the nurse's station. I follow him.

I peer into his room, leaning forward just enough to go unnoticed. He is sitting against the wall just beyond the door. His lanky legs are pulled up to his chest, and his bent arms rest in between them, curled up like a frightened and abused animal. I'm paralyzed as I watch him in such distress. My insides swell, my nose begins to sting, and my throat tightens. My self-control seems to be weakening, but I talk myself through it, "Breathe."

I walk a few steps to the opposite wall where the nurses' windows surround the station. I lower myself below the window and lean against the wall so that I am directly across from Robert. He still hasn't moved. I pull my knees up to my chest and cradle them with my arms; my eyes focused on Robert as I rest my chin upon my knees. I feel every pump of blood pushing through my heart; my hearing is heightened so each heartbeat is magnified. I deeply connect with Robert's sadness. He looks desperate and abandoned. By the way he is curled into a tight ball, I believe he has been ridiculed and humiliated. My heart aches. I can't stop thinking he has lost whatever was keeping him alive; a final blow that pierced his inner soul. And then my mind screams, wanting him to hear me.

Get up Robert! Don't give in! You can win! Run! Run, Robert! Don't let them catch you! My head feels as though it's about to explode. Buzzing creeps into my ears, getting louder with every passing moment, and then my mind goes blank.

I find myself in bed covered with two blankets. At my bedside, Chad sits in a chair. I don't know exactly how I got here, but I recall being helped down the hallway. I open my eyes and connect with Chad's. I can see the clear, blue ocean with dancing waves sparkling through his gaze. He smiles at me. Mesmerized, I don't return the gesture. I think he might storm me with questions, but he doesn't.

I move onto my side, facing Lottie's bed. I bend my knees slightly, so I feel less exposed under the blankets. I place my hands on my pillow and rest my head upon them. I stare out the window, and Chad moves his eyes there too. I shift my eyes to the clock with one swift glance. It's almost four. I think about Robert as I continue to stare into the clouds. I'm not sure why I had decided to keep watch over him, but I did. And nobody could alter my watch outside his bedroom door.

eighteen

Carol introduces me to another shrink doctor. I follow him to one of the conference rooms where I usually meet with Dr. Ellison for therapy. As soon as he unloads his briefcase with some inkblot pictures, I know what they are. I had taken a psychology class last year and learned about the Rorschach Inkblot test. I roll my eyes. *Is he kidding me?*

Dr. What's-his-Name explains the test. I have no intention of giving him the pleasure of analyzing my life with a few answers to some freaky pictures. He pulls out the first picture. I tell him it looks like an eagle because it truly does. The second picture is somewhat similar to the first, so I say eagle again. He writes a few words and moves on. The third inkblot looks nothing like an eagle, but I say it does. I do the same with the fourth and the fifth before he puts the inkblots down and looks directly at me for the first time.

"I can see you are not going to cooperate," he says exasperated, looking over his glasses that have slipped so far down his nose they teeter on the edge of his last attached skin cell.

"Why do you think that?" I taunt. "Do you see something other than eagles?"

He stares at me for a moment more. "I am going to continue through the pictures. If you see anything other than eagles, speak up."

When he continues, I give answers like tomato and boot but nothing I think might alarm him. He shows me the second to last picture, and something stirs inside me. One blob looks like a young girl lying on a bed, and the blob next to it looks as though the mother is trying to comfort the girl. My throat and chest tighten. Dr. Inkblot must notice my reaction because he asks me if my father ever abused me.

"What?" I scream. "You are sick!"

I want to throw a dagger through his heart. I want to jump over the table and grab him by the throat, but I am too concerned with my next breath. The inkblot is not my father, it's me, trying to cover Liz with an afghan as she lies dying on the couch.

Snapshots begin to flash, one right after another, filling my head—a vivid picture of Liz being dressed and taken from her bed, then the car, and then the driveway. I see a flash of myself at my parents' bedroom window and then a flash of Frances walking up the steps. Flashes of a bed and under the covers are the two of us, Liz and I, but the next flash shows only me, alone. *She's gone!* I want to scream, but I can't.

My breathing stops after a cry escapes from my lips. I hear a loud buzzing in my ears as dizziness swells my head. The room closes in on me and then expands quickly. My grip on the chair weakens. Unable to force my lungs to exhale, I fall limp in my chair.

Later, Dr. Ellison tells me my medication is to blame for my fainting spell and that she has cut back the dosage, but I know better. I haven't told anyone what I had seen before I fell unconscious, but I believe the flashing images are to blame for sending me into oblivion.

THE SECOND WEEK on the fifth floor is never ending. Dr. Ellison probes my psyche for information that I simply don't have. She's relentless, usually carrying on the entire hour, keeping me from joining the others in the art room for arts and crafts, which is where I'd rather be than answering questions. I spent two days staring at the wall, refusing to talk, before realizing my tactic was more of a punishment for me than Dr. Ellison, who caught up on charts as I gave her the silent treatment. Today, I give in.

"I don't know how to answer your questions," I say, avoiding the insane quiet of the last two days. Dr. Ellison closes the binder she opened in preparation for my silence. Just the thought of her being one up on me drives me crazy.

"Answer honestly. When I ask a question, you need to tell me what you are thinking, not what you think is safe to say. You can tell me anything."

"I am telling you everything," I say, knowing I'm not because she can't possibly understand everything like she says she can.

"Are you willing to talk about your family today?"

"Like what?"

"Well, let's start with one sibling." I tense afraid of what she is asking. "You choose," she says, relaxing my nerves.

"Maybe Frances?"

"What can you tell me about Frances?"

"She's the oldest."

"How old is she?"

"Thirty."

"Does she live around here? Do you do things together?"

"She lives..." I search for reasons why I shouldn't answer, carefully thinking through the question, knowing nothing good ever comes from quick answers, "in Plainfield," I say.

What now? After Frances, then Jim, and then she'll want to know about everyone else. I don't want to sit in silence but talking means revealing things she won't understand, like Chad asking why we don't hug, or Carol asking why I don't eat, and then on and on. These are things I can't explain; it's just the way they are.

"Everything is confusing," I say, placing my hands over my face.

"What's confusing?" Dr. Ellison asks, reaching over the

table, slightly pulling at one arm, wanting me to uncover my face.

I put my hands back in my lap. "I don't know, just everything. Please can I go?"

"What is confusing you?"

I sit back, wanting to go into silent mode. I want to show her I can be just as persistent and stubborn and relentless as she is.

"This. This whole thing. I don't even understand why I'm here. I don't need to be here. I'm eating aren't I? And you said my kidneys are fine, so why can't I go home?"

"You are here because of why you chose to stop eating."

"That's easy," I say, straightening up in my chair and firmly planting my feet on the floor in frustration. "I was on a diet, that's all. My mother got freaked out about it. God, I swear it's nothing more than that."

Dr. Ellison goes quiet, letting me calm down, and when I do, I realize I have said too much. I know quiet is good, and I have broken my own rules, setting myself up for torment all because of this stupid therapy session. I race back through the last ten minutes, noting what I had said, analyzing what could come of it. Losing ground had not been my intention. *Quiet is good.*

"We'll talk more tomorrow," Dr. Ellison finally says after ten very long minutes.

I get up to leave, and Dr. Ellison opens my binder. I wonder what she is writing. Maybe she is writing something fascinating about Frances being thirty and living in Plainfield. *I doubt it.*

GROUP AND ONE-on-one sessions, along with other activities throughout the days, finally earn me enough signatures to have visitors.

My parents are the first to visit, and it's awkward. I don't have anything to say. Nor do they, although my mother is much better at trying to keep the conversation going than I am. My father, on the other hand, gets himself a cup a coffee before entering my room. He sips on it as my mom and I try to make conversation. When his coffee is gone, my dad gets up from his chair, throws his cup away, and puts his hands into his front pants pockets and jingles his coins. He does this a lot at home when he's bored and waiting for my mother to finish whatever she is doing before they go somewhere. He finally leaves to pace the hallways, making me less anxious.

I have mixed feeling about my father. I think all of us do. When he's home, I feel like he'd rather be somewhere else than around us, and yet when people from outside our family speak of him, I feel like I am wrong. I answered the phone once to hear his secretary on the other end; the only time I can ever remember anyone, including my father, calling from his work. She introduced herself. I had never heard of her, so I figured she had never heard of me, but she had. "Oh, Anna," she said. "You are the ninth child, right? I've heard so much about you." I was totally taken by surprise. I handed the phone to my mother. That was about four years ago. I always wanted to ask my father about his work since then, but because I was unsure if he'd willingly explain his work or selfishly disregard my questions, I stopped myself from doing so. I figure he is good at whatever he does because of his college education. My mom reminds us that most people didn't go to college back in her day, so when my dad called her on the phone to ask her out on a date, she was thrilled.

My brothers occasionally mention camping and fishing trips with my father when they were young, but otherwise, I know very little of him. He provides for us, in a survival kind of way. I have a roof over my head and good shoes on my feet, as my mother often reminds us. "And good doctors and dentists," she adds, as if this is the most important detail in growing up. Since I'm on the fifth floor, I suspect survival consists of more than pink gums and well-made shoes.

By the end of our visit, I persuade my mother to smuggle a mirror onto the fifth floor the next time she visits. I want to actually see what food lingers in my teeth or how terrible my face looks. She agrees. I admire this side of my mother's personality—trusting her kids without question.

nineteen

I am more accepting of Chad and Carol and their efforts to get me to talk about my past, but still there is little to offer. Carol is prompt with the everyday schedule of taking my weight and blood pressure. I become angry stepping on the scale, seeing my weight creep up, knowing the fifth floor is gaining control. Carol seems happy with my progress. But for me it feels like a kick in the gut, losing a battle I don't plan to lose. So when I step from the scale, I decide to play the game with new rules.

Ethan, as I predicted, is more than happy to eat a piece of bacon or a portion of my sandwich at every meal. We become table buddies with a system of handing food under the table or casually passing it right in front of everyone's eyes while the nurse in charge is busy helping other patients. It becomes so systematic that I have to monitor myself carefully so not to mess it up. The other teens have become my allies, although there was never a time we all swore to it. Even Robert, who seldom looks up from his plate, has somehow given me a vibe that he is part of our inner circle.

Turns out that after a few days of giving my food away piece-by-piece, my weight gain halts—stuck on 95.2 for two days. Carol checks the numbers twice to make sure they are right. *Crap!* If I don't counteract Ethan's love for food with a new plan, I know Carol will figure it out. The next morning, my alarm buzzes at six thirty, and I hurry to the bathroom. Cupping my hands to fill with water, I drink as much as I possibly can. I jump back into bed pretending to be just waking when Carol enters the room at seven. She's pleased with my weight gain as she charts 95.5.

I have to pee so badly it's painful. I walk in the bathroom like nothing out of the ordinary, but when I get the door closed, I am almost doubled over. I don't want Carol becoming suspicious, but with her standing right outside the door, it's nearly impossible managing the flow, stopping it at the right moment so what's in the bowl looks typical of every other morning. I can barely straighten up, but I manage to pull my pajama bottoms up and walk out. Carol walks in with her chart. *Holy Moses! Is she ever going to leave!* She takes my blood pressure so slowly I want to rip the cuff off my arm and the stethoscope from her ears. Even her movements seem slowed.

Holding my legs together tightly, I don't think I can make it the few steps I need to take before wetting myself. I pause, waiting for a wave of relief before I bolt. The pee pours out of me before I am fully sitting on the seat. After what seems like five minutes, I listen from inside the bathroom to make sure Carol hasn't returned. I turn the faucet on full force, hoping it might mask the flush. I wait until the water tank fills before putting on my game face in case someone is near when I open the door. I walk out, undiscovered.

I improve my strategy by the next day, waking at six forty-five to drink water and then waiting fifteen minutes after Carol leaves before turning on the shower to mask the sound of the flush. Jonny Love, who is always up early walking the halls, participates in my routine by stopping by my room at quarter to seven just to make sure I'm up.

"Psst! Psst! Anna, you up? It's six forty-five."

I crack open the bathroom door. "Yeah, I know. Thanks."

Almost a week in and my weight gain stops, so I figure I won't be able to engage in this charade too much longer. Tonight, after giving half my dinner away to Ethan, I sneak over to the water fountain and gulp water, hoping to add to my morning weight, but it backfires completely. At around seven, I pee what I think to be the appropriate amount to satisfy Chad.

"Hey Chad," I whisper into the nurse's station where he is writing in someone's chart. He looks up. "I used the bathroom." My face reddens. I have gotten used to telling Carol and Virginia and even Isaac without reddening, but every time I flag down Chad about my bathroom business, I am absolutely mortified

"Great. I'll check it in a minute."

I join Addy in the lounge, watch TV, and hope he will check it sooner than later. I don't want Lottie to use the bathroom with my pee in there. I never know how she might react. I wouldn't put it past her to come out yelling that someone left a potty chair in her bathroom. The thought makes me sick. *If anyone finds out, they'll...Oh God, Chad... hurry, please.* ESP, I guess, because Chad makes his way down to my bedroom.

Ten minutes pass. *It's taking too long.* My stare leaves the TV and settles in the direction of my room. The way Chad is walking toward me tells me something is wrong. He sees me looking his direction. He doesn't say a word but motions with his finger for me to come with him. *Holy crap! This cannot be good.*

We reach the bedroom, and Chad points to one of the chairs ordering me to sit. Moving the other chair to mirror mine, Chad sits down, our knees almost touching. I don't want to look at him, but he orders my eyes on his. My face swells and my chest tightens. I am embarrassed to be caught doing something this humiliating. *This is not happening. Why couldn't this be Carol or Dr. Ellison sitting across from me? Anyone but this gorgeous man.*

"You know why I've asked you here, correct?"

I hadn't heard Chad's voice this stern before. I nod

without a word. Silence fills the room. *What? Does he want me to explain? No way.* Tears swell around my eyes. *Control!* I demand of myself. I lower my eyes, trying to hide my weakness. I tightly grip the armrests of the chair as I try to regain my composure, but it is nearly impossible when my legs stiffen involuntarily.

"Look at me, Anna," he demands.

I straighten my back, trying to appear confident.

"This is not going to continue. I put a call in to Dr. Ellison, and she is aware of this conversation. She planned to speak to you tomorrow anyway, but as of right now, this stops." Chad's voice softens. I sense the gravity of how he feels being played this way. I am ashamed I let him down and embarrassed that he and the others were analyzing my every move. *I hadn't fooled anyone. I am the one being played.*

"This isn't a game, Anna," Chad says, as if he had heard my thoughts. "Our immediate goal is your physical health and that means proper nutrition and weight gain. Focusing on your weight will only delay finding the real issues of why you are here, which by the way, is our second goal."

I listen but act as though I'm ignoring him.

Chad leans back in his chair, placing his folded hands in his lap. "Anna," he says, after a long moment of thought, "if you want to be treated like the young adult you are, then you'll need to play the part."

I have no doubt Chad chose his words strategically because he has me thinking. I stop the nonsense of water drinking and food swapping, mostly because of complete humiliation in thinking I could get away with it. But I figure nobody needs to know my reasons since "I'm playing the part." The part of eating to gain weight is so difficult that it gnaws at me day after day. I've known for some time what I must eat in order to get a signature but playing the part means doing it without being reminded.

I stop fussing about drinking numerous calories against

my will. I thought this would be easy since no one listened to my complaints anyway, but it's not. I want to scream every second it's in my hand. I want to dump it, spill it, anything but drink it, and the thought of my tactics failing is driving me crazy.

"Play the part," I keep telling myself. But after a week of being followed to the bathroom and watched while eating and drinking, I can't hold back one second longer when Holly hands me my pills, and I find an extra pill in the cup.

"Four," I say disgusted, taking a look at the pills.

"It looks like Dr. Ellison ordered you a new medication."

"Why?" When Holly doesn't answer right away, I test the waters further. "For What?"

"For your appetite, Anna. And it will help you feel less bloated after you eat."

I think about hiding it under my tongue just to keep up with my strategy, but I give up the idea after thinking it through. A while back, Robert tried hiding his medication, I assume, because every morning a nurse heads into his room with a needle.

"I'm not taking it," I say, handing the cup back. At that exact moment, Dr. Ellison enters the unit. I take the cup from Holly and swallow all four pills.

When I reach 96 pounds, I am no longer weighed in private. Each morning, I line up in the lounge area to have my blood pressure taken, my weight charted, and down my medications along with all the other patients. I am very self-conscious to be part of this charade, but if role-playing a responsible individual means meeting these ridiculous requirements, then I guess I have no other choice.

Although Gretchen's room is next to mine, and Addy and I have some things in common, I am more connected with Ben. We begin hanging out together on the fifth floor. There isn't much room to explore, so we just sit in the hallway and talk—sometimes on my watch outside Robert's door. I wonder if Robert likes having us here, hearing us chat. I hope it comforts him to know he's not alone.

It's hard not to notice all the scars on Ben's body, especially since he's wearing shorts today. Looking at his arms and legs make me wince more than once. Some scars are so deep; I wonder how they managed to close on their own. I want to ask how he got them, but I'm not sure how. I wish I could just spurt it out, but I can't trust that Ben won't think I'm stupid for not knowing where those kind of scars come from. My stomach knots and my heart races just thinking about it. I prepare the best I can, hardening my soul in case he thinks strangely of my curiosity.

"Do you mind if I ask where you got all those scars?"

"When I was four, my mother and I trampled over barbed wire during our escape from Vietnam."

I take a breath, relieved by his casual manner. I want to ask about his father, but I don't. I want to ask if he has brothers or sisters, but I don't. I want to ask why he is here, but I don't. "Where do you live?" I ask, playing it safe.

"In Chicago. My mother and I rent the upstairs of a two flat." He doesn't say, but I guess it's small with barely anything inside.

"Why are you here, Anna," I freeze, surprised by Ben's question, "sitting by Robert's room?"

My chest opens in relief but tightens again when I think about Ben's question.

"Because...well...Robert has nobody else."

Ben and I lean against the wall across from Robert's room, quietly staring at nothing in particular. I wonder what it would feel like to share my deepest secrets with him and have him share his with me. I want to believe we would understand each other. I want to believe Ben, at this exact moment, is staring at nothing too, pondering the same thing.

twenty

"Hi Ruth," I say, entering the art room. I quickly loosen the large tray that pushes her securely against the wheelchair's back, making sure she has enough breathing room. "Is that better?" I ask.

Ruth is an older woman who arrived here less than two weeks ago. I guess she is around sixty years old. Her hair is thick and a beautiful gray. It stands straight up high from her forehead because she is constantly moving her hand forcefully through it. She is thin and frail and looks so sad that my chest swells each time I see her. Her eyes are lifeless, and puffy bags underneath show exhaustion beyond sleepless nights. Her skin appears soft and not as wrinkled as I would expect from someone her age, but salty streaks from crying form lines down her face. I never hear so much as a whimper from her, so I guess she cries when no one is around.

When she first arrived, her lipstick and blush were so thick it was hard to notice anything else. I assumed her husband, who visits twice each day, tried to make her presentable like she would have done for herself had she been able. I heard her father was the founder of a successful dairy company, not that this matters much to me, but it gives me reason to believe that Ruth had always been meticulous and well kept, unlike her frazzled appearance on the fifth floor.

Earlier in the week, Ruth stripped herself of her gown and was sitting in her chair completely naked. Addy and I ran to her aid as others laughed. I hoped Ruth hadn't heard, but I couldn't be sure. The thought of such disregard by the others made my heart wrench. Addy and I covered Ruth with her gown the best we could until Virginia and Isaac arrived to take care of the situation. Since that day, I have felt a special bond with Ruth, and I promised myself, if I ever found out who laughed at her, I would never speak with them again.

I sit down next to her, ready to work on a collar for Oreo. Nearly six weeks have passed, and this coming weekend is my first home visit, which has me both excited and nervous.

"Good Morning," Ben says, sitting next to us. "I see they still have you tearing pages from phone books," he says to Ruth.

"They do, and it's ridiculous," I say, annoyed the art teacher can't find anything better for her to do.

Ruth is frustrated with the tedious work, and I understand why. She is too smart for such a senseless job. Looking at her, I see her intelligence through the way she watches, taking in information for when she may need it. She follows the rules, ripping out clumps of phone book pages at a time. Her body heaves and jitters as her unsteady hands work endlessly at it. Sometimes she grabs too many pages, making it too thick to rip.

"Let me help you," Ben says, tearing several clumps of pages from the book, reminding Ruth not to take too many at one time.

I turn toward the art teacher, who's busy helping another patient. "Does Ruth really need to rip a phone book apart?" I had asked this question a few days ago, and she had said it was a good stress reliever. *Yeah, right!*

"Let me worry about Ruth, Anna."

"But you're not worrying about her. If you were, she would be doing something else. She's not dumb, you know. She can do something other than tear a phone book." I try to act like I am having more of a conversation than an argument, but with the way my insides feel, I know I won't be able to hold back if she doesn't listen. And then it gets worse because my comments are ignored.

"Tell her, Ruth. Tell her you're not dumb. Tell her you can do more than rip a stupid phone book."

Ruth doesn't even look at me. She drops the phone book and moves her hands to her forehead and begins pushing her hair back. I look at her with sorry eyes. *How could I have done this?* The art teacher opens the door and calls for Carol, but I am already headed toward the door to leave.

"I'm really sorry, Ruth," I say as I pass.

Ben picks up the phone book and begins to rip it in two. "I'll tear it for you," he says.

Carol meets me at the door. "You want to talk about it?" she asks.

"Not really."

"Personally, Anna, I think it's nice that you care about Ruth. She needs people like you. How about you finish your project? I think Ruth would like that."

I want to refuse, just to save face, but I head back in. Ruth seems calmer already. I assume it's Ben's gentle voice and caring ways that have made her this way, since I too feel calmer watching him.

"Let's put this phone book to better use," Ben says, tearing out a full page. He folds the paper in several different ways; he's made a paper crane. He places it on Ruth's tray. "It's for you," he says. "It represents everything good."

I want Ruth to say something, but she sits quietly. I pull my chair closer to the table and continue working on Oreo's collar. Ben pulls several pages from the phonebook and hands a few to Ruth before he starts folding another piece. Ruth pushes hers aside. She focuses on the paper crane and then Ben, watching him fold. She seems calmer, even more than before.

I AM WAITING for my parents when I see Ruth's husband

wheeling her down toward the exit. "Where are you going, Ruth?" I ask, looking at her and then to her husband for an answer.

"We're going to another place where you'll feel more at home. Right, Dear?"

I like the way Ruth's husband answers me by talking to Ruth. "Bye," I say smiling, trying to keep her from knowing I will miss her.

Ruth looks up at me like she's going to say something, but she doesn't. There's no need really. I know what she wants to say. Tears I controlled moments ago trickle down my cheeks. I want to hug her, but I don't because I can't.

"You're welcome," is all I can do.

MY FIRST WEEKEND away from the fifth floor is awkward. I had become accustomed to my routine and my friends and the nurses, and it scared me to leave the security of these hallways. I think about the days I planned and schemed to flee from this place, and now I am scared at the thought of leaving.

My mother and father come early Saturday morning to get me for the day. They plan to take Bridgett and me bowling in the early afternoon, and then a barbeque at home with the rest of the family for a week-early Mother's Day celebration. That's how my mom explained it anyway, but I know they are coming to see me. I think about Chad and Carol questioning me about things like showing love and hugging and other stuff I think is weird to talk about. If not for these talks or saying good-bye to Ruth, this kind of thing would never have crossed my mind, but now I'm questioning why it's so difficult for everyone in my family to think this way.

The warm sun is welcoming as we drive toward home, but as we get closer, the once familiar streets seem somehow different. Oreo is first to greet me when I walk through the door. She seems double in size even though she is years past the puppy stage. I wrap my arms around her neck, hugging her tightly. "How's my pup?" I say in a high-pitched voice. She wags her tail, and only now do I realize how much I have missed her. I take off her chain and tags and buckle her new leather collar around her neck. It fits perfectly. She shakes her head, getting a good feel for it, and then follows me upstairs, glued to my side.

Bridg comes from her room, and she also looks different. She looks a foot taller and skinnier too. She is only thirteen, but somewhere in the last seven weeks she has grown up. She holds herself with such poise that she looks graceful walking toward me. Her hair is neatly trimmed and brushed— different from the stringy mess she typically has hanging from her head. I often laughed at our blatant differences. If not for living in the same house and sharing the same last name, nobody would guess we are sisters. She loves to read and I hate it. She laughs when watching afternoon cartoons, while I like watching *Little House on the Prairie*. She is tall and I am short. She stays up all night and I like morning best.

It's uncomfortable when we look at each other. I don't know what to say, and I can tell she doesn't either.

"Bowling should be fun," my mother interjects, letting us both off the hook.

I venture down the hallway and into my bedroom. The bed is made neatly, and everything is clean and put in its place. Jingles, with his fur completely worn and a green button in place of one eye, is sitting in the middle of my bed, positioned so he seems to be looking in my direction as I enter my room. I am sure Bridg did this to welcome me home. Part of me wonders if she knows I secretly clung to him every night before being taken to the fifth floor. I think about the cards and letters and posters she sent with my mom to give to me over the past weeks, and although she would never say it, I know Bridg cares.

Sitting on my bed, I feel comfort and sadness at the same

time. My bed is where I laid my exhausted body in the weeks before the fifth floor and where I woke crying and terrified from nightmares.

IT'S STRANGE TO be bowling; it's something I've never done with my parents. I wonder why on Earth anyone would like this game. Throwing a heavy ball down a strip of waxy floor does nothing but bring back memories of being picked second to last to the fat kid in gym class. I have no athletic ability and bowling shows it off.

Every roll is worse than the one before it. Holding the ball up toward my chest, like I know what I'm doing, I swing back and let it go—right into the gutter. To make matters worse, I actually have to turn around and face my family who awkwardly smile, looking in three different directions, none of which are at me.

My father says, "Good try." Two words I don't recall him ever using. It's the walk of shame over and over. My dad tries to show me how to hold the ball so it doesn't roll into the gutter. His arm takes a full swing back, but before he lets go, he slips on the floor with the ball still attached to his fingers. Bridg and I can't stop laughing. I win with a score of 67, and my dad takes second with 62.

Back at home, my sisters bring salads and desserts, and my dad proudly pulls burned chicken from the grill. I feel as though everyone is watching in anticipation to see if I am going to eat anything. I do, of course, but only enough to satisfy them. Back at the hospital I am measured, weighed, poked, prodded, and everything else under the sun, but there is no way in hell I'm complying here. Earlier, Virginia had handed my mother my medication for the day when we left the unit. I had it in my possession by the end of the elevator ride down and down the drain as soon as I got home.

I'm scheduled to return to the fifth floor by eight, so everyone leaves around seven. Had this been a month ago, surely I would have needed to be forced into the car or maybe I would have made a run for it. It's different now. I'm accepted as an individual on the fifth floor, unlike growing up in a large family, and it makes me feel good. I still hate most of what is required of me, especially swallowing pills and being coerced into talking about things I don't want to recall. But part of me feels safe behind the closed doors. I notice a sense of pride developing as I work for signatures, accomplishing one task at a time, but it's more than that. I think bonds might be forming. And strangely, it is these connections that worry me most.

The door latches behind me as I enter the unit, erasing my earlier thoughts of wanting to return.

"Stand here and I will find somebody who can check you in," Isaac says, pointing to the wall right outside my bedroom.

Gretchen walks toward me; her thighs rubbing together causing her shorts to rise up her legs. "You'll need to take everything off," she says. She had informed me of these strip searches before, but I still think she is exaggerating.

"I'm serious," she says. "They'll make you take your clothes off, and they'll search you for drugs and stuff."

"They can't do that, Gretchen," I say.

"Well, I'm just saying the next time I'm searched, I want it to be Mark. Don't you think he's hot?"

"Even if they do what you're telling me, they wouldn't let a guy do it."

"Why not, most guys think I'm sexy."

I give Gretchen a blank stare.

"I'm just kidding," she laughs.

Bonnie, a nurse I hardly know, shows up at my door.

"Good luck," Gretchen says as I walk into my bedroom with Bonnie.

"Okay, Anna. I need you to remove everything.

"Everything? You're kidding, right?"

I'm more horrified than I've ever been in my life. Bonnie

watching me makes me feel completely violated as I strip and place my clothes on the bed. She makes sure I have nothing taped to myself or hidden in my underwear like I'm an inmate returning from the yard. Then she checks my clothes.

"I'm not a prisoner," I say, disgusted.

But I am a prisoner. And all the ways I had convinced myself that being here was right became a thing of the past. *I need to get out and get out fast.*

BEN COMES BY my bedroom to ask about my family visit. We walk toward Robert's room together and sit against the wall outside his bedroom.

"I want to know everything," Ben says.

We laugh when I mention my dad slipping on the floor and laugh harder when I mention our final scores.

"What did you do?" I ask.

"We went to the lake and walked around talking."

"About what?"

"Vietnam and my dad."

My stomach flutters wanting to ask. "Where is your dad?"

"He was killed in the war—two days before my mother packed a suitcase and escaped with me."

I want to know more, but my conscience doesn't allow it.

"Here, I brought you something," he says, handing me a book.

Nothing is written on the front hardcover, so I look at its spine. In black letters it reads, *To Kill a Mockingbird* by Harper Lee. I open it and see it's been recently checked out from the Chicago Public Library.

"It's for you...to keep," he says.

"But it's not yours to give."

"I've checked this book out so often, it's practically mine." He reaches for it, wanting me to hand it back over.

Without hesitating, he opens to page ninety-eight and begins reading like he has read this page many times before.

"When he gave us our air-rifles Atticus wouldn't teach us to shoot. Uncle Jack instructed us in the rudiments thereof; he said Atticus wasn't interested in guns. Atticus said to Jem one day, 'I'd rather you shot at tin cans in the back yard, but I know you'll go after birds. Shoot all the blue jays you want, if you can hit 'em, but remember it's a sin to kill a mockingbird.'

"That was the only time I ever heard Atticus say it was a sin to do something, and I asked Miss Maudie about it.

"'Your father's right,' she said. 'Mockingbirds don't do one thing but make music for us to enjoy. They don't eat up people's gardens, don't nest in corncribs, they don't do one thing but sing their hearts out for us. That's why it's a sin to kill a mockingbird.'"

Ben's voice sounds like music as he reads the words. I don't completely understand why he has chosen this passage, but I am sure it has some significant meaning for him. He gently closes the book. He looks as if he is somewhere other than against the wall outside Robert's bedroom on the fifth floor. He stands and I remain seated. His eyes soften.

"I have scars all over my body, Anna, ones that should have me hating this world, but I don't. I will never kill a mockingbird, a Boo Radley, nor a single living thing. Like you, I have been born to bring hope and to see good in the hearts of others. The only difference between you and me is that you don't know it yet. Your scars run as deep as mine, except yours have been imprinted on your soul. Someday you will see the truth and be able to use your scars to help others, but only after your soul no longer bleeds. This book, Anna..." Ben hands the book over and I take it from him entranced by his every movement, "is for you. Keep it." And without another word, Ben leisurely walks down the hall, leaving me alone.

I sit stunned, watching Ben turn the corner and then out of sight. I am completely confused and intrigued by his words, more bewildered than overwhelmed. I get up and walk slowly back to my room, turning around once to make sure Ben hasn't returned. Lying on my stomach at the foot of my bed, I tuck my pillow under my chest and open *To Kill a Mockingbird.* I read the first sentence and close the book and stare at the blank cover, unsure if I should keep reading.

I begin again, *"When he was nearly thirteen, my brother Jem got his arm badly broken at the elbow..."* and continue until two thirty in the morning.

twenty-one

I wake tired and angry. My eyes are crusted as though I had been crying. I stayed up half the night reading at the end of my bed, trying to catch as much light as I possibly could from the hallway outside my bedroom door without disturbing Looney Tunes. Today will be like every other Sunday, slow and boring. Although rigorous schedules of the weekdays are exhausting, weekends are worse because there are no group meetings or scheduled activities to keep me from thinking about nightmares and other unwanted thoughts.

There are no scheduled weigh-ins or blood pressure checks, but lucky me, Dr. Ellison's orders make me the exception. I follow Virginia across the hall to the laundry room. I wonder if someone has ever dropped dead from a heart attack on the weekend. I guess the nurses would really take some heat. Thinking of the unfortunate timing for the poor soul is kind of comical, even though I know it shouldn't be.

"Hop on, young lady, and we'll get your weight."

I am not in the mood for Virginia's happy spirit, but I do as I am asked just to get it done. I look away, asking Virginia not to share the numbers with me.

Back in my room, I use the bathroom. Virginia charts the amount and flushes it down. I am sick and tired of this whole measuring and charting thing. I've complied with it since Chad warned me about trying to tamper with the samples, but today I'm angry just thinking about it, much like I felt my first few weeks here.

"Is there something on your mind, Honey?" Virginia asks.

"Not really."

"You seem kind of out of sorts today. Talking about it will make you feel like a hundred percent again."

"I'm just tired," I lie. *A hundred percent, my ass! I haven't felt a hundred percent since Gabe used to swing me around by my ankles when I was a little girl.*

"All righty, breakfast is in twenty minutes. I'll see you there."

Virginia leaves, but I am too wrapped up in thinking about what just happened to notice. *Gabe...swinging me by my ankles?* The thought zipped through my mind, exploding into a flash, but it was more than just a flash; it was a moving picture, like when you flip through a hundred pages to see a stick person dance. I concentrate. I'm five or six. Standing in the middle of the living room, I anticipate the thrill. Gabe grabs my ankles and quickly pulls them from underneath me and up toward the ceiling as my body cascades down toward the floor. Hanging upside down, I laugh and laugh. He swings me around in a circle until we are both dizzy. He lowers me down to the floor, reaches for my hands, and pulls me up quickly, springing me into the air before landing on my feet.

"Are you coming to breakfast?" Gretchen asks, peeking into my room and startling me.

"Be there in a minute."

I make my barely slept in bed and tuck my book into my nightstand drawer so my klepto roomie can't make it her own. What Ben said about never killing a mockingbird makes more sense now, but I'm hoping I can grab a seat next to him at breakfast to ask what he meant by deep scars and changing people. Is he comparing himself to Atticus Finch or Boo Radley, the poor, ridiculed, shy kid who had saved Jem's life? I scan the room but don't see him. Assuming he's gone again for the day, I'm disappointed having to wait until later to get answers.

The day drags endlessly. Addy and Ethan are gone on home visits. I empathize with how they probably felt yesterday when it was Ben, Jonny Love, and me away for the day.

Jonny Love spots me on the exercise bike and comes over. "Hey, Anna. Want me to cover for you?"

Jonny Love amazes me sometimes. I had never mentioned that Dr. Ellison only allows me ten minutes per day on the bike because she's overly concerned about calories. Just like I had never told him about drinking water to gain weight, but somehow Jonny knows these things.

"Okay," I say, even though I don't need the cover because Isaac doesn't bother with these little details like Carol and Chad.

"Are you looking forward to Mother's Day next week?" Jonny asks.

I scrunch my nose. "Why? I'm not a mother."

"I'm just figuring all girls look forward to Mother's Day, kinda like a wedding day."

"I guess," I say, having no idea how to respond to him.

"I'm taking my mom out. She says she wants to go somewhere fancy."

"Where are you taking her?" I ask, wanting to find out what kind of restaurant Jonny can afford.

"Pizza Hut."

I laugh only because I think Jonny is kidding, but he's not. He smiles, ignoring my laughter. I feel awful. Jonny is quirky without a doubt, but he's a nice boy, and I would never hurt his feelings.

I try to redeem myself. "I love Pizza Hut, too."

"Ah, it's okay if you do or don't. My mom loves it, and that's what's important."

"Whatcha guys doing?" Gretchen says.

I was hoping to hold Gretchen off longer than mid-morning. She follows me around on the weekends when we're here together. I'm grateful Jonny is with me because he'll be the distraction I need; besides, he doesn't seem to mind Gretchen acting like a twelve-year-old. I worry she'll start blabbing one of her boyfriend stories. I hurriedly bring up something before Jonny Love because if he asks her about Mother's Day, I am afraid of what I might hear.

"Hey, Gretchen. What was it you were making in crafts on Friday?" I ask this because it's the only thing that comes to my mind in time. She begins telling us right away, excited to explain in great detail the leather bag she made for herself. When Jonny Love starts in about leather and cows and nature, I nonchalantly head to the water fountain for a drink and sneak away.

Lunch comes and goes. Robert is sitting on the couch in the TV room. I know the nurses have demanded he sit somewhere other than his room because he would not be here on his own terms. He is staring at the TV with his arms tightly crossed. I can tell he's uninterested in what's on, and I can't say I blame him. The old people always seem to take charge of the TV on weekends, and we let them because we stand our ground during the week when we insist on watching *The A-Team* and *The Cosby Show*, or if we've earned a late night, *Magnum P.I.*

Virginia finds me on the couch next to Robert. She hands me a milkshake instead of an Ensure. When Carol first told me of the switch a couple days ago, I thought Dr. Ellison was finally coming to her senses. I had stupidly thought that swapping drinks meant progress and progress meant home, but spending about thirty seconds with Carol killed my idea of progress.

"Dr. Ellison changed your Ensure to a milkshake," Carol had told me.

"That's it? No Ensure?" I said, straightening up.

"You'll still drink Ensure in the evening," she said, disappointing the hell out of me.

"I'm eating," I huffed. "Why do I have to drink this stuff anymore?"

"Have you thought about asking Dr. Ellison for yourself?"

I tried the same thing with Chad, but basically he said what Carol had said, so I gave up.

"Want to indulge with me?" I say, holding up the cup toward Robert, "Then maybe we'll both get thrown outta here."

Robert responds with a very faint chuckle. I look at him in shock, trying to act calm. I sit back against the couch, staring at the same damn TV as Robert. I am speechless. Somehow Robert and I have made a connection. My mind races with questions. *Should I keep talking? Look at him? Stay quiet? Leave?* My breathing becomes shallow. We must look like a pair of puppets with our eyes popped wide-open and set in one direction. My cup and mouth connected by a straw and Robert with arms tightly crossed, neither of us moving a muscle.

Virginia appears from out of nowhere to retrieve my empty cup. She reprimands me when she sees it's only half gone.

"I'm going to give you two minutes to drink up; that should be plenty of time." Her voice is so sweet, even her scolding sounds nice. I am more than happy to drink down my shake and quickly hand the cup over. "Now that's more like it, young lady," she adds.

I get up to leave, but not without first getting up the nerve to look at Robert. "Well, it's been nice talking to you. We'll have to do this again sometime."

Robert continues his stare in the direction of the TV, but again from deep within his throat, there is laughter. I smile.

It's three o'clock, and although we don't have quiet time on the weekend, I decide to go to my room to be alone for a while. The unit door opens and closes with day and night shift staff coming and going. I haven't seen Lottie all day and suspect she is on a home visit. Realizing I have never seen her with a visitor, I wonder if she has a family.

I take out *To Kill a Mockingbird* and thumb through the pages. I turn to page ninety-eight and read the passage just as Ben had last night. I walk to Ben's room, book in hand, to sit outside his bedroom door in case he returns early from his visit. Although we're not allowed in each other's rooms, I peek in just to make sure he's not in there. My heart stops. His bed is stripped of its sheets. His side of the room is completely empty. Although I had never seen any posters taped to the wall, his room always showed his presence. *What happened? Where is he?* I want to scream his name loudly so he will hear me from somewhere in the unit, but I know it's no use.

"What the hell!" I hysterically shriek. "Where the hell is Ben?"

"Whoa, Anna, calm down," Isaac says, walking toward me. "I thought you knew Ben left for home today."

"No I didn't!" I shriek again.

Mark, another MHT and the one Gretchen thinks is sexy, comes toward us from down the hallway. I want to throw Ben's book at the two of them to scare them out of my way, but I know better than to throw a fit on the fifth floor. I had seen patients taken down faster than the blink of an eye, and I myself had been victim to Chad's grip once and didn't see any reason to experience that again. Using both my hands, I forcefully throw *To Kill a Mockingbird* onto the floor. I slide down against the wall, pull my knees to my chest, and lay my forehead on my knees. A few tears run down my cheeks before I wipe them away, regaining control.

Isaac sits down next to me. He whispers Mark away, easing my tension.

"I'm sorry you didn't realize Ben left today."

I want to stay silent, but I have to ask, "Why didn't he

tell me he was leaving?"

"I'm not sure. I thought he had. He's known for a week, but it would have been up to him to tell you, not us."

When Isaac puts his hand on my back, I involuntarily recoil from his hand. We sit against the wall quietly for what seems like an eternity. I tell Isaac I'm heading back to my room. He hands over *To Kill a Mockingbird* before I walk away. It reminds me of Ben handing it to me last night when I sat against the wall like Isaac is now. Walking toward my room, a few more tears run down my face.

Isaac's knock wakes me abruptly. I look at my clock. Six thirty. I sit straight up.

"What time is it?" I ask.

"Six thirty."

"In the morning?"

Isaac laughs. "In the evening. I let you sleep through dinner. Daniel and I are taking a group out for a walk at seven. I want you to join us, but first," he says, pointing to a tray of food, "eat what you can."

I knew it was too good to be true to be allowed to miss dinner altogether. I nod, letting Isaac know I'll be ready. I sit still on my bed as the events of earlier today resurface: Ben's unannounced departure, the emptiness of the unit, my connection with Robert, and reading into the wee hours the night before. All of it seems surreal.

After eating a couple bites, I push the tray away and venture into the bathroom to see if I look somewhat presentable. I open the cabinet doors under the sink and dig around in my big box of sanitary pads for the mirror I have hidden from the nurses and Lottie; the mirror my mother smuggled onto the unit inside her purse. I glance in it and see tired, bloodshot eyes. I brush my hair and teeth and splash water on my face. I hear the group gathering outside my room, so I quietly replace my mirror under the sink and hurry from the bathroom. I grab my jacket and walk to the unit's exit. Addy and Ethan are back from their home visits, making me happy to have someone else to walk with besides Gretchen.

"What's up Addy?" I figure Isaac asks because Addy is quieter than usual.

"Nothing, really."

"Looks like your boyfriend broke up with you," Gretchen chimes in.

I have never heard Addy talk about a boyfriend, but I think Gretchen is right by the way Addy reacts, crossing her arms and rolling her eyes.

"Hey, Addy. Did he?" Ethan says. *My God, am I the only one that doesn't know about her boyfriend?*

"Shut up, guys, I'm not talkin' about it."

"Sorry, Addy. I just think you should know he's an idiot for doing it," Ethan says.

When neither Daniel nor Isaac intervene, I suspect they're gathering information like me.

We all stare at the elevator doors, urging them to open.

"All right, the night is ours," Daniel says, breaking the ice.

It's rather chilly when we exit the building. I zip my jacket closer to my chin and so do Addy and Gretchen. Jonny Love and Ethan cross their arms and shiver, probably regretting their attempt to look cool by not bringing jackets.

"Man, it's freezing," Jonny says, tightening his arms around his middle.

"You can't say I didn't warn you," Isaac teases.

"C'mon, it's a typical Chicago spring. Get used to it," Daniel adds.

"You're all wimps. It's warm out here," Ethan laughs. His fat, I imagine, keeps him warm, but for the rest of us, the wind chills us to the bone.

"Can we do the trail?" Gretchen asks.

"It's getting dark, guys, so let's stick to the sidewalk,"

Isaac says.

Daniel agrees, probably just to avoid a debate on which one we should do. Gretchen and Jonny Love are disappointed, but I'm not. Not tonight anyway. I want to get this over with and back upstairs.

"Awww...the exercise trail would have been more fun," Gretchen whines.

I don't blame her for complaining; the trail is more fun because of the apparatus stations set up alongside it. We compete fiercely, especially when the MHTs get involved. I have won twice for running across the balance beam without falling off.

"Borrrring," Gretchen continues as we stick to walking around the hospital grounds. We all ignore her, so she catches up, skipping along next to Ethan.

Halfway around, we spread out a bit. Isaac and Daniel walk behind the five of us, herding us like cattle. Gretchen and Ethan are a few feet in front of them and Addy, Jonny Love, and I are up front, keeping a quick pace trying to warm ourselves.

Gretchen flirts with Ethan, whispering one of her sex stories, and because the wind is at my back, I can hear her every word. I roll my eyes. Ethan listens only because he craves friendship so badly he takes whatever he can get. He tries to change the subject at least three times before asking about Ben. Gretchen perks up, more than willing to fill him in.

She speaks softly about the events that took place on the unit earlier in the day regarding my breakdown. She doesn't mention my name, but I sense her pointing at my back. *She can blab all she wants for all I care. I deserve it.* I threw Ben's book to the floor acting like a brat but only because I was so angry with him for leaving without telling me. There would be no way to get ahold of Ben, ever. *I don't even know his stinkin' last name.* My mind is in overdrive. The wind is whistling so loudly I feel as though I could scream into it and no one would hear me. But I don't scream. Instead, I run...

I have no intention of running when I start, but something propels me forward, maybe the wind. Whatever the reason, when I round the corner, out of Daniel and Isaac's line of sight for a mere second, I take off running faster than I have ever run before. I don't have a plan of where to go; I just keep going until I see a loading dock tucked away in the back of the hospital. There are a couple of trucks pulled up to large openings in the building. I don't see anyone manning them, so I curve around and run toward one of the trucks. Only now do I notice Addy and Jonny Love running behind me. I throw myself behind a set of big rig tires and so do the other two. My breathing is out of control, and for a moment I think I am going to vomit. In the distance I hear Daniel's voice yelling our names and his running footsteps coming closer. The three of us hold our breath until we hear him pass. I turn around and rest my back against the large tires of the truck.

"What the heck!" Addy frantically whispers from where she and Jonny Love are hiding.

"Why the hell did you follow me?"

"Fuck, Anna, you took off sprinting as though an armed madman was chasing us. I figured I'd better run if I didn't want my head blown off!"

Jonny Love begins to nervously laugh. I do too and then Addy.

"We are so far up shit's creek," I say, trying to think straight.

I want to stay hidden to avoid the humiliation of being found, like a child playing hide-and-go-seek, except this isn't a game. This is real. How can I possibly explain this one away? *I ran to escape my thoughts.* I realize there is no turning back; no second chance to rethink my decision to run. This dock, this truck, this set of tires I'm leaned up against is nothing but a sinking ship, and I'm the bloody captain.

"Hey, Anna," Addy whispers, "we better get the hell out of here."

We walk toward the sidewalk, and in my panic, I initiate a plan. "When they catch up to us, act like we were simply running around for fun, trying to keep warm. We have to be in this together, okay?" I say.

We make sure the coast is clear for our return to the main walkway. The three us of quickly get to the sidewalk and begin walking leisurely, chatting as though nothing has happened. About thirty seconds pass before Mark and Daniel approach us, frantic and out of breathe. *Shit, backup.*

"What's wrong?" Addy says, trying to act casual, but by their silence and the look on Daniel's face, we know better than to speak another word.

We are immediately sent to our rooms on our return to the fifth floor. The stone-cold reactions from Daniel and Mark were so awful on the elevator ride up that I am grateful for the solitude of my bed. I have no idea what's to come, but being sent to my room, I sense, is not the end of it.

Lottie is fiddling around on her side of the room as though she is packing, but there's no suitcase in sight. My nerves have me so wound up I begin talking to her.

"How was your weekend?" Lottie stops for a second and stares at the wall.

"Good, good, fine," she answers, back to her packing. Her voice is deep and distorted like a devil. *There is something radically wrong with this girl.* I feel bad having never made an effort to get to know her. Although after nearly killing me, why would I?

"Did you visit your family today?" I ask, trying to give the impression that I'm interested in her instead of worrying about the trouble I've made for myself.

"Going in three days." Lottie's voice is barely audible with the way she gurgles through her words.

"Where are you going?" I reply, trying to stay engaged in

this strange conversation.

"In three days," she says.

I give up. I feel kind of sorry for Lottie. I wonder why she is here and if she has family who cares for her.

I take a shower, hoping to sooth my nerves. I check the closet and my drawers, making sure nothing of mine has found its way to Lottie's side of the room, before climbing into bed. I stare at the ceiling, imagining the buzz in the nurse's station. Dr. Ellison has probably been called and my mother. By now, I'm sure the whole unit knows of my "attempted escape." They would understand it wasn't an attempt at all had I been given a chance to explain.

I bury my head deep into my pillow, trying to escape my thoughts, when Isaac walks in. His look shows how disappointed he is in me.

"You'll put these on tomorrow instead of your clothes," he says, very matter of fact. He drapes two gowns across the footboard of my bed. He turns and leaves like he'd rather be any place but here near me. I wonder if Isaac and Daniel have gotten reprimanded for letting us run off.

I hope not, but just in case, I intend to set the record straight first thing tomorrow morning.

twenty-two

$\mathcal{C}$arol is in my room early. "Let's get your weight, Anna." Her disappointed tone makes it obvious she has gotten word of last night's outing.

I step onto the scale without a word. Carol has nothing to say either. I feel terrible having her so disappointed in me. And then I think of Chad. I will be most ashamed around him.

Carol charts my blood pressure and pulse. "Why don't you use the bathroom?" she says.

Because I'm not a little kid. I keep quiet, knowing it's my best defense; besides, she'd probably disagree with me about the kid thing.

Carol pulls up a chair, and I sit on my bed. "I hear you had a hard time with Ben leaving yesterday. How about we talk about it?"

I'm at a loss. I was preparing to explain my run instead. "I'd rather not," I say.

"Well then, I should tell you what to expect this afternoon," she says, changing the subject. "With the exception of group meetings, you'll spend the day in here. Your meals will be brought to your room. And Chad and I will be here too, for your one-on-one sessions. Around three o'clock, you, Dr. Ellison, Chad and I, and Isaac and Virginia will meet in the conference room so we can better understand what happened last night."

"Fine," I say, shrugging my shoulders like I care very little about what she has said. I fear if I say too much, my mother's name may be added to the list of people waiting for me in the conference room.

"And Isaac talked to you about your clothes."

Tears form in my eyes. I pray for control. "You really don't understand."

"You're right, I don't understand, not completely anyway, so I'm interested in hearing your side of what happened." Carol's voice finally reassures me that I am not the worst person in the world. Still, I can't offer her any information, not now anyway.

I head to the bathroom to take a shower. I put on clean underwear and a bra and crawl back into my pajamas, which consist of a T-shirt and shorts. Carol said no clothes, so I'm walking a fine line pretending pajamas won't be considered clothes. I cover up with the two dreadful gowns. I feel like a prisoner on house arrest, except I figure it's worse being confined to a small room than an entire house.

When I exit the bathroom ready for the day, gowns and all, my breakfast has already been delivered, placed on the same rolling cart from my first days on the fifth floor. I'm disappointed I missed the chance to interact with whoever brought my meal. It's only eight in the morning, and already I'm experiencing separation anxiety.

"This is ridiculous," I say aloud. *I ran for no longer than thirty seconds. I returned. No one was hurt. This is the most ludicrous act of punishment for something so minor.* I want to scream.

I lift the lid to my breakfast and decide I'm in no mood to eat. *They can throw me behind locked doors, take away my clothes, and force me to live with a lunatic, but they will not force me to swallow this food. Let them put tubes down my throat; see if I care.* I am so angry I kick the cart away and it topples over, spilling my tray and food all over the floor. "Well, at least now I have an excuse not to eat it," I mumble under my breath.

I'm nervous, thinking I've caused more trouble for myself, but since no one comes to my aid, I assume the commotion has gone unnoticed. I pick up the cart and tray and try to scoop the food onto the plate so it looks like it did moments ago. Except for a couple hairs I peel off the toast, it looks somewhat undisturbed. I replace the lid and roll the cart to where it was.

Lottie enters the room. My heart skips a beat with excitement that I have some human contact, even if she is completely bizarre. She fiddles on her side of the room, going from drawer to drawer, unfolding and folding her clothes. I wonder if she is truly leaving on Wednesday. I ask again, craving conversation to avoid thinking about what's to come.

"Hey, so you're leaving soon, huh?" I ask.

"Yep, Wednesday." But it sounds more like, "Yeeep, Wennnnnssday."

"Who's picking you up?"

"My mom."

Thank you, God! I pray under my breath. *She has family.* "Do you live with your mom?"

"Yaaaaah."

"Where do you live?"

Lottie either grows tired of my questions or truly is unaware of where she lives, but regardless of which it is, she stuffs the rest of her clothes into a drawer and walks out of the room. I wish I could follow her, but I can't.

It's time for arts and crafts, but I won't be there. I wonder if Dr. Ellison will come to my room at our usual meeting time today. But by twenty after nine, I figure she's not coming. I sneak a quick peek out my door but see very little commotion.

Oh my God! Is this ever going to end? I wait for ten o'clock, eager to get out of my room.

I hear a faint knock on my door. It's Gretchen.

"How's it going?" she whispers.

"Fine," I answer.

"Are you guys in trouble?"

"What do you think, Sherlock?" We both quietly laugh, more from nerves than humor.

"What's going on out there? Are Jonny Love and Addy under room arrest too?"

"Yeah, but I can't sneak over to their rooms without getting caught."

We both scoot into our bedrooms when we hear someone coming down the hall. When the exit door opens and then closes, we assume our posts.

"Is Dr. Ellison here?" I ask.

"She's in the nurse's station. She's talking to Carol. Seriously, I watched their faces, and they don't look happy."

"Crap!" I sigh.

"What happened after we took off running last night? Did you and Ethan run at all?" I ask, trying to get a heads up on what to expect later.

"Hell, Anna. We didn't know what you guys were doing. You took off like a bullet. It kind of spooked me. As soon as Daniel and Isaac realized what happened, Daniel took off running after you. Isaac stayed with us, and we came back here. He radioed up here and talked to Mark. We were almost back when Mark radioed Isaac. He said that Daniel had the three of you in sight and that the police had been notified not to come. Then Mark said he was on his way down to meet with Daniel.

"I was actually scared for you guys. We got up here, and it was weird. Everyone was already in their rooms with the doors closed. The few visitors that were here before we left for our walk were already gone. Ethan and I were told to go to our rooms, and we did. I cracked my door and listened. I could hear a lot of craziness in the nurse's station before you got up here, but as soon as I heard the exit door open, I closed my door. I heard Isaac tell you and Addy and Jonny Love to go to your rooms. I wanted to knock on your door last night, but I figured I'd better not. The whole thing actually freaked me out."

"Yeah, me too," I admit.

Gretchen begins to ask where we ran to, but again we hear footsteps, so we bolt into our rooms for a second time. I act as relaxed as I possibly can when Carol gets me for group. As I pass, older patients stare at me like I have committed some terrible crime, and I'm reminded of a movie I was forced to watch in junior high about a woman who is stoned to death after she's ostracized by society. It scared me so much that I've often thought about that horrible death. Now I'm questioning which is worse, stones or stares.

I get past their stares and into the dining room, but I still feel awful. I am thankful Addy and Jonny Love are also dressed in gowns but ashamed to be sitting in the same room with Isaac and Carol. I look around secretively. The room seems empty without Ben here. Robert is in his usual spot looking at his hands, making everyone believe he is unwilling to interact, but I know better. I catch a small glimpse of a smile from him when he sees me covertly observing the group.

We are all unusually quiet. Holly walks in with a new girl, and all the attention on me goes directly to her. They sit in the two empty chairs. Holly introduces Cassandra. She seems to be my age or maybe a year older. She has the perfect shape, one that I could only dream about. Her jeans fit flat against her stomach, without any little bulge that I swear I'd still have if I were fifty pounds lighter. They're also the perfect length, unlike mine that are constantly too long. Her height is perfect too, about 5'6". She looks around, focusing on no one in particular. I imagine she feels how I felt on my first day. She has taken Ben's place, and it angers me again to think he disappeared into thin air without saying good-bye. The mere thought of it has my pulse racing.

We circle around introducing ourselves, the same as weeks ago when I was first introduced to everyone. To no surprise, Gretchen has more to say than the rest of us. Robert says nothing. Ethan, Addy, and I both tell nothing but our names, and Jonny Love, who seems to be oblivious to the fact that he is dressed in a gown, enjoys the introductions.

"I'm glad you're here," he says. *Are you kidding, Jonny? Of all the things you could say...She's not glad, I'm not glad, nobody but you is glad to be here.* Jonny Love's intentions are genuine but silently lashing out at him through my thoughts feels good.

Group drags. There is not one mention of last night. I figure there will be enough talk about it later this afternoon; besides, it's nobody's business anyway. The focus is on Robert today more than ever.

Holly, who works closely with him, begins. "I would like all of you," she says looking directly at each of us, "to share ideas with Robert on how to feel comfortable sharing his thoughts."

Robert didn't ask for this, but hey, he's got to start doing something other than stare at his hands if he ever plans on getting out of here.

Gretchen, very immature-like, tells Robert she'll be his friend. *Yeah, girlfriend, I bet.* I don't hear what the others have to say because I am concentrating on what I should say, if anything at all. The idea of Robert and me having secret conversations, even if they are just throaty laughs, makes me feel connected to him more than anyone in the group. I don't want to ruin what we have, but in the past weeks I have been expected to add something to group discussions. Ben would have had the perfect words for Robert, perhaps a speech to change his life around, but Ben's not here. I can no longer count on him—nobody can.

I take a quick glance toward Robert. He doesn't seem impressed with the suggestions others are giving. *Why should he? We don't know what he has been through. Who are we to judge what will help him and what won't? Maybe he was* kidnapped. *How could I possibly know what that feels like?* Everyone's eyes are on me. I don't want to play a part in this dreadful conversation, but I know I have to.

"Does anyone know my middle name?" Blank faces stare back at me. "Does anyone know Robert's middle name? How about the names of his brothers and sisters or if he has any at all? How about where he goes to school? How about pets? Does anyone know if he has a cat or a dog or a hamster? I don't. I don't know a single thing about Robert's life because he hasn't told me anything." I look over at Robert. He hasn't moved a single muscle. "Robert, I don't know what to say to you because I don't know anything about you."

I imagine Robert feels as uncomfortable as I do with everyone staring at us. Holly seems shocked by my tactic, but by the look on Carol's face, I don't think she is at all surprised by my response, though I am not sure why. It is unlike me to spill my guts, but I was not about to destroy the connection Robert and I have. There is an uncomfortable quiet. I look to Gretchen. *Now would be a good time to start blabbing.*

NEITHER MY BED nor my chair is a comfort when I return to my room. I move my nightstand about two feet from my bed and sit on the floor between them. I curl my knees toward my chest, lean against the wall, and close my eyes. Being here, between my bed and nightstand, feels all too familiar.

I am a small child tucked against the wall by the side of the piano, opposite the staircase in my house. My legs are curled up tightly with my head hidden deep in the emptiness between my knees and chest. I hear the murderer searching through the upstairs rooms as he kills my sisters and brothers and parents. I hear their screams before he shoots each one. Everyone is dead, and the house is quiet. I am alone. I tuck farther into myself, trying to appear as small as possible. The wall pushes me forward into the open space of our living room. I am unprotected and alone.

The killer comes closer. I close my eyes tightly, hoping that if I can't see him, he can't see me. I feel his breath on the back of my neck. I lift my head from my chest and knees. I look at him. His face is rugged, and his clothes smell of dirt. He shows no remorse or empathy toward me.

"I am going to kill you." He laughs.

"You can't."

"Why?" The killer laughs again, smirking at how helpless I look.

"Because I am going to open my eyes."

And when I do, the killer disappears.

I lie awake, paralyzed in my bed and badly short of breath. I try to minimize my breathing so if the killer is here, he can't determine where I am. I scan my room without moving a single muscle but my eyes. My bed is under the window. Bridgett's is across the room. Next to my bed, maybe two feet away, is Liz's bed, empty. It occurs to me it has been empty for some time now. I hear Bridg breathing. I look to the doorway and see my mother's closed bedroom door. I must call to her but without disturbing my older sisters in the next room, afraid I might be called a faker.

I move my body ever so slowly in my soaked bed. It takes many calls before my mother hears me and comes to my rescue. She's upset that I have wet the bed again. She strips the sheets as I lie on the floor in the fetal position, trying to capture some warmth. When I nestle into bed with clean pajamas and sheets, I feel safe with my warm blankets wrapped around me and my mother at my feet.

She whispers, "What was your dream about?"

I don't say a word. I can't. To tell what's happened would bring it back, and the thought of it scares me. I close my eyes tight in hopes to forget it.

"Please, Anna, tell me. It will help. It will make you feel better."

I hear desperation in her pleading. I suppose my mom

is scared too.

CAROL'S VOICE STARTLES me, and I jump up from where I have hidden myself between the bed and nightstand. My back and legs are stiff as I straighten out. I quickly look at the clock, almost one.

"Did you fall asleep down there?" Carol asks lightly. I meet her smile with one of my own, hoping it discourages her from asking questions.

"No, just deep in thought, I guess"

"About what?" She pulls up Lottie's chair, and I know she is here for our one-on-one session.

"Just thinking about last night," I fib. I've learned to say something or risk being worked into a frenzy about things I don't want Carol to know.

"I would like to hear your side of what happened."

"I don't know, Carol. I just wanted to keep warm, nothing more than that." *Damn! Why can't I tell her I don't understand why I ran? Maybe I ran to get away from myself or the bits and pieces of pathetic memories I can't control from flooding my thoughts.* I am completely confused.

"I don't think you were running to keep warm, Anna. You are using that as an excuse to take the easy way out of what you are truly thinking and feeling. You know exactly why you ran. You may not be able to put your finger on it at this moment, but if you try to describe what happened, I can bet you'd be able to sort it out." Carol pauses, probably hoping I'll add something significant, but I have nothing.

"I understand, Anna. I want you to know that. I don't understand exactly why you ran, but I do understand how difficult it can be to sort things out, especially on your own." She takes a deep breath. "Thirteen months ago, my husband died. He fought hard, and in the end, he finally succumbed to his illness. Eventually, I did too, but I fought longer. I refused to let go. I wouldn't let his illness out of my sight. I cursed it and blamed it for everything. I gave it the power to control my day and my thoughts. I separated from friends and family, and worse, I separated from the one man who had brought tremendous happiness to my life."

Her eyes flood with tears as she tries to compose herself in front of me. I can barely hold it together just hearing her voice strain and the way she's pausing between sentences trying to steady her words. *Why is she telling me this?* I want to scream for her to stop, that I don't care about her husband, but I do care. I want to know why she's sad. I want to know what happened.

"Dave and I were married for just a few years, but they were the best years of my life. We loved each other. And when he died, all I could remember was his death and the illness that had taken him away from me. I wanted to run, and in a way I did. I ran from those who love me. It took a lot of strength and support to take back my power. I began to remember the good times Dave and I had together instead of the one tragic event that took him away. I will never forget him, Anna. I will always love him, but I had to trust others. I had to forgive myself for thinking I wasn't there enough or I hadn't done enough to save him."

I try with all my heart to stop the flow of tears, but I can't. I cup my hands around my face. Carol is crying too.

"I couldn't save Dave. There was nothing more anyone could do. It was his time, not mine."

I throw myself onto my pillow face down.

"Forgive yourself, Honey," she whispers.

Forgive myself for what? I want to scream, but instead I focus on controlling my tears. I'm not crying for Carol or her husband. I am crying for Ben and Robert and even Lottie, who I hope makes it in the real world. I cry for Ruth, trapped in her wheelchair, because I fear her husband will die first, leaving her defenseless and alone.

Carol pats my arm. I flinch, pulling away slightly but

allowing her hand to stay.

"You're a special girl, you know it? There aren't too many people I would tell that story to, but you, you've got something. I can't quite put my finger on it. It's almost as if you can feel a person's soul from the moment you meet them."

I bury my head deeper into my pillow, trying to drown out what she is saying. *How dare she think I am going to believe her nonsense? She doesn't know a damn thing about my life, not a stinkin' single thing.* I forget about trying to stop my tears because I can't. And when I'm done, I can't remember a time I've cried so hard.

CHAD IS SPEAKING with another patient outside my bedroom door. My anxiety worsens with every passing second. *I can't face him.* I like the way he interacts with me, making me feel like I have a lot to offer; something I never get being born the ninth kid, and now I've gone and messed it all up. How can he ever expect me to do better than my best when my best is my worst? Sitting crossed-legged in the middle of my bed, I'm staring at my hands, just like Robert, when Chad walks in. My only hope is that he starts talking, asking questions, anything but silence.

"I hear you ended your week with a bang," he says.

His choice of words humors me, but I know it is not meant to, so I stay put trying not to move a muscle.

"C'mon, Anna, let's get this over with." He nudges me to get up so we can go to the conference room together, but I don't budge.

"I'll go alone. I don't need you as an escort," I mumble.

"Anna, let's go!" he says.

I knew from the beginning Chad would neither avoid the issue nor let me hide from the truth. I follow him to the conference room with confidence, telling myself to stay calm, but with everyone already seated around the large table, my nerves take over, sending me scrambling for my chair.

Dr. Ellison speaks first, "Do you know why we're here?"

Are you kidding me? How stupid do you think I am? Of course, I do! Or maybe I don't. Have I won a ticket out of here? Oh shit! Maybe I have. What if I'm sent to a place crazier than this one? "Um-hm," I grunt in answer to her question.

"We have already discussed with Addy and Jonny what happened on last night's walk. The only one we haven't heard from is you."

I can hear Jonny explain, "Yeah, she took off and I thought, what the heck, it's a cool way to stay warm, so I ran too. But I swear, we didn't mean anything by it. You know, no harm done." And then Addy, "Hey, it scared the shit out of me the way she took off. I figured I better follow or end up dead." Part of me wonders if anyone here really spoke with Addy or Jonny Love like Dr. Ellison says.

Dr. Ellison pulls me from my thoughts. "I would like to know your version of what happened last night."

With every passing second I become angrier than the moment before, feeling as though I am here for a sentencing.

"I was cold, and I thought running might warm me up," I lie.

"Why did you hide from Daniel and Isaac?" Dr. Ellison asks.

It's obvious Addy and Jonny Love spilled their guts, so I decide not to hold back. I narrow my eyes and look directly at Dr. Ellison. "If you're the only one to ask all the questions then why does everyone else need to be here for this ridiculous interrogation?" I say, slamming the accusation toward her.

She's quiet for a brief moment, making me uncomfortable. "Are you finished explaining what happened, then?"

"Oh my God, I didn't do anything wrong," I say, placing my elbows onto the table, widening my hands as if to say, I give up.

"This is what we expect of you for the next few days. You will be limited to your room except for group time," she continues.

"No kidding!" I sneer. My words are completely ignored.

"You will be allowed no visitors or phone calls. No signatures will be given on your chart. No street clothes. Thursday, if all goes well, you will be allowed to follow your regular schedule. Do you understand?"

"Sounds fun," I sarcastically respond.

"Dr. Ellison," Chad says, "Anna hasn't eaten lunch today..."

"Nor breakfast," Carol adds.

They've got to be kidding. Tattling? I lower my eyes. I felt much braver tossing my food aside when I didn't have anyone watching, but now I am scared of what Dr. Ellison might say.

"How about the milkshake?" she questions the group while eyeing her chart.

"No," Chad answers.

"Stop talking like I'm not here."

Dr. Ellison places her chart on the table and looks over at me, sending me vibes to explain myself. When I don't say a word, she turns to Carol.

"Keep me updated. If necessary, I will have an IV ordered."

"Delightful," I add, rolling my eyes.

I'M BACK IN my room for only a few minutes when Chad comes in, milkshake in hand. "You have twenty minutes," he says, handing over my drink.

"I don't need twenty minutes." I suck it down and hand the cup back to him. "And save yourself some time and don't come back to chat 'cause I'm not talking." My snap is harsher than I intend it to be, but I don't care.

"I'll be back at four. You can decide then," he says,

leaving.

Chad has a way of avoiding confrontation, and it irritates me. I want to yell and scream, and I want him to yell and scream back, so I can hate him.

Shit! I'm going to be sick. I run to the bathroom and the entire milkshake comes purging from my gut.

twenty-three

The backyard smells of dirt. Fog drifts in, surrounding me. A fence, the chain-link kind, stretches between the two yards, separating me from the other side.

"Anna, Anna," Bridgett calls. I hear her crying, but from where? I cannot see her.

"Where are you?" I yell, calling out in every direction. I can barely see the hill that leads to the willow tree. I scan the branches, searching for my sister.

"Bridg!" I scream.

"Anna, Anna, help me."

I see her, clinging to a branch. I grab at the fence and start to climb, but it sinks with my every step. Bridgett's screams pierce through the fog, urging me up and over the fence in seconds.

"Hang on!" I scream, sprinting across the yard.

Snap! The sound sends everything around me into slow motion for a quick instant. The fog rushes away at lightning speed, and once again, I am sprinting toward the willow.

"Bridg! Bridg!" I scream. I kneel by her side. I turn her over. It's Liz. Her face is covered with dirt.

I wake to the snap of the exit door, reminding me I'm on the fifth floor. I lie motionless in a cold sweat. It's dark except for a crack of light coming from the doorway. I want to call for my mother, but she isn't here. I pray for some kind of commotion from the hallway, but nothing. Slowly, I reach for my clock, moving it ever so slightly. I look closely. It's three twenty-five. I put the clock under my blankets instead of returning it to the nightstand in case someone is under my bed waiting to seize my arm.

I have already waited too long to use the bathroom. If I wait any longer, I'm going to have an accident right here in my bed. I sit up feeling light-headed, regretting my decision last night of refusing to eat. I close my eyes, hoping my dizziness and fear will disappear, but both remain. I pull myself from my bed and walk toward the bathroom. The room seems lopsided as I try to regain my balance with every step. When I make it to the commode, I grab on to the sides to stop myself from falling off. I slowly stand and pull my pajama bottoms up when I'm finished. *I need to make it to my bed.*

Buzzing fills my ears. I reach for the sink. In the distance, I hear my head crack against the countertop and then silence. I'm completely down on the floor when I come to. One side of my face is flat on the cold tile floor, and for a second, I can't feel anything but its chill. And then my head begins to pound. Pushing myself to a sitting position, I slide to the back corner of the bathroom, behind the door, and lean against the cold wall. I curl my knees to my chest and lay my forehead on them, and immediately pain bursts through my head.

I struggle to listen for sounds outside the bathroom door, but nobody seems to be around. *I must make it to my bed before I pass out again.* I crawl around the bathroom door and grab at the footboard, but my hands refuse to grip it. My body is twice as heavy as moments ago. My efforts to stand are forced back down, so I crawl around to the bed's side. I lean forward against my mattress, and knowing I have made contact with something stable helps me relax for a mere second. The room is spinning, making it difficult to precisely locate where I need to be. My hand finds my pillow, and I climb toward it. I curl up somewhere on top of the bed, not caring to pull the sheets over me. The room continues to spin even with my eyes closed, but having found a place to rest, I feel safe.

"Anna, Anna." I hear from a distance.

"Anna. It's time to get up." Carol shakes me awake; something she typically does not need to do. I come to. My head is pounding. I struggle to sit up. I want to hold my head, but Carol might notice. I cover the lump on my forehead with my bangs.

"Are you all right?"

"Yeah! Just tired, I think," I try to assure her, but I know my weak voice is unconvincing.

"Are you sure?"

I push myself up, letting my legs hang over the bed. Feeling for the floor, I steady my hands on the mattress, letting it hold most of my weight. The bed sways to the left then to the right. I shake my head attempting to keep up with the bed, but my head throbs, and the center of my forehead pounds. Carol's hands are on me, guiding me back.

"I want you to lie down, Anna. Take it slow." Her voice sounds muffled.

I fall backward, pushing myself up toward my pillow with the heels of my feet. *Oh yes, this is better.* A cold stethoscope shocks me. And then the pumping of the airbag tightly cuffed around my arm. *Hssssss!* Pump again. *Hssssss!*

"Put this under your tongue," Carol says.

The thermometer drops from my mouth with my lips unable to grip it. Carol pushes my hair away from my face and touches the soreness. I try to act undisturbed by the pressure, but my face tightens, giving me away.

"How did you get this bump?"

"I hit the sink."

"When?"

"In the night. I'm tired."

"Did you fall?"

"Um-hm."

Carol brings the covers up toward my neck. It only takes

moments before I am warm again. I drift off to sleep, knowing Carol is near.

"Wake up," I tell myself. "Wake up." I open my eyes slightly. Dr. Ellison is sitting on the side of my bed, nudging my leg. I have a pounding headache, and all I really want is to close my eyes and sleep.

"Anna, open your eyes."

I barely get them open before Dr. Ellison shines a light in and away from them.

"You had quite a fall."

Nodding so she knows I'm listening, I close my eyes, needing sleep.

"You can rest in a minute, but right now I need you to focus."

I open my eyes again.

"I want you to follow my finger without moving your head."

I follow her finger up and down, right and left, and she seems satisfied. She examines my bump, and without thinking, I push her hand away.

"It's pretty tender, hmm?" she asks.

"Yes," I say, more alert now with each bothersome poke and prod. She picks up the blood pressure cuff from the bed and wraps it around my arm. I pull away, trying to explain that Carol has already done this. She smiles softly, not listening to a thing I say. I close my eyes, letting her finish.

Carol returns with a needle, and automatically I think it's an IV.

"I don't need that," I say, protesting at the sight of it.

"We need to get some blood to see what's going on with you," Dr. Ellison explains.

"I'm fine. I feel much better now," I lie.

Neither Carol nor Dr. Ellison listens to my ineffective fib. Carol reaches for my arm to put the rubber band securely around it. I allow it simply because I don't have any fight left.

Besides, it's pointless to resist. So why bother? I close my eyes, wincing when the needle goes in and again when it's pulled out.

"I'll be back in an hour to check on you. Until then, I want you to rest," Dr. Ellison says.

I glance at the clock that has somehow regained its position on my nightstand. It's almost ten. I wonder if anyone will miss me at group. It doesn't matter because I am too tired to think about it.

I wake to Dr. Ellison's voice. "Anna," she says loudly, "wake up."

Almost two hours have passed. My head feels much better, but I still have a headache. A tube hangs from a stand down to my hand. Dr. Ellison pushes my lunch into the room. I manage to get up and sit in a chair since I really don't want to be lying in bed all day like I'm sick.

"Careful. Sit up slowly," Dr. Ellison says.

I detect sympathy in her voice and wonder if my injuries are worse than I think. She takes a quick look in my eyes and seems to be pleased with the results. She pushes the lunch cart closer to me and pulls up a chair for herself. I sit in my chair careful not to disturb the IV and pull the tray closer, acting as though I am complying with an unspoken request to eat. Actually, I'm hungry and want to eat.

Dr. Ellison opens the binder filled with chart paper, logs of all our conversations, and whatever else she has in there. It's thick, reminding me of how long I have been here. She writes something down.

"How are you feeling?" she asks.

"Fine."

"Tell me what happened last night."

I tell her as much as I can recall: the trip to the bathroom, the buzzing in my ears, hearing my head hit, crawling back to bed, and the room spinning. I leave out the nightmare part because I figure it will lead to a pointless conversation.

"You fainted because your iron is very low." She looks at her chart again. "You haven't eaten since the night before last...," she says, flipping through a few more pages, "except for a milkshake." She looks at me wanting answers.

"I vomited it," I say, more embarrassed by the action of vomiting, than admitting it.

"Did you make yourself vomit?"

"No," I say, annoyed.

"Starving yourself is not an option. You need to eat."

"I know. You've already told me."

I am so angry with her matter-of-fact, you-will-do-as-I-say attitude that I want to scream. I want to believe she cannot force me to eat, but she can, and it frustrates me more. I know if I don't do the actual chewing and swallowing, she will do it for me by forcing needles and tubes into me. I shove the lid off the plate of food. I really want to take it and throw it across the room, but I have used my last chance; this I know for sure. I let out a big huff, showing my anger and frustration and humiliation. I pick up the container of yogurt.

Anger from within me wants out, but I have no idea how to untangle the mess brewing in my gut. I bang my yogurt and spoon back on the tray. "I hate this!" I yell, pulling my legs up on the chair and wrapping my arms around them. The pull of the IV heightens my anger. "And get this stupid thing out of me." I tuck my head into my knees and cry.

An eternity goes by, and I hate that Dr. Ellison is still here. My nose is draining buckets. I need a tissue, but I refuse to reveal my reddened face and runny nose. Dr. Ellison must notice my constant sniffles because she hands me several tissues. Ignoring her, I take them and begin to blow. I feel the tissue box on my chair next to my feet. I take several more and get myself cleared up as much as possible before unwinding my body. My head is pounding, and every one of my movements makes it worse. I turn my eyes toward my tray, deliberately avoiding any eye contact with Dr. Ellison, and reach for my yogurt once again. Curled with one leg up near my chest, I begin to eat. Except for my head, my insides feel better than before.

Dr. Ellison holds out. I recall my first visit to her office. Her patience is greater than mine, and I trust this hasn't changed.

"Can I have some aspirin for my head?" It's ironic I ask, because until I came to the fifth floor, I had never swallowed a pill, and now I down them every day. Everything seems like a choice at first, but there are no choices in this place. If you don't eat, they'll insert a feeding tube. If you don't swallow your medicine, they'll inject it. If you don't comply, they'll confine you to your room. Chad was right from the beginning when he said this isn't a game. There are no cards to be dealt. There are no tokens to be moved or points to be earned; therefore, there are no winners and no losers.

I think about the odds of leaving this place. *How does it happen? What do I need to do? If there is no game to be played and no winners, what possibly could be my ticket to the outside world? Without a game, there is no strategy needed to play. How did Ben walk away from these walls?*

I think back to Dr. Ellison's words, "When I know you are ready, you can go home." *Ready for what? What does being ready look like?* I want to ask, but I can't. Something stops me from wanting to know.

I am so preoccupied with my thoughts I hadn't heard Dr. Ellison respond to my question about getting some aspirin. I look at my plate. I have eaten the yogurt and two pieces of toast, and I'm hungry for more, but there is nothing more for me to eat. I have no doubt Dr. Ellison would be more than pleased to have more brought in, but I am not willing to give her this kind of satisfaction.

"What's on your mind?" she asks.

"Please, get this out," I say, pointing to the IV.

"Everything should be back to normal by tomorrow, if

you continue eating. Until I know for sure, I want it to stay in." She thumbs through a couple pages in my chart. "And as long as you continue to gain weight, there is no reason to chart your input and output any longer. Deal?"

"Deal." I say, trying to hide my excitement.

Carol comes in a few minutes after Dr. Ellison leaves and shoots medicine into my IV.

"This will make your head feel better," she says.

"Thank you." I smile.

The hours drag before Carol returns with an Ensure. I drink it slowly, remembering yesterday's purge.

"You look better already. How's your head?"

"Better," I reply.

She comes in for a closer look at my bump, and I push my hair back willingly.

"Yes, much better," she agrees.

She sits so we can chat.

Should I ask? I want to know, sort of. I take a deep breath, "What did Dave die from?"

"He had cancer."

Unsure I want to hear anything more, I fumble with the can of Ensure, bring it to my lips, and finish what's left.

"We never got a chance to talk about your family visit," Carol says. "So how was it? What did you do?"

I tell her about the bowling experience. We laugh just like Ben and I had.

"What else?"

"We had a barbeque."

"Was everyone there?"

"Three of my sisters and a brother," I reply.

"Name all your sisters and brothers." Carol eagerly gets her fingers ready to count as I name each one, much like other people do when they find out I come from a large family.

My stomach knots at the thought of naming my siblings.

I have been questioned before and looked at with odd expressions from those who want to know why the number of ten kids doesn't match the number of fingers standing when I'm done naming everyone. Carol notices my hesitation, so she starts.

"Okay, we've talked about Bridgett, and you have mentioned Marie and Frances. And is it Jim? He's the one who stopped in right after you came here."

"What do you mean?" I ask, completely confused by her remark.

"Jim, right? He's your oldest brother?

"Yeah." I am reluctant to ask how she knows this.

"Two days after your mother and Dr. Ellison brought you here, Jim came here to find out what was going on. He needed to know that you were okay. Well, as he said, 'This isn't just anyone; she is my little sister.' He was very concerned, Anna. I could tell he cared very much."

"Did I talk to him?" I search my memory. It surfaces. "I do remember." I smile.

"I do too," Carol chuckles. "He wanted answers."

"Okay, so Bridgett, Marie, Frances, and Jim. That's four, and you make five. Who am I missing?"

I cannot help thinking she already knows everyone who hasn't been named, but I pretend that she does not. I continue her count, like I have most of my life, acting like it's nothing out of the ordinary to have so many siblings. "Gabe, Meg, Kyle, and Timmy."

My nerves get the better of me, so I hurriedly add, "I have four brothers and four sisters." My chest tightens. My belly fills with air. *Breathe, Anna. Breathe.*

"I'm kind of tired of talking," I say to Carol.

I'm left alone. I lay on my bed. My body feels paralyzed, but my brain feels like it's surging electricity. The constant flow of the unit door opening and closing reminds me that I have gotten halfway through another day.

Facing Chad will be tough. I treated him badly yesterday when he came back to my room to talk. I ignored him, wanting to show how angry I was. Later, he came back with my dinner and then again with my Ensure, and to show him how stubborn I could be, I didn't touch either.

Chad says hello to someone as he passes outside my room on his way to the nurse's station to get ready for his day. My stomach turns thinking about him reading my chart. He'll know I fainted and smashed my head because I stubbornly pushed away last night's food. I figure it's a good idea to present the best me I possibly can for today. I get up from bed, hoping to look less than totally pathetic when he comes to my room. Wheeling the IV stand to the bathroom is completely humiliating, but looking like I've been sleeping all day seems worse. I rummage around for my mirror and finally get a first look at my forehead. *Whoa! This thing is huge.* It looks as though the bump is raised a foot off my forehead. The bruising around it makes it look like I've been beaten with a club.

I finger-comb my hair, forgetting about my IV until it pulls at me. I cringe, realizing how pathetic I am with this hanging from me. I wish I could just pull the damn thing out. I open the sink's cabinet to hide my mirror, but the IV line catches on the corner of the cabinet door. "Damn it!" I fumble for the mirror, accidentally hurtling it higher into the air. It falls to the floor unbroken but hits with enough of a bang to be heard outside my bathroom door.

I freeze. "Please, please, please, let no one be outside my door," I beg under my breath, panting in fear that someone has heard. I steady my breathing, knowing I must stay calm. I quietly move my ear to the door, hoping to hear silence on the other side. I hide the mirror back inside the box but this time taking careful measures not to disturb my IV. I brush my teeth and comb my hair before nervously exiting the bathroom, thinking someone will be there waiting to question the noise.

I open the door, acting as though everything is normal. Relief spills over me when no one is in the room but Lottie, folding and unfolding her clothes.

Wanting to busy myself, I pull out *To Kill a Mockingbird* and thumb through it until I find the paragraph Ben read. The time we had together seems surreal. If not for this book, I would second-guess his presence. He was not like the other kids, and this had initially attracted me to him. He wasn't tough and acting all cool. He didn't present a greatness that was easily recognized, but his uniqueness was undeniable. He was gentle and kind; a lover not a fighter. I had carefully watched the effect Ben had on other patients. Some were pulled in by his genuine manner, while others didn't know what to think of him. He walked around the unit helping anyone who needed it and then was gone before he could be thanked. I noticed this time and time again, and it intrigued me. He was always there, but never there—kind of like a spirit.

Chad's knock startles me. "Sorry." He smiles. "Am I pulling you away from your thoughts?"

I straighten up and smile, hoping for his forgiveness.

"I'm here hoping you want to talk. Should I stay or go?"

"You can stay, I guess," I say, scared to admit I want him here.

"How are you?" he asks, looking more at my forehead than my eyes. His face contorts like he feels the pain that comes from smashing into a countertop.

"Good."

"Missing our one-on-one session yesterday should give us a lot to talk about today," Chad says, making himself comfortable in Lottie's chair. He pulls a pen off his clipboard and finds a usable piece of paper.

"Let's make a list of the events of the last few days. This way we can pick one to talk about." He looks up at me.

"My family visit," I say, trying to avoid all the stuff that happened afterward.

Chad writes it down.

"Your excursion around the hospital building," Chad says. I nervously laugh at his choice of words. "Ignoring me last night," he adds.

My face reddens. "My nightmares scare me," my voice cracks.

Chad stops writing mid-sentence. I have no idea what made me say what I did, but I said it, and I have no idea how to explain it, but it's out. Chad's eyes somehow offer a feeling of safety, keeping me from looking away.

"When did you have a nightmare?"

I turn my eyes toward the window. My throat tightens. A rubber band squeezes around my chest. *Tell him. It will be all right. No, it's crazy. I can't.* A picture flashes on the windowpane. It is Liz, or maybe Bridgett.

"Always!" I spurt out. My breath relaxes. My chest loosens a tiny bit. The image on the glass is gone.

"Anna, look at me." The back of my chair feels like a wall pushing me forward. I look to Chad.

"What are you nightmares about?"

Seconds seem like minutes.

"They're very scary." I look away. A memory flashes of when I was a child. "I can't get to her to help her," I say frantically.

"It's okay. You're safe." He pauses. "Who can't you help?"

"Bridgett. I can't help her," my voice cracks. I beg myself not to cry.

"Tell me more about Bridgett? Why does she need your help? What happened to her in your nightmare?"

"I can't tell you." I try to shake away the memory.

"Yes, you can. It is your nightmare. Think back. You are trying to help Bridgett. Is she in danger?"

"Yes. She can't breathe." The childhood memory sparks

again. "No, I mean I don't know. She can breathe, I think. I can't remember. I can't tell you." I try to force my nightmare back down inside me. My chest tightens. I blow out a long and drawn out breath, realizing only now I had been holding it for far too long. "I can't tell you," I say again.

"It's not that you can't, it's that you won't. The words are there, Anna. Look for them. Why do you need to help Bridgett?"

"I don't know."

"Where is she?"

"In a tree."

"What is she..."

"I'm sorry, Chad. I don't know," I interrupt, lowering my eyes.

"That wasn't easy, was it? Anna, look at me," he says, waiting. "Give yourself credit. It takes a lot of effort to recall a time when we're scared." Chad takes another look at my forehead. "Heck, I would have passed out just thinking about hitting my head." He smiles, and so do I.

Dinner is pushed into my room, and I'm surprised at how quickly time has passed.

"Why don't I leave you to eat on your own?" Chad winks.

I agree happily. The feeling of Chad's trust in me feels good. It makes eating a bit easier too. I lift the lid off my plate. The smell of food instantly confirms how famished I am. And without anyone watching, I cram the food down.

twenty-four

I wake with more energy today than yesterday. The sun is shining, and the room seems brighter than it has in a long time. My headache is gone, and my bump, although more discolored today, has gone down considerably. Carol knocks while I'm in the bathroom. Her disturbance doesn't bother me.

"No need to measure," she calls from outside the door.

"Okay." A smile stretches across my face. "Can I throw this thing in the garbage?" I yell from inside the bathroom.

She agrees and in it goes. Carol takes hold of the IV stand as I exit the bathroom. "Let's get this out."

It takes less than a minute to pull the needle from my hand and get it cleaned up. A feeling of independence comes over me even though I am reminded of my room confinement when Carol and I walk across the hall to take my weight. She leaves me to shower before breakfast and get ready for the day. I take a long shower, inhaling the smells of the Ivory soap and lavender shampoo.

Breakfast is waiting for me when I exit the bathroom. Carol is here moments later. She is not as willing to let me eat alone as Chad was last night. I am not as hungry as yesterday, making the food less appetizing. I don't care to eat what they have given me, but with Carol here I have very little choice. If she insists on being here for breakfast and lunch, I will find a way to pass on dinner. I think how I might manage this without losing Chad's trust. I drink the orange juice, eat my toast and half the scrambled eggs, but leave the sausage sitting on the plate. I fear being defeated in a game that I am beginning to suspect is nonexistent.

Dr. Ellison walks in just as I am placing my napkin on the plate. I straighten up. *Crap! Why now? There must be hidden cameras in the room.* I look around, considering this for the first time. Dr. Ellison's presence does something to me. She has the power to order tubes and needles and unwanted tests—that commands respect. She glances at my plate for a mere second. My heart skips.

"Feeling better I see."

I nod, confirming her assumption.

"Scoot forward," she says.

I scoot to the edge of my bed and hang my legs over the side. Dr. Ellison takes her flashlight and shines it in and away from my eyes.

"Any headaches?"

"No," I answer.

"Walk to the window and back, please."

I want to die inside. Having Dr. Ellison watch me walk to the window is bad enough, but turning around and walking toward her is worse. It reminds me of the whole bowling ordeal, making me feel as though I'm walking the walk of shame once again.

"Hopefully, this will eliminate your light-headedness," Dr. Ellison says, handing me a small cup of three pills.

The thought of swallowing them aggravates me. They leave a thick residue in my throat, causing me to gag as I choke them down. What started out as a happy day is turning into the same old disappointment.

"What upsets you about taking medicine?"

"I don't like taking drugs, that's why," I answer. "And I don't need them."

"They are helping considerably, and hopefully you won't need them for a long period of time."

Hopefully! If she thinks I'm willing to swallow these pills after I get out of here, she's nuts.

"Chad mentioned that you are having nightmares."

I knew this was coming. There are no secrets, and I hadn't expected Chad to keep last night's chat to himself. Still, I feel a bit disappointed that he didn't.

"Sometimes." *More like every night.*

"It is important that you talk about your dreams, Anna. I can help you sort them out so they are not as frightening. You may find that reliving and discussing them in your conscious mind will help separate them from your subconscious."

I lift my eyebrows in confusion.

She smiles. "Basically, talking about your nightmares while you're awake can stop them from happening while you sleep."

"I don't really remember them," I lie. The truth is, I want my puzzling nightmares to fit together, but at the same time I am terrified of what the final masterpiece might reveal.

"Do you ever dream about Elizabeth?"

I'm shocked. *Why is she asking about her? She has no right to ask about my dead sister.* I try frantically to act unmoved by the subject, but the quiet in the room as Dr. Ellison waits for my response prevents me from ignoring her question.

My stomach churns. The taste of leftover residue from the pills causes me to gag. *Oh God, I'm going to vomit.* I feel them coming up. I look for a way out. Dr. Ellison allows me access to the bathroom. I throw my head down toward the commode and gag again, but nothing comes up. I realize I have my head pushed into a two-person toilet. Sickened by the thought, I quickly sit back on the floor and concentrate on keeping my meds down. If they come up, Dr. Ellison will not hesitate to prescribe my medication to be injected. The thought of a needle piercing my skin daily makes me shudder, so I concentrate harder. It works because I lose the feeling of sickness.

Reentering the room and facing Dr. Ellison is embarrassing, but she continues like we haven't missed a beat.

"Do you remember how old you were when Elizabeth died?"

Oh my God. I can't do this. Why won't she stop? "I can't talk about her."

"You were seven, almost eight. When death happens at such a young age, it is very difficult to understand." *Please! Stop!*

A quick image emerges. It's Frances; she's walking up the stairs to the living room.

"It was a long time ago. I'm seventeen, and I understand it perfectly fine."

"I agree, and being older will help you explain what caused your sister's death."

Another flash. This time it's an image of the swing set I played on as a child. *Oh, please, no.* My chest becomes unbearably tight. My senses are intensified. I can see Liz swinging from the top bar. I hear laughter, then her silence as she hits the ground. She looks lifeless. I take my fist and press it hard into my chest, hoping it will release the pain.

"Stop, please," I beg, my plea barely heard. "Dr. Ellison, I am asking you, please don't make me do this."

Ignoring my request, she continues, "You sister died of a brain tumor when she was ten, isn't that right?"

A gasp escapes my lips. I struggle for breath. *No it's wrong, all wrong. I killed her.*

Dr. Ellison's mention of a brain tumor lessens the flashes of my sister's fall. I had accepted over the years since my sister's death that pretending it was a brain tumor was easier for everyone than thinking about what really happened.

Dr. Ellison waits until I calm down before she continues. "You need to say Elizabeth's name."

Distorted flashes rip through my mind. I feel an odd presence.

"I don't mind waiting. Take your time." Her voice is distorted, sounding unfamiliar.

Oh my God! Why is she tormenting me like this?

"Her name is Elizabeth," she repeats.

No! It's not! Her name is Liz.

I swallow hard. I cannot get my tongue to formulate the letters. I try again. "Liz," I whisper.

IT FEELS GOOD to be back with the others during group. I notice Addy and Jonny Love are in their regular clothes. I guess their sentencing was less severe than mine, and I don't understand why. They ran too. I didn't tell them to do it; they had made that decision on their own. Cassandra seems to be fitting in just fine. She's not as vocal as Gretchen, but not as quiet as Robert, so I guess she's conforming to what she must do while locked up here. I can't understand why people cooperate so quickly without sorting through their options. I think about this for a moment and wonder if I have it all wrong. *Maybe Ben's willingness to cooperate and conform led to his release.*

Suicide is mentioned, and whoever is speaking gets my attention. It's Cassandra.

She's telling about her attempt to kill herself by cutting her wrists. I notice the bandages peeking out from beneath her long sleeved shirt. How had I missed this before? As she continues talking openly to the group, I contemplate how it is she can possibly trust everyone enough to spill her guts about something so dreadful. She doesn't seem to be embarrassed by her attempt.

I would be more embarrassed by the fact that I didn't succeed. I think to myself. *What am I thinking? What the hell is wrong with me? Would I really be more terrified of failing even at death, than I would be of surviving?* And because I think my answer is yes, for the first time I am truly aware that something is radically wrong with my thinking.

Cassandra's voice is weak when she reaches the events that took place right after her attempt. "I could hear my little brother playing in his bedroom as my wrists were bleeding. He was making zooming noises, moving his trucks back and forth. The same sounds I made a hundred times when he insisted I play with him. Something about the noises scared me into believing I was abandoning him just like our mom did. I couldn't do it; I couldn't leave my brother alone. I'm the only mother he has. And then I just started screaming for my father. I woke up in the hospital, and now I'm here. That's about what happened."

Everyone is quietly listening, much like we did when Ben spoke. Tears run down Cassandra's face. Carol comments on how proud she is of Cassandra for trusting the group enough to tell about herself. Others chime in.

"I'm glad your father heard your screams, otherwise we would have never met." Cassandra smiles at Jonny Love. I look for a confused look on her face after his remark, but there's none. Maybe she gets him.

"Were you scared?" I ask, surprised by my willingness to voice such a question. I can plainly see the others are stunned too. No one hesitates to look at me, hanging on my question and waiting for Cassandra's answer.

"When I cut myself?" Cassandra asks back.

"Were you scared..." my chest pulls, "to scream for help?"

"I didn't think about it, I guess. I was more frightened thinking about how hurt my brother would feel believing I didn't love him enough to fight for him."

"How does your brother feel about what happened?" Carol says.

"I think he's angry with me right now, or maybe just scared. I hope to make him understand that I'm living for him."

"And how about you?" Carol continues. "Are you living for yourself?"

For an unknown reason, my emotions stir with Carol's question. Cassandra answers, but I don't hear a word of it. My thoughts are explosions of flashes.

Returning to my room, I find it empty. Lottie is gone. A sense of loss comes over me. Lottie was crazy, but she was *my* crazy roommate, not Gretchen's, not Addy's, but mine. And now she is gone. She's just like all the others who left. I fling myself on my bed. I think about Jim leaving when I was five and Frances when I was six, and then...then Meg and Gabe. My body tenses with anger.

"I hate you! I hate you!" I scream a half dozen times into my pillow. I tuck my fists under my chest. My blood is pumping much faster than normal. *It's not Lottie's fault for leaving.* I bury my head deeper into the pillow, silencing any chance of being heard.

"It's not her fault!" I scream. My heart aches. I turn my head toward Lottie's bed. "Quit being a baby, Anna," I whisper to myself. I get up out of bed, ignoring my urge to curl up and sleep. "Accept it."

I strip the sheets from my bed so it's as naked as Lottie's bed. If not for the posters and pictures and letters hanging on my side of the room, it would appear no one roomed here. I decide to make some changes. I move the two beds so they stretch out perpendicular to the window, so I can reap the benefits of a window as much as my new roommate, whomever she may be. I keep my desk against the same wall and move Lottie's against the wall where my bed used to be. Both nightstands sit next to the beds, mine to the right, Lottie's to the left. I carefully take down my posters from the far wall to rehang them on my new side of the room. I tape the poster from Marie in the center of the others because I like it best. It's of a kitten that is barely hanging onto a tree's limb. The caption above it says, "Hang in there." I hang the rest and stand back making sure the posters are straight. *Perfect.*

Confinement or not, I don't care. Without even taking a peek outside my door, I nonchalantly walk across the hall to get new bedding for both beds, and this time I grab as many blankets as I can possibly hold. I make my new roommate's bed first, hoping she's a young girl I connect with—maybe like Cassandra. Having taken six blankets for myself, I lay five of them directly on top of the mattress to give it as much cushion as possible. Then the fitted sheet, then another blanket, and a quilt I finally snagged. There are only two quilts on the unit, so some other lucky stiff and I will be sleeping in comfort tonight.

Looking around at the new layout, I feel a sense of ownership and pride. I fling myself backward onto the bed, testing the comfort level, satisfied when I don't hear the crackling of the cheap mattress underneath.

"Tomorrow, I will dress in my clothes, and everything will feel right."

At my desk, I take a puzzle from the drawer that my mother brought me weeks ago. The cover shows two cats sitting in a basket. I never opened it, believing I would be gone from the fifth floor before I could ever put three hundred pieces together. How wrong I had been. I string together the border pieces first, smiling when I've finished the frame.

twenty-five

The sun shining in through the window and the glorious comfort of my newly made bed make a world of difference to this morning. I can't wait to shower and pull on my jeans and T-shirt. I jump from bed like it's Christmas morning, knowing the long awaited anticipation has come to an end.

I look at the almost finished puzzle. I worked on it all day yesterday, taking breaks for lunch and dinner and visits from Chad and Carol. I thought after Dr. Ellison's conversation with me, both would bring up my nightmares again, but they hadn't, and I was thankful for the casual conversations they brought to the day.

My shower is quick. I exit the bathroom with a dance in my step. My teeth are brushed, my hair is brushed, and oh, the luxury of my jeans and shirt. I hurry to breakfast, wanting to be near the others. I don't care who I sit next to today as long as it's a warm body with a beating heart. It turns out the beating heart next to me belongs to Ethan, who quickly sits down after I am seated. I think he has missed the extra servings I had provided during mealtime. I feel bad thinking how disappointed he will be when I don't offer him anything, but there is no way I'm taking a chance of losing privileges again. *That's for damn sure.* I don't even lean over to explain to him for fear Isaac might think I'm passing food. I make a mental note to clarify things with Ethan before lunch.

The conversation is light. We all dismiss the last three days as never happening. Instead, we talk about outside friends. Gretchen, of course, brings up a different boy's name. I don't know how she keeps all her stories straight. I can only hope her stories are made up, because if they're true, she is sure to become pregnant within weeks after she leaves here. I notice Cassandra doesn't say much. She is more of a listener, making comments only when it pertains to her. Aside from her suicide attempt, she seems put together. I have a feeling she has always been a responsible, fun-loving girl who was given too much to deal with at too young an age. She reminds me of Ben. I look around. It's very possible all of us sitting at this table were dealt the same hand.

I AM AS thrilled as ever to be in the art room choosing the project I want to create. In the past, I chose to make things that could be finished within the hour, thinking that I would be gone the following day. But after three days of confinement, I forget my wishful thinking. I choose to make a hot plate for my mother. The wooden pallet is already provided. I select about a hundred small tiles to glue to the wood, mostly blues and purples and some white and yellow and a variety of other scattered colors, too. I arrange them into several different designs before choosing the one I want. I smear deco glue over the wood and carefully push the smooth, granite-like tiles on one by one. I eyeball the pallet from different angles, making sure it has even edges and balanced corners, so it doesn't look like the piece of crap I brought home from ceramics class last year. The entire hour passes quickly before it is ready to set aside for tomorrow.

Looking at it has me thinking about my mother. I think about all the times she has come to visit me. There are no hugs exchanged between us, which according to Chad is unusual. Regardless, she comes every possible chance she can. I wonder if Chad has changed his thinking since he has seen her commitment to me. And Bridg—it occurs to me that my parents are forced to leave her at home alone when they are here with me. Like years ago when they were forced to leave me for Liz. A teardrop falls onto one of the tiles and rolls off to the side, giving me my first indication that I am crying.

Not now! I beg of myself. But it's too late. In what seems to be slow motion, tears fall upon tile after tile; their colors blend into a mass of black surrounded by rays of vivid yellows. I keep my head down, hoping to go unnoticed. I push my project aside, wanting to protect my mother's gift from being ruined. My heart swells. An image flashes, then two, and then another. I see myself standing by my mother's bedroom window tucked behind the drape, a car backing down the driveway, and inside on the back seat rests my dying sister.

I push the hotplate farther away and lay my head on the table, enclosing my face tightly in my arms and opened hands. Pounding hammers and voices of those around me become distant as buzzing fills my ears. I fight to keep the room from going black.

Why can't I stop this? I question myself over and over, struggling to find answers. Searching, my mind strays. I hear Ben's voice surround me. *"Scars... imprinted on your soul."* I feel Robert's desperation. Then Cassandra, her words ring through my ears. "I was more frightened thinking about how hurt my brother would feel believing I didn't love him enough to fight for him." I think of Liz. *Did she too try to live for me?* The rubber band squeezing my chest tightens with every thought. *She loved me. I know she loved me.*

The art teacher sits in the chair next to me, whispering for me to lift my head slowly. She thinks I'm on the verge of passing out, so I try to act like this is my only issue. She doesn't need to know about my flashes because frankly, it's nobody's business. I lift my head slowly according to her wishes. She comments on the beautiful tiles I have chosen for my project, which makes me feel as though I'm two years old and needing the extra encouragement. I contemplate throwing it out, but looking at it, I can't. My mother, who I know will cherish it, deserves at the very least this much.

THE REST OF the day drags just like the last three days. Group presents the same old problems. Listening to Gretchen's boy troubles has me wanting to scream. Addy hasn't let up on her tough attitude, and honestly, I am sick of it. And Jonny Love, well I'm not really sure why he is here or even if he cares where he is as long as he's happy. Ethan on the other hand, I have to admit, seems to be toughening up. He's learned some real skills that will be of use to him in the outside world. I wish someone would tell him that losing weight would be a plus. Take about fifty pounds off, and he might be quite a looker. And Robert, sitting quietly without speaking a word, is processing mounds of information. I can sense this about him. The way he shifts his body and his head every so often gives me hope. He is a kind-spirited soul, a little like Jonny Love, but more of an intellect.

And then there is me. I guess it wouldn't be fair if I sat around analyzing everyone but myself. Feeling as free as a bird at the day's beginning, just because I dressed in jeans and a T-shirt, had not turned out as such. The familiar latching sound of the unit's door, which I thought I'd grown accustomed to, only proved that I was locked in. But it's worse than that, I figure, because the only freedoms people really have are their own thoughts, and I have trapped mine securely within my soul. I have come to learn the reasons why I'm here and have done nothing to accept them as my own. I am not here because I stopped eating or ripped a test in two or decided one day I just didn't have the energy to move forward. I am here not because I lost every battle with the outside world, but because I have lost every battle within myself. And because of this, somewhere along the way, I had come to believe I could never truly be free.

I THOUGHT I would be happier sitting in the small conference room for my one-on-one instead of my bedroom like the last three days, but really I don't feel happier. So much for the easy conversation from yesterday, because today I can tell, Carol is following Dr. Ellison's lead and questioning me about Liz. She's trying to make it sound like we are having normal chitchat, but I know where the conversation is heading. Actually, I feel a need to share. I want to tell her about the flashes and nightmares and the thoughts I can't seem to control, but my mind and body seem to be at odds with each other. When I try to tell her just a little something, my throat closes as though my air passages are being knotted, threatening my life.

I assume Carol senses my frustration because she puts her hand on my arm.

My first thought is to pull away, but I resist. Instead, I accept that she may be able to help.

My heart begins to race. She moves her hand down toward my wrist, and I am not sure, but I think she is feeling for my pulse.

"Anna, let me help you..."

"Carol," I interrupt. I am about to say something important, but suddenly I can't remember what it is. My face heats, and a painful sting radiates inside my nose. My throat constricts, causing me to tense. I shift in my chair trying to release my breath. The room begins to spin.

"Shhh. Imagine your throat opening. Breathe," Carol whispers. She faces me, our knees almost touching. Her hands are on top of my hands, forcing them to lay open on my knees. I blow out a puff of air and take it in ravenously. I do this several times before each breath gracefully makes its way to my lungs.

"Carol...," I close my eyes begging for it to come, "I'm sorry I left her out."

"Who?" Carol asks.

"You know. When I counted. I'm sorry."

"You're right, Anna. I do know, but I want you to tell me."

"Liz," I say.

Carol taps my leg, wanting me to look at her. "It's okay."

"It's not okay."

"Why?"

"I don't know what to say when asked what number kid I am. I was the ninth, but if she doesn't belong anymore, I'm the eighth.

"What makes you think Liz doesn't belong anymore?"

Carol's question has me wanting to stop. The sting in my nose returns, and my throat is fighting to stay open. Carol is telling me again to breathe and focus on my throat opening.

"Because, Carol," I say, frustrated she doesn't get it, "she's..." A vague image flashes in my head.

"Try again," Carol says. "Liz is...what?"

I close my eyes, hoping to stop the second flash from coming, but I can't. "Nope. Nope. I'm seriously done talking," I say, putting my hands in front of my body like I'm ready to push at anything that gets in my way. Carol waits for me to give in, but there is no chance I will.

"Chad asked me to remind you about his switch with Brian tonight," Carol finally says after the long pause.

I am thankful for the reminder. Chad had told me about his schedule change a week ago. He said he wasn't thrilled about the dreaded night duty, but he was pleased that Brian would have the pleasure of meeting me.

I hadn't told Chad that I sort of know Brian. Not that I have any clue what he looks like, but I know him very well by sound. He has a light step and seems to be happy. I know this by the way he strolls into our rooms at night, sometimes quietly whistling Beatles' songs. I would think the night shift would require more quietness, sneaking from room to room, making sure everyone's in their rightful place, but apparently not. I am awake most nights on his hourly rounds, pretending to be asleep. I hear him opening and closing bedroom doors way before he gets to mine. I like knowing someone is around. When he reaches my room, he clicks the flashlight on, shines it into my face, clicks it off, and turns on his heels to leave. Even though I have never met him, I get the feeling Brian is a kind person, and someone who would probably jump from his skin and go screaming down the hall if I were to jump out from behind my bedroom door and scare him. Chad doesn't know it, but I look forward to meeting Brian, too.

WHEN I DON'T see Robert in the lounge area, I make my way to his room to check on him. I find myself sitting just outside his bedroom door instead of across from it. He is sitting against the wall, near the inside entrance of his room. I sense his need for company; maybe we both need it. His silence gives time for my thoughts to run wild. I think about Cassandra and the way she seems put together. I suspect she'll be gone soon. Being here is probably just procedure—suicide attempt, hospital bed, fifth floor, and then home to her brother and father. And yet I don't believe she conformed to anyone. I think about her words from yesterday. Somehow I understand where they came from—deep within her soul. She had given up, not given in. Cassandra had figured out how to give up the feeling of abandonment to celebrate her life with her brother. Ben had done the same. He had given up hatred and reaped the power of love. And Carol, she'd given up self-pity to claim her self-worth.

It occurs to me that maybe Ben's parting words told his story, just as Robert's face tells his. I look over at Robert. His stare is pitifully blank. I have no idea what has happened to him, but it must have been horrific. I can't stand seeing him this way any longer.

"Have you ever read *To Kill a Mockingbird*?" I ask, expecting Robert to answer, but he doesn't. Not right away, anyway. I sit back against the wall to think, and from the corner of my eye, I see Robert respond with a slight nod, indicating he has. My eyes brighten. I had expected Robert's answer to be no, but what I got instead was an answer, I realize now, I should have expected all along.

I'm not sure if I had any real intention when I first asked Robert if he'd read the book. I sit forward, staring at the blurred wall. I swallow hard and take in a long breath. "You remind me of the mockingbird, just wanting to sing your heart out and bring good to others. But it's like when someone shoots at the mockingbird, you too have been hurt by people's cruelty. It's like that sticks and stones and other baloney...names do hurt.

"Robert..." I stop, blinking a few times to let my vision clear. I'm left staring at the door frame in front of me. A stream of visions enters my thoughts. It's Kyle and Timmy climbing the stairs. Trailing behind is another sibling, but I can't make out who. They follow Frances upstairs to the living room. I see myself watching all four climbing toward me. Tears swell in the corners of my eyes, blurring my vision again. I want to stop, but I need to finish. Not so much for Robert but for myself.

"Sometimes really bad things happen to really good people."

A teardrop frees itself from the corner of my eye. Robert's legs stretch out as he repositions his back higher on the wall, uncurling the rest of his body. He reaches his long arm toward me and places his hand on top of mine. Tears stream down my face.

Sometimes really bad things happen to really good people. Ben understood this, and by using the mockingbird, he was teaching me to search beyond other people's ignorance. Atticus Finch understood this, too. He wanted Jem and Scout to hear the mockingbird's song. He wanted them to listen to the truth of an already convicted Tom Robinson and recognize what Boo Radley had to offer. Ben wanted the same for me.

"I'm sorry, Robert, for whatever happened to you." Robert wraps his fingers around the back of my hand. I know he is listening.

TONIGHT MY PARENTS arrive exactly at six. I suppose my mother has been worried with the absence of my phone calls and her visits. She stays in my room for the full two hours while my dad strolls in and out of my bedroom, pacing the hallways and drinking several cups of coffee. He's done this for the last few weeks, so I figure my parents worked out this plan to make my life easier. I am grateful for my mother's presence, but I just don't have much to say. Maybe today has taken its toll on me.

My thoughts have been unpredictable all afternoon with flashing images I don't understand. I wanted to skip dinner, but without that option, I had forced it down. Brian was on dinner duty, and though I was sure he was up to speed with my rations, he didn't push the matter when I left my plate half untouched.

My mother and I continue random conversations until visiting hours end, saying our good-byes. She walks toward the nurse's station to find my father, but part of me wonders if she's hoping to speak with one of the nurses. I could tell she sensed something was different tonight. Maybe it's the last three days of confinement, or maybe not, but I feel it too. Something seems out of the ordinary.

My dad peeks into my room to say good-bye as I am already heading to the bathroom to change into my pajamas. My mom waves again from behind my dad, and they walk out together. I listen for the exit door to snap shut before continuing on my way to the bathroom, listening for its familiar sound because of something I noticed earlier. When I had been talking with my mom, the constant snap, as visitors came and went, confused me. Each time the door closed, the sound of it seemed distant, as if the door were miles from my bedroom. My parents exiting the fifth floor did not change this unfamiliar sound.

I am in bed before eight thirty. Longingly, I look at the empty bed stretched out alongside the opposite wall. An unusual awareness stirs within my innermost core. I think about Chad checking on me throughout the night, and a sense of relief and safety reassures me. I hear the tick of my clock as it lulls me to sleep.

I wake to a piercing scream.

twenty-six

 My nightmare plays out like an eight-millimeter black and white film.

I am a small child standing in a room, partly hidden by a drape that doesn't belong hanging from this wall. An old, gold colored couch sits in the middle of the room, facing a large window that looks out onto the backyard. I realize I am in the living room of my house. Someone is playing the piano that sits to the right of the stairs leading down to the foyer. Her blonde curls stream down her back. She stops playing and turns to face me. I tightly close my eyes, but laughter compels me to open them again. I stare at her. Liz stares back, her smile brightening the room.

I wave. She giggles and then I do, too. She presses her finger to her lips to hush our giggling, but I am so happy she is here that I cannot stop. She points toward the stairs with her other hand. My eyes shift to follow her gaze. The front door opens and then closes, snapping shut. I sense something is wrong. Frances appears on the stairs first, then Kyle and Timmy and—Liz; she is following behind. I cannot see the grim faces of the others because I pay close attention to Liz. Her angelic face is glowing, her smile is wide, and her few freckles sparkle like specks of sand. I giggle, jumping in excitement. Liz, again, puts her finger to her pursed lips to quiet me. The room becomes very still. An odor of dirt comes from underneath the drape and surrounds me.

The film crackles, and I can hear the reel jump forward,

grind to a stop, and then rewind back to the same frame. This time it moves forward in slow motion. Completely tucked behind the drape, I am no longer a little girl jumping and laughing. I have aged, almost an adult now. Unable to step beyond the drape's protection, my spirit child is lifted from my soul and into the open room. I watch myself portrayed as a child observing those ascending toward me. Liz follows quietly behind the others, climbing each step slowly. My breathing falls silent as I continue to watch myself from behind the drape. I recognize my innocence, see my smile, and hear my giggle. Frances is begging me to stop, but I am absorbed with the presence of Liz, who is nearly at the top step, and I ignore my eldest sister's plea.

My inner child holds her arms out in excitement to greet Liz.

"I have waited so long for you to come home." Hearing the echo of my innocent voice disturbs my focus from behind the drape.

Frances' voice booms through the room at a thunderous level, "Liz is dead! Don't you get it? They're going to throw her in the ground and cover her with dirt!"

I pray for the film to skip ahead, knowing I can't bear to watch. I know what plays out next because I was there. I look for an escape, but I am motionless as the film resumes.

On the couch just a few yards away, sits a seven-year-old girl changed from what she was just moments ago. Her innocence has vanished. Her vulnerability is so fragile and her grief so complex that her mind forms gaps severing reality. Deeply wounded, she frantically holds onto life as her mind plummets toward death.

I push the drape aside, stepping away from its protection and into the open room. I cannot take my eyes off my inner child. I walk toward her, watching my every step for precision. As my focus heightens, those around me become translucent; some even disappear.

I sit on the couch next to this little girl and pull her into my open arms. The commotion subsides. The only sound that can be heard is the whimper of a seven-year-old child. This child I must protect because only I can understand her pain. I feel the swelling in her chest as her delicate body begins to choke itself. Air becomes a precious gift she never before understood. Intoxicating smells intensify, and monotonous buzzing in her heightened hearing grows louder.

My adult voice, though quiet, fills the room, "Breathe, Anna." She looks to me, searching for reassurance. Her eyes tell a story that can no longer be kept secret. I sense her distress to move forward. Her face distorts as she fights to take a breath.

"Breathe!" I scream.

The first scream has me sitting straight up in bed listening for where it might be coming from. It takes only seconds before I realize it's me. Again, my screams rip through the room. I should stop; I want to stop, but I can't. Chad pushes through my door, switching on the lights and racing toward my bed. I'm aware he's entered my room, but the film continues in my mind. The images are no longer snapshots of my childhood, but rather a constant strand of memories.

I start a series of screams, trying to escape the explosions firing through my head.

"Anna! Hey! Look at me." Chad's hands are on my arms, forcing them to my sides, but I have a new power I cannot explain, making it easy to fling his arms away from me. I throw my head back on my pillow, gaining power behind every kick as I involuntarily push at anything in my way. One good strike, and Chad is shoved away. Then another and my bed pushes away from the wall nearly a foot.

Another scream erupts, but this time I cannot control the words I have kept secretly hidden inside for so long.

"I hate you! I hate you. You left me! I needed you, and you left me!"

Two other men join Chad.

"Let's get her bed away from the walls," Chad says. "Anna, calm down."

A nurse arrives. I am trapped with so many surrounding me.

"Anna, you need to stop now." Chad has his hands tightly around my arms, pushing them into my mattress.

I should stop, but I can't force myself to do it. Every scream, every kick, every twist and turn of my body feels glorious. My legs are being pulled and pushed, triggering another wave of violence to free myself from their grip. One leg escapes. The instant it's free, I send it slamming against someone or something before it's caught midair going in for another violent strike. Forced to the bed by someone's powerful hold, I can no longer move my lower half. I try to move my upper body, but I am completely pinned. Then a sharp stab to my thigh has me screaming in rage. Strands of memories lessen as I fight to keep them from disappearing.

"No!" I scream. "Oh God, please let me see her."

"Who, Anna? Who do you want to see?" Chad urges, shaking me.

He thinks I'm half asleep, but I'm awake and aware of everything. I look at him, focusing on his expression. Something is wrong. His blue eyes have lost their sparkle and they are filled with worry. His tight grip loosens. He looks directly into my eyes, panting heavily.

"You're awake. Calm yourself," he says.

His eyes turn warm, but he gulps air like a boxer who has just won after fifteen rounds. My breathing matches Chad's, though I gather I'm the loser of the match since I am flat on my back.

My bed is rolled away from my room. My clarity fades, frightening me. The hallway lights are brighter than normal. The doors to the other bedrooms seem to be in the far distance. I can hear voices, but I am not sure from where.

I squint trying to see through the bright hallway lights. Two distorted images push me farther down the hall, *and then she comes into view. Walking to the side of my bed, as clear as day, is Liz.*

I have no concept of time when I wake. I am in a different bed but have no memory of how I got here. My head is pounding, and I can feel blood pulsating through my temples with every heartbeat. I try to move, but I am securely strapped to the bed. I lift my head slightly and see wide leather belts with massive two-prong buckles binding my ankles and wrists.

Someone sitting in the corner of the room leaves, and moments later Chad, Carol, and Dr. Ellison are at my bedside. They are speaking, but I can't make out what they are saying. Their bodies are swaying back and forth similar to the room. Memories of my childhood surround me. Pictures of myself as a child appear on the walls and ceiling, some in flashes, others in constant motion. I close my eyes, but the scenery doesn't change. Loud buzzing fills my ears. I assume it's Carol who turns my head to one side as I gag and then vomit. Immediate relief surges through my body for a short time as I fight to stay awake. I am slipping in and out of consciousness before I am overcome with blackness.

Standing in my parents' bedroom, I hide between the window and the long drape that hangs down to the floor from the rod above. I look out onto the driveway below through one of nine windowpanes, waiting and watching. In one framed glass, a reflection of a swing set appears as Liz tumbles onto her head. Then a reflection of our bedroom materializes on the next pane. Liz is dressed in her shoes and coat as she lies silently in her bed. My father's reflection appears. He lifts his daughter from her bed and places her into a hospital bed. Machines are hanging from the walls, and from her tiny body hang wires and tubes. Her head is wrapped in white cloth. She rests underneath an old tattered afghan. I close my eyes to rid the images from my view, but each reflection remains visible.

My mother, she is there by Liz's hospital bed and so is my father. I am there too, but my parents can't see me. I pull the afghan closer to Liz's chin. A doctor enters the room and explains to my parents about some brain tumor and an operation.

I touch a windowpane with my fingertips, touching Liz's face.

"I'm going home soon, Anna."

I jump up and down in excitement.

My father leaves the room to continue the conversation with the doctor. My mother stares at Liz with a confused look.

"Look." Liz smiles, pointing to the corner of the hospital room. I look to where she is pointing and then smile. I recognize Her. She's the Lady in the stained glass window at church, except prettier.

Liz's arm goes limp and falls to her side, but her smile remains the same. She turns to face her Mother. Her words sound heavenly, "I'm going home."

"No! Please, no! Don't go! Don't leave! I'm sorry! I didn't mean to kill you! I couldn't catch you!"

My eyes flood open like a bursting dam. I gasp for air. My high-pitched screams fill the room. "I'm sorry! I'm sorry. I didn't mean it. Please!" I beg, repeatedly screaming toward the ceiling.

"I hate you!" I scream louder. "I will always hate you! I'm sorry! Forgive me! I didn't mean to kill you!"

The tight squeeze of the restraints holds back my need to run from my screaming. I toss my head in resentment, but Carol catches hold of it. She and Dr. Ellison are at my bedside talking to me, but I ignore their attempts to console me. While my head is forcefully held in place, I wriggle one of my arms free from its restraint and swing it toward Carol's hold. Wires tangle around my arm before Isaac arrives, pressing my arm down against the mattress. I suck my lower lip into my mouth and bite down hard in an attempt to lessen the storm raging inside me. Carol plugs my nose, closing off my air passages. I hear the beeping of machines I hadn't noticed before.

My chest swells. Blocked, pressure builds. Forced to pull my clamped teeth from my lip, I gasp for air. Dr. Ellison has a large needle brought to her.

"No! Don't! Please stop!" My demands are denied. My muscle stiffens with anticipation as the needle plunges into my right thigh again. With no possible escape, my emotions overflow into frustration. My screams become pitiful cries.

"I don't hate you. I have never hated you. I wanted to die for you. I prayed for you to live. I will never hate you."

And then, I guess from the drugs, my legs begin to twitch, then my feet and arms and hands. My screaming picks up speed as my heart races. The machines sound a different alarm than moments ago. Spasms jerk throughout my body. I scream for help, not from anyone around me, but from Liz. I beg her to touch my hand. I beg for her forgiveness. I beg for her love. The strain in my muscles suddenly relaxes. The walls close in on me. My eyes flutter, but I refuse to close them. My attention is on one particular corner. I recognize Her immediately.

Her dress is beautiful. A pale veil cascades down around Her shoulders. I am spellbound by Her aura and beauty. She is standing in the corner of the room just like She had as Liz lay resting in her hospital bed. Her heart is filled with such glory; burden lifts from my body. Tranquility fills my soul.

"Do you see Her?" I ask, trying to point with my restrained hand. The three standing over me look to the corner and then back at each other confused. I don't repeat myself. There's no need because they can't see Her, just as my mother couldn't years ago. My lids weaken. If I don't speak soon, I won't be able to at all. I attempt a deep breath, but only a whisper crosses my lips, "She is here, watching over me."

twenty-seven

Dr. Ellison urges me awake. My eyes flutter open then shut again.

"Anna, I am going loosen your restraints. Can you hear me?"

I nod, fluttering my eyes again. I can't seem to wake myself.

"I want you to lie still."

Each restraint is loosened and then unbuckled, unbinding me from their tight grip. Too heavy to move, my arms and legs remain in their restrained position.

"Can you drink some water?" Dr. Ellison asks.

I slightly shake my head no.

My arms and legs are being rubbed; I suppose to wake me. I wonder who besides Dr. Ellison is in the room.

"Let's roll her to her side," Dr. Ellison says.

"Anna, I'm going to roll you to your left." Chad's voice is so loud he must think I'm deaf. I attempt to roll myself, but with the small amount of strength I have, the task is impossible; besides, something pulls at my chest warning me to be careful.

"Hold on," Chad says, "you're hooked up to a couple machines." He rolls my dead weight to one side. "Take a few sips," Dr. Ellison says.

A straw is placed in my mouth. My tongue feels swollen. I take a few swallows before one goes down too fast and I cough, spewing it out. Dr. Ellison takes the opportunity to check my lungs while I'm on my side half choking to death. The straw returns to my lips, and I manage a few sips before Chad rolls me to my back. He buckles the restraints, but they're looser than before.

"I want you to rest, Anna. I'll be back in a few hours to check on you," Dr. Ellison says, mentioning something about the monitors before she leaves the room. The bleeping has me fixated on its rhythm. My body, heavy with exhaustion, gives in to sleep.

Again, I wake with absolutely no concept of the time or day. The windowless room is dark. A restraint lays snugly over my abdomen and another across my forehead which I don't remember from before. Machines are still beeping with a synchronized sound. The room's door must be cracked open because a stream of light, on the only wall I can see from my restrained view, takes the shape of a slightly opened door. I have to pee and the pressure of the heavy belt over my middle is making the sensation painful. My moan brings Chad into the room. There is no time to waste.

"I have to use the bathroom." My voice is horse so I try to repeat myself, but Chad obviously understands.

"Let me get Virginia," he says.

"Hi, Darlin'," Virginia says, nearing my bedside.

"I have to use the bathroom," I say, grimacing.

"Sure thing, Honey." She unbuckles the restraint around my waist. "I'm going to slip a bedpan under you, and then you'll feel much better."

"I want to use the bathroom." I clear my throat to rid my voice of its raspy sound. "Please, Virginia."

"Not yet, Sweetheart. I promise this won't be so bad." She places the bedpan underneath me and gives me privacy.

When I finish, I call for her. With my hands restrained, I realize I have to drip dry. I am completely embarrassed as Virginia drags the bedpan from underneath me and takes it to a nearby bathroom, I assume, because I hear a flush within seconds.

Chad enters so quickly after Virginia leaves that I figure he must have been waiting right outside the bedroom door. My face reddens again.

"How are you feeling?" he says.

My head is pounding and my body is stiff, especially my right thigh where I was stabbed with needles.

"Can you get these off?" I ask, pointing with my eyes toward my wrists and ankles.

"I'll unbuckle this one," he says, releasing the restraint from my head. "I'll leave this one off too." He slides the abdomen restraint off and down to the side.

"I want them all off."

"Not now, Anna."

"When?"

"As soon as I get word from Dr. Ellison."

When I hear this, I don't question him any further.

"My leg feels hot."

"I think ice will help quite a bit," Chad says, examining my right thigh.

And though I hate the thought of pills, as Chad leaves for the ice, I ask him to bring something for my head.

The ice sends chills up my spine, but the relief from the pain feels so good I don't care. I lift my head as Chad pops in two pills and lifts a small Dixie cup to my lips. I swallow them down.

"What day is it?" My voice crackles.

"It's Saturday," he says, and looking at his watch adds, "and almost six in the evening."

"What happened to Friday?" I blink several times clearing my focus. "Why are you here on a Saturday?"

Chad smiles. I focus on his eyes, and I am reminded of not too long ago when they were heavy with worry. There is no need for him to answer my questions. We both know the answer. I suspect we'll talk about Friday sooner or later. And

Chad—he's here today because of me. I quietly sink back into sleep.

CHAD'S VOICE WAKES me. He and Virginia are in the room.

"It's time to unhook you, Honey," Virginia says.

I have no idea what she means until she tugs at wires connected to my chest.

I push my eyelids open for a mere second and see wires everywhere. There looks to be a hundred of them. "What are those for?" I ask, closing and opening my eyes attempting to see straight.

"This one shows us your heart activity."

"Sorry, Darlin'," she says, pulling my hair from a sticky pad on my head. "And this here shows us your brain's activity."

"EEG," I say, closing my eyes.

"That's right." She sounds impressed. *It's not rocket science.*

"That's got to feel good," Chad says, removing the four restraints holding my ankles and wrists. I want to open my eyes to look, but I'm too dizzy.

I slide my feet slowly up toward my butt, bending my knees, and then losing my strength, they fall like dead weight. I cautiously work the kinks from my arms and shoulders. I am stiff, but my soft muscles immediately begin to regain some strength. I open my eyes in an attempt to focus, but everything is fuzzy. I turn toward Chad. There are two of him. I am seeing double so severely I don't know the real him from his double.

"I'll order you some dinner," Chad says. He lifts the rails on both sides of the bed before he leaves me alone in the room. I look around. Things double into fours, making me feel nauseous. I close my eyes to avoid vomiting.

I smell food before Chad enters the room. He lowers one of the rails and pushes the all-too-familiar cart on wheels by my bedside.

"Can you sit up?" he asks.

I slowly push myself up, keeping my eyes tightly shut.

"Are you feeling all right?"

"Yeah."

"Open your eyes, Anna."

I act as if nothing is wrong when I open my eyes and see four of him.

"Sorry about the hamburger. I've put in a new order, but until it arrives I want you to take a few bites."

I see four hamburgers on the plate. I attempt to take hold of one, but I have no idea which one to take hold of, so I take my chances reaching for all four hoping to get lucky. When I bring it to my mouth nothing is there. I go in for another try, but as I do Chad pushes the tray away, already assuming something is wrong before I tell him I am seeing double.

Chad helps me lay back down. He walks just beyond the door and asks someone on the other side if Dr. Meyer is available. I know the name. I see him on the unit a couple days a week, usually working with older patients.

Dr. Meyer examines my eyes, asking me to look every which way while he shines a light into them, and then he feels a need to listen to my heart. I think it's an automatic for doctors to plug their ears with their stethoscopes and listen to a beating heart no matter if it's a broken toe to be examined or seeing double. Dr. Meyer unplugs his ears, charts something, and looks at me with eight eyes.

"You're going to be okay," he says, looking at my chart again. "You have a lot of medications in your system needing to be worked out. By morning you should be as good as new."

I close my eyes, wondering if I had been given more than two shots.

After Dr. Meyer leaves, Chad stays only long enough to make sure I drink water. "I'll be here on Monday. Until then, please behave yourself." He chuckles, closing the door behind him.

"Chad. I'm scared." I expect him to ask me why or of what. I don't know how I will answer him because I honestly don't know myself.

He heads back over toward me. "You've been through a lot, Anna. It's normal to feel frightened."

"Leave the door open tonight, okay?"

"Wide open. And I will be right outside your door if you need me. Now try to sleep."

Chad again heads for the door. Opening it to its full potential, light floods my room. Silent tears stream down the sides of my face. Before long my abdomen is convulsing with each sob. I let out a gasp. It feels good to cry, really cry. I think back over the past few days. Friday is missing, but the others are vivid. I recall the nightmares and screams. I recall my dying sister's face and the beautiful image of the Lady. I recall childhood memories I thought were lost forever. The tears soak my pillow, but I don't care. I remember waking to a soaked pillow after unsettling nights, unable to recall the events that had caused me to cry. Tonight my tears are real, for a real reason, real events, and real memories.

MY EYES ARE practically swollen shut when I wake. I'm on my stomach with my hands tucked under my pillow. I have no recollection of when I made the switch from my back, but all the heaviness from yesterday's wires and straps and tears are gone, and it feels good to move freely. I scoot to the end of my bed to get around the railings that have been holding me hostage like a two-year-old child. With my feet planted on the ground, I look around, seeing the room for the first time from all angles. Dr. Meyer was right. My double vision has disappeared and so has my dizziness and nausea. My bed is right smack in the middle of four boring walls. The machines that were hooked to me earlier are now in a corner with the cords wrapped around the bottoms ready to be rolled away.

No closets, no bathroom, not a thing but four boring walls. *Quite the accommodations.*

There is no commotion outside my door, giving me the opportunity to peek out. A couple of nurses on the other side of the window are busy looking through charts and other stuff. I figure it's around four in the morning by the looks of their tired faces. *Sunday. Right? Nobody better tell me different, or I'll lose it.*

I go unnoticed, stepping farther into the open area. *Ah, I know this place.* After leaving Dr. Pins' office when I first arrived on the fifth floor, I had noticed these empty rooms and wondered what they were used for. I guess the last few days have given the other patients in the unit reason to no longer speculate their use. And the bathroom, I know it will be to my right before I look. I had assumed the nurses and MHTs used it when I first saw it.

I look through the glass to see if I can see Robert's room on the other side of the nurse's station, but it's too dark. I head to the bathroom and see the lounge through the front glass. I glance at the clock on the wall above the TV. Almost five. The door that leads to this back room stays locked and can only be opened by a buzzer in the nurses' station.

I use the bathroom without turning on the light, hoping to scoot back into my room without being noticed. I wash my hands before I flush, knowing the sound may send a nurse to investigate my activity. *One, two, three...*I take a breath, push the handle. *Flush.* Acting casual, I exit from the bathroom, heading around the doorway and disappearing into my room; my heart beating heavily. I jump to get into bed, forgetting about the railing, and hit my knee. *Crap! Crap! Crap!* I want to yelp, but instead I limp around to the end of my bed, jump in, and scramble under the covers. I rub my knee forcefully, hoping the friction lessens the pain.

"Is everything okay in here?" a night nurse calls, startling me. Quickly lying back, I tense, unsure if I should pretend I'm sleeping or admit it was me out there.

"I had to use the bathroom."

"I don't want you leaving your bed without help. Do you need anything?"

"Yes. Water, please."

The light switches on, forcing me to squint. Coming into view is a large black lady whom I have never seen before. Her graying black hair is pulled so tightly into a bun that her eyes look stretched. Her teeth are whiter than white, enhancing the brightness of the room. She looks old, but by the sweetness in her voice and the sparkle in her eyes, I rethink my guess.

"I'm Trudy," she says. She points to the cup on the cart.

I pull the straw and lid off and drink, tapping the bottom hoping to catch every last drop.

"Look at you, child. You're thirsty, aren't you?" Trudy leaves the room and returns with another Styrofoam cup filled with water.

I barely say thanks before lifting it to my lips, gulping it down.

"Girl, you got to slow it down. You'll make yourself sick drinking too fast like that."

She may be right, but I don't stop until the cup goes dry. "Can I have more, please?"

Trudy smiles. "Yes, you're thirsty all right. I'll bring you more in five minutes and not a moment before." *And not a millisecond after.* "You let what you have inside you settle some. I'll be back, don't you worry."

It is the longest five minutes of my life. My stomach is in knots at the thought of my thirst. She returns with a much larger cup filled to the brim with water. My hands shake as I reach for it, believing I won't get it to my lips fast enough. Trudy doesn't let go until I have a strong grip around the cup and it's pressed against my lips. I suck half of it down before I can control my thirst and savor the rest of it. I take the cup away, gasping for air.

"I want you to remain sitting up for a few minutes 'cause I want no vomiting on my watch," Trudy says playfully.

I nod in agreement and attempt to say thank you, but I burp in between my words.

"You are very welcome." She laughs. "You sure are a sweet thing, aren't you?" *She's obviously not up to date on my chart.*

I feel okay, so I lay down as soon as Trudy leaves, thinking about what she has said. I once was a sweet girl. I think back to the days when I giggled at the silliest things. It was my smile most everyone commented on—how happy it made them feel. I cringe thinking about the events that took it all away.

Maybe there's a chance to get it back.

Staring at the ceiling, I wait for Sunday morning to arrive. When it finally does, I don't feel any different than hours ago. The commotion in the nurse's station is welcoming, but my loneliness stays unchanged. Virginia comes in bright and early, dragging a vitals cart behind her. I don't complain having my blood pressure and temperature taken. *But c'mon, how much more information can they possibly need after having me tied down and hooked up for the last three days?*

"You're looking good this morning," Virginia says. "How are you feeling?"

"Fine."

"Did you sleep well?"

"Yeah."

"Your mom will be here tonight."

"Okay."

Virginia gives up, realizing my one-word answers hint that I want to be left alone. Deep in thought about nothing has me confused. I can't place my feelings, and it bothers me.

Holly rolls in breakfast.

"How's Robert?" I ask, not sure if I really want an answer.

"He's good. He's worried about you, though. He sat in the TV room for most of Friday and Saturday and a few times right outside the back room door."

I should be excited by Holly's news, but for some reason I'm not. "Tell him I'm fine, would you?"

"Are you...fine?"

I truly don't know how to answer Holly's question. I figure I didn't die from the last ordeal, so I guess I'm fine, but fine doesn't really explain how I feel—neither does great or miserable or anything in between.

"Yes," I say, figuring it's the most logical response to put a stop to our conversation.

"I'll tell him, then." She smiles, leaving me to stare at my breakfast.

I force enough food down to satisfy Virginia, but when she looks at my tray an hour later, I think she contemplates asking me to eat more. Lunch is the same. I don't really care if I gain an ounce; I'm just not hungry. My stomach feels full or empty or maybe neither. I have only taken a few bites of the toasted cheese sandwich and barely a sip of milk when Virginia puts her foot down and sits with me, insisting I eat the strawberry yogurt, which has gone warm, making it even harder to swallow. I feel bad about giving her the brush-off earlier, so I eat the yogurt without complaining.

Alone once again, I venture out to use the bathroom. Still in my pajamas, I feel unkempt and gross. I wash my hands and finger-brush my teeth the best I can. I wet my hands again and pull them through my hair, trying to rid myself of bedhead. Splashing cold water on my face releases the tautness I feel from the saltiness of my tears. I dig into the corners of my eyes, removing crusty, leftover sleep. I want to look somewhat presentable, but I question for whom or for what reason.

Instead of heading back to my room, I walk alongside the nurse's station to a large screened window. Besides the muffled voices of the few nurses and MHTs who are visible through the glass, quietness surrounds me. I sit in the corner of the six-foot window ledge. It is the perfect sitting area for my size. I stretch out my legs, and still there is plenty of space if I decide to lie down flat. It is nice to have a different view of the outside world from the one outside my room. I find the exercise path below. My thoughts lead me to the last time I was outside the hospital. It has been a week since I took off running for no apparent reason other than it felt right at the moment. A lot has happened since then.

I close my eyes and envision Ben walking alongside aisles of library books until he finds his favorite. I imagine him pulling it from the shelf and gently rubbing his hand over the cover before he opens to his favorite page. I think about his gentle ways and his acts of kindness. Unexpectedly, I don't miss Ben as I think about him. I hope he is well where ever he might be—helping the hopeless would be my guess. I try to smile, but instead I cry. I am not crying for Ben or me or anyone. I don't curl my legs to my chest or block my face with my hands or lower my chin. I simply look out from five floors up, allowing my tears to fall as they wish. There is no discomfort in my stomach or legs or arms or any body part at all. There is no buzzing in my ears or blackness before my eyes. No flashes, no images, no momentous thoughts.

The back door is buzzed open and the sound comes from the distance it should. There is no echo or distant sound that so often skewed my hearing before. I notice Robert and Holly only when they are close enough for me to sense their presence. I take my eyes off the outside and turn toward them.

"Robert wanted to make sure you were fine. He asked to see you."

I look from Robert to Holly and back to Robert.

"Thought you two might like to spend some time together," Holly says before leaving us alone.

Robert props himself up against the window's ledge opposite me. With our outstretched legs, his feet reach to about my knees. His eyes have a touch of life that hadn't been there before.

"Did you really ask to see me?" I tilt my head to one side looking cockeyed at him.

He smiles. "That, I did."

His voice is masculine, much more than I thought it would be.

"You mean to tell me that your first words on the fifth floor were heard by someone other than me?" My smile grows with each word, and Robert's smile matches mine.

"If it's any consolation, my first word was Anna."

We don't say much after that. We both turn our heads toward the outside and watch. I am glad Robert is here, but my loneliness continues to invade my world. I wonder if this has been Robert's feeling for so long—knowing a great big world exists and we can't find us in any part of it. My tears fall again.

"Robert?" I ask, turning to face him. "Will we make it?"

"Yes, Anna. That, we will."

I try to smile but realize there is no need to fake it. Robert moves his legs so that they surround the outsides of my legs. He gently squeezes, protecting mine with his own. Again we move our gaze to the window, and from the fifth floor we look beyond the screened window that protects us from the world outside that awaits us both.

This time it is Robert who turns toward me. "I did have a pet—a guinea pig named Charlotte." He looks back toward the outside. I think back to the conversation during group when I spoke on Robert's behalf. I smile.

twenty-eight

Holly comes for Robert by the time my dinner arrives. I remain on the window's ledge as the sun sinks into dusk. Several walkers and riders appear on the trail below, probably getting some fresh air after their long day. The sky dims, and the dark heavy screen covering the window makes it difficult to see the commotion below as cars buzz in and out of the parking lot. I try to catch a glimpse of my mother's car below. Frustrated by the screen blocking my view, I begin to pick at the heavy mesh hoping to create a tiny hole to get a better look, but it's impossible. *It's here for a reason—to keep me securely inside and hidden away.* Just thinking about it has me wanting to cry or rip the secured screen from the window. Not knowing which one would make me feel better frustrates me more. I slap at the screen with the back of my hand, testing its strength or maybe my strength. The instant sting takes away the ache in my gut for a few seconds, and the release feels good. I place the back of my hand against the screen; this time rubbing my skin over its rough surface.

I don't feel the pain at first, but as I dig in deeper, I feel the tiny cross wires of the mesh rip at my skin. With each back and forth motion, I hurt myself worse, but I don't stop. It feels good to feel something after feeling nothing. Isaac enters the back room through a glass door that connects to the back of the nurse's station instead of using the buzzing door. He's dragging an office chair behind him—the comfy kind that swivels and rocks. I quickly move my hand where I hope it will go unnoticed. A sting begins to radiate from my knuckles.

"Hey, Anna. Let's get some food in you. Want a ride?" Isaac says, standing behind the chair, waiting for me to hop on. I'm not interested, but he is so nice I don't have it in me to disappoint him.

Grasping underneath the seat, Isaac zigzags me back to my boring, nothing-on-the-walls room where my tray of food waits, cold and unappetizing. I position myself on my bed, keeping my hand hidden from Isaac's line of sight. I don't expect him to stay while I eat, so when he does, I awkwardly maneuver the fork with my left hand.

"It's been a tiring couple of days for you, to say the least," he says, rocking in his swivel chair as I take a bite of stone-cold mac and cheese glued together by the sauce. "How was your day?"

"Fine."

"Describe fine for me, Anna. I've got to write something in your chart and 'fine' just won't do it for Dr. Ellison. You don't want to get me fired, do you?"

I look at Isaac just to make sure he's kidding. A big smile stretches across his face.

"I'm not sure. I don't feel sad or happy, I guess." I try to zone in on how I feel, knowing I will be drilled tomorrow. Virginia and Isaac tend to let me off the hook now and then, but come tomorrow, there will be no chance that either Carol or Chad will accept a "get out of jail free card" from me, and as for Dr. Ellison, I better be prepared for the third degree.

"What do you remember most from the past few days?" Isaac continues.

I want to ask him why I can't remember Friday and parts of Saturday, but not wanting to hear his answer, I decide the time is not right. I simply don't want to think about anything at the moment, but knowing Isaac won't leave until I chat about something and eat at least half my dinner, I fish around for anything to talk about.

I uneasily put down my fork and pick up my spoon. It's harder to control than the fork, but I attempt to carefully move a spoonful of canned peaches to my mouth without giving away my awkwardness. Slurping to try and catch the juice running down my chin doesn't help.

"I remember screaming...and being tied down."

"Do you remember what you were screaming about?"

I think back. I remember my tormented screams and my frustration of being restrained. I remember the rhythmic bleeping of machines and drugs being pumped into my leg, but now it all seems so surreal.

"Honestly, Isaac, I really don't."

Virginia pops her head in my room. I am surprised to see she is still here. "Your mom's here to visit, Darlin'."

Isaac chimes in, "Well, I have to say, it's your lucky day." I know he is referring to visiting hours saving me from finishing our conversation and this nasty dinner. "I'll tell you what. I'll talk with your mom for a few minutes while you finish up your peaches and..." looking at my glossed over macaroni and cheese, Isaac shifts his eyes to something more appealing, "mashed potatoes."

Knowing my mother will be buzzed into the back room is humiliating. I am uncomfortable to have her see me here in my dirty pajamas at six o'clock in the evening. Earlier Virginia offered me a gown, but I couldn't bear the thought of slipping into yet another one, so I refused. I try to imagine my mother's thoughts as she walks past my old room to this back room—double secured and bleak.

I hurry and finish what I can of my dinner when I hear Isaac nearby. He glares at the tray and then at me before removing the tray, leaving the vanilla milkshake behind on the cart.

"I want this finished by the end of visiting hours."

He is justified in his disapproval, but still his warning

embarrasses me with my mother here.

Isaac leaves his chair in the room for my mom, but I end up sitting on it while she takes a seat on my bed. I swivel it so my right hand faces the wall, not wanting to bring attention to my hand. The sting is worsening.

"Are you okay?" my mom asks.

"Yeah," I reassure her, rocking back in the chair.

"I got a call Thursday night about what was happening. I heard your screams in the background. It was awful, Anna; I haven't slept since."

I look over at my mother. She looks exhausted and aged. Her hair is whiter, and it looks as if she's gained weight. She had been here only twice this week, and apparently everything had taken its toll—first the news of my attempted escape and now this. Her face shows worry, much like the expression I had seen years ago after my sister's death. It's funny how this memory reappears just by an expression on my mother's face. I cannot stop thinking I have disappointed her in some way.

My mother continues her one-way conversation as my thoughts take a turn for the worse. I am not where I am needed most—at home making sure all is good. "The Little Girls"—Bridg and me—this is how we were referred to after Liz didn't return. "The Little Girls"—I was responsible for so much more than before. I had once been the middle child of three, pushed into the obligations of the oldest of two after Liz's death. My position in the family had changed overnight. I didn't quite fit between Bridgett and Marie, who is eight years older, or my brothers Timmy and Kyle. The divide in our family had happened many years ago, separating Liz, Bridg and me from the older seven. Without Liz's return, the gap became more pronounced. My mom had lost Liz to death and now me because of it. I had failed miserably at protecting my little sister, something Liz, had she lived, would not have done.

"Anna, what am I going to do with you?"

My mother's comment pulls me from my thoughts, and I smile. She often asks this when I am happily trying to make life perfect for everyone around me.

"I really wish I knew, Mom." I contemplate what I want to say next, and then I just go for it. "I'm really glad you're here," I say. It is beyond awkward to let these words pass over my lips. I wonder how it is possible to feel completely vulnerable by merely a sentence.

She hesitates, searching for words, questioning if she should look at me or smile or simply nod her head in agreement. "Wild dogs couldn't keep me away," she says.

We continue our visit with nothing more than small talk. By the time visiting hours end, I desperately need to inspect my hand—now pulsating systematically with my heartbeat. I close the bathroom door behind me and inspect my hand for the first time. *Shit!* The skin is ripped badly. White pus is oozing from my knuckles, and a patch of skin is missing from the back of my hand, right in the center. I run cold water over my entire hand, attempting to stop the burning sensation and get some relief, but the sting and redness worsens each time I pat it dry. The soap is worse. The second it touches my riddled skin, the cuts seem to burst into flames, so I quickly put my hand back under the cold water, rinsing it off, keeping it there until there's a knock on the bathroom door.

"Are you all right in there?" Isaac says.

"Yeah. Can you wait?" I call back, gathering up the courage to ask for help. I pat my hand one last time and open the door, trying to act like what I have to show him is no big deal.

"What's up?"

I show Isaac my hand.

"How'd this happen?" he sympathetically questions, looking from my hand back to me.

"I'm sorry," I begin and then tell him the truth.

Isaac takes me into one of the doctor's room and has me wait while he gets Virginia to inspect my hand more thoroughly.

"Oh, Darlin', why would you hurt yourself like this?" she says, carefully tilting my fingers in every direction to get the best possible view of each separate wound. She guides my hand to the examining table, placing it in a small bowl containing some kind of solution. The sting is painful but worsens when she dabs my knuckles with hydrogen peroxide. I close my eyes thinking it will help, but it doesn't

"Hold still."

"My God, are you ever going to be done?"

"I've got to do this, Sweetheart, if we don't want infection setting in."

"Seriously, I'd rather have the infection," I hiss. Virginia ignores me. By the time the bandages are wrapped around each finger and most of my hand, I want to cry. I am embarrassed for hurting myself on purpose. Virginia asked why, and for the life of me, I can't figure it out.

Isaac comes into my room to say goodnight. "Tomorrow morning we'll get you back to your old room, but for tonight I want you to sleep tight with no worries. Is that a deal?"

"It's a deal," I say.

To my surprise and his, I ask Isaac to close the door. Lying in complete darkness actually feels good. My hand is throbbing, but I try to ignore it. Something tells me that I will not be reprimanded for my actions like I would have in the past, but still I am self-conscious of harming myself.

It's been a long day, longer than any I can ever remember. The emptiness of my thoughts and the loneliness I feel are more than I can bear. Isaac said to sleep tight. I think I will do just that. I move to my stomach, letting my arms rest along my sides. I let the darkness close in around me, knowing tonight I will sleep undisturbed.

twenty-nine

It doesn't take long to stir out of sleep. I venture out from my room. I tap on the glass, startling Trudy. She opens the same back door Isaac used yesterday.

"Well, you're up early. It's not quite five yet." Her grandmotherly ways put me completely at ease.

"I'm ready to move back to my room. Can I, please?"

"Well look at you, all bright eyed and bushy tailed. Let me see what I can do. You give me a minute here to make a phone call or two."

Trudy goes behind the glass. I keep my eyes on her every move. I figure the only person she's calling this early is Dr. Ellison to get permission for my return to my old bedroom. I like the way Trudy doesn't seem to have a care in the world that it's an ungodly hour to be disturbing my doctor's sleep. She senses my craving for some normalcy, which makes me her first priority and Dr. Ellison's sleep second. Her smile tells me I'm a freed woman.

My room looks larger than it did before, although nothing has changed. My bed is back in its original place, and the other bed is still empty. The idea of returning to a new roommate hadn't occurred to me until now, and I am glad to be alone.

"Let me cover your hand so it stays dry. Did I guess right? You want to take a shower?"

I stick out my bandaged hand and smile.

"You sure are a sweet thing, aren't you?" Trudy covers

my hand with a plastic bag and some medical tape.

The shower is incredible. Trudy checks on me several times just to make sure I haven't drowned. When I tell her I'm okay, her laughter lingers as she leaves the room. Even if I tried to explain the feeling of hot, steamy water falling over my body, or of brushing my teeth, or of dressing in clean clothes, and of combing my hair, my words could not justify how happy I am walking from the bathroom.

I'm at my desk placing the last fifty or so puzzle pieces into their rightful spaces when the entrance door begins to open and close. The daytime shift will be here soon, bringing Carol and Dr. Ellison and everything in between. I put the last puzzle piece perfectly in its place. I admire it, proud of myself for completing it. I look at the box's cover and then the constructed three hundred pieces. Although both show the same picture, they seem different. Whereas before I was looking at two cats sitting in a basket, now I see it as two kittens playing, looking as if they have been up to mischievous acts. Memories float into my thoughts—mischievous memories of long ago—of climbing walls and building forts. These are good memories, and ones I can place and call my own. Carol enters my room as I pull the puzzle pieces apart, placing them back into the box.

"How does it feel to be back in your room? And cleaned up?" Carol has a great big smile on her face and is bubblier today than ever, probably happy to be freed from the back dungeon too.

"Good," I answer for lack of a better explanation.

"Breakfast will be ready soon. I'll see you there in a few minutes."

EVERYTHING AND EVERYONE seems different at breakfast. Gretchen asks me right away what happened, and of course, everyone sitting at the table goes silent waiting for my response. When I say nothing, Ethan saves my neck, jumping in at the perfect time to break the ice with a question for Jonny Love.

"So, Jonny, how'd your home visit go?"

I'm sure home visits were already discussed last night, but I'm grateful for Ethan's interjection. *Yep, Ethan's going to make it on the outside.* Robert willingly sits at our table. That doesn't seem to surprise the others, so I guess he's included himself over the past few days, and they are over the shock. I wonder if he has taken to speaking to anyone besides me.

I am looking forward to finishing my mom's gift in the art room, but Dr. Ellison has me in one of the small conference rooms by nine o'clock sharp. The conversation is grueling, and I just want it to end. She isn't wasting any time while things are fresh in my mind, I suppose.

"Do you prefer to call your sister Liz instead of Elizabeth?"

"Yes. Nobody really calls her Elizabeth."

"Your mother tells me the two of you were very close. What sort of things did you do together?"

"I can't remember..." *Give her something.* "Actually, we used to build forts together, but it was a long time ago."

"True, but you still remember it. We all look back on memories, and I want you to look back on good memories, too."

Dr. Ellison goes quiet for a second too long, indicating she's preparing me for a tough question.

"Do you remember screaming that you hated her? Were you referring to Liz?"

I nod my head in remorse, feeling guilty at my unkind words about someone I had loved so much. "Yes. I didn't mean it, though."

"Look at me, Anna." Dr. Ellison is relentless in her questioning, and I know if I don't look directly at her she will not continue until I do. "It's okay that you said what you did. And if you're thinking it now, it's still okay. You're grieving. It is normal to have these thoughts. You should know that you also cried out many times how much you loved her."

"I did like her," I say, not being able to consciously force the word love into the open for others to hear.

"Yes, you did, and you still love her. It's all right to be angry by her death."

"I'm not angry. It was a long time ago," I mutter, becoming frustrated by the conversation.

"Do you feel like she betrayed you?"

I shift my eyes away from Dr. Ellison. "I cannot do this anymore."

"Yes, you can. Do you feel as though Liz betrayed you? That she left you?"

"I'm seventeen. I know she didn't decide to die."

"You were seven when she died. Did you feel at the time of Liz's death that she left you alone?"

The way Dr. Ellison rephrases the question makes it easier to answer.

"She died, so I guess she did leave me, but it wasn't her fault."

"Do you think it was someone's fault that she died?"

"I don't know! Why are you asking me these questions? I told you, I don't remember!" I yell.

Dr. Ellison lets my breathing calm while she charts. She finishes and closes the binder. She looks at me with little emotion. "Do you feel a need to cool off in the back room?"

"What? No."

"Then I expect you to compose yourself." She continues, her compassion returning. "You have every right to be angry, but you'll need to open your mind and let me help you resolve your anger. I understand you would rather avoid my questions than answer them. You are unsure of how to handle the past, and it frightens you..."

"It doesn't scare me," I interject.

"You may not think so, but nightmares are telling. I am speaking of things you already know either in your conscious or subconscious mind. You are ready to work through your past, Anna. Quite honestly, I have never seen anyone more ready than you, but you are going to have to trust that we can do this."

I nod, indicating I'm willing to try.

"We're finished for today, but our conversation will be the same tomorrow and the next day and the day after that and as many days as you need."

BY DINNERTIME, I just want to curl up and sleep, to make it all go away. After leaving the conference room, my day hadn't gotten any better. My one-on-one with Carol was not as grueling as Dr. Ellison's, but still she pushed for answers I didn't know how to give and others I didn't care to mention. Chad stopped by my room during quiet time to tell me he needed to register a new patient, so not to expect him until much later, after dinner some time. I had barely scraped by lunch, eating just enough to get nothing more than a look from Isaac, and I secretly hoped Chad would stay too busy to check on my dinner. Part of me hoped he would stay busy all night, and the other part wanted answers about the last few days, especially Friday.

I pull myself from my bed knowing dinner is being served and wanting to avoid one of the MHTs or nurses coming for me. I walk toward the dining area. The hallways are empty, like my insides. Flashes are now non-existent, but conflicting emotions are now my driving force. I take my tray of food and seriously contemplate sitting alone, but knowing I'll be obligated to explain myself, I sit in my usual spot with the others. One look at my meal and I feel ill because my stomach just can't take it. I wish this whole eating thing had never been an issue in the first place. Addy's eating a mouse's portion of food, and I've seen Gretchen not touch a bite when she's had a bad day.

What about me? What about my bad day?

It seems strange that just a short time ago mealtime consisted of planning and scheming to clear my plate. *What had I been thinking?* I look over to Ethan. He actually looks thinner. A salad and fruit cover his tray instead of his typical burger and fries. I think back to breakfast and lunch. I don't recall him eating bacon or any greasy food.

"When did you start ordering salads?" I ask.

"Two weeks tomorrow."

"Are you on a diet?"

Ethan's grin shows how proud he is. "Yep, lost eight pounds as of today. Lifting weights too."

"That's great." *Was I attempting to push food on his plate when he was dieting? Had I been so wrapped up in myself that I hadn't noticed or considered his feelings?*

"Isn't it?" Jonny Love adds.

"You keep this up, you'll give those idiots back at your school something to worry about. One false move and you'll pound them into the ground," Addy says.

I believe Addy is right. Already Ethan's face is clearing, revealing his good looks. His bigness is becoming tallness, making him seem more confident. Even his voice seems manly instead of nerdy.

"Ethan, I'm sorry if I tempted you with food when you were trying to lose weight. I wasn't thinking...I...I'm really sorry."

"Don't worry about it. I could have refused it."

I chuckle to myself, imagining what it would look like if Ethan were to take Addy's advice and pummel anyone who bullied him. I look at Ethan again. *Won't happen. He's way too nice.* I smile, truly happy for him. If nothing else, he deserves this much.

I glance over at Gretchen. She is staring at Ethan, quietly adoring him with dreamy eyes. Maybe I've been too critical of Gretchen. It's possible she just wants to belong.

We're just about finished eating, and still Chad hasn't

been in to check on me.

"Are you sewing your shirt tonight?" Jonny Love asks Addy.

"Uh-huh. Isaac said I could. I'm almost done."

"You sew?" I ask, making it sound more like an insult than a question.

"Yeah, I do!" Addy reacts to my question sarcastically, making me aware that I have insulted her.

"Sorry, Addy. It's just that you never mentioned sewing."

"True, but I don't know much about you either, so I guess it makes us even." Her tone catches me off guard, so I react without thinking.

"Well, what the hell do you want to know?" Our voices go unnoticed by others sitting at the surrounding tables, but Ethan, Jonny Love, and Cassandra become as quiet as Gretchen and Robert.

"Are you fucking with me?" Addy ridicules. "In group today we asked what the hell happened to you, and you didn't make a single comment about the past few days. We were all going crazy with worry, and you decide not to tell us a single damn word. And Robert over here..." she says under her breath, glaring at Robert then back to me, "is as closed mouth as you. He's the only one who gets access to see you, and we couldn't convince him to share what was goin' on in that back room if our lives depended on it. And furthermore, I love to sew and I'm damn good at it."

I have never been more relieved than the moment Chad enters the dining room to check in on me. "What's up? You sure are a quiet group," he says. *The hell we are.*

No one seems to move a muscle until Jonny Love decides to lighten the mood with his typical free-spirited way of life. "Just trying to clear the clouds from the sky," he says, moving his hand as though he is clearing the clouds away from above us.

Thank you, thank you, thank you, Jonny Love. We all

laugh, including Robert whose laughter is nothing but a sudden chortle, but all the same, it is heard by all of us.

TONIGHT CASSANDRA, JONNY Love, Gretchen, and I decide to sit in the dining area while Addy sews away on her shirt. I pretend to be reading the teen magazine Gretchen slid under my door over a week ago. I think about my bad luck today with Dr. Ellison, Carol, and Addy; it's all one giant mess. Chad hasn't come looking for me since dinner, so I figure tonight can only get better. I look over at Addy. She looks completely absorbed in her sewing. It surprises me she is allowed to use scissors, but I figure someone must trust it's not a problem. Although with Isaac and Daniel peeking in every three or four minutes to check on us, I can hardly say we are unsupervised.

"Hey, Anna, you want to cut my hair?" Gretchen asks.

"Sure," I say, putting down the magazine. "Do you mind if we use your scissors?" I ask Addy.

"Go ahead." Addy continues sewing, paying little attention to us.

"I'll be the lookout like in the old movies." Jonny Love watches the door.

"You shouldn't, Anna. You'll get caught," Cassandra says.

"Sit here," I tell Gretchen, pointing to a chair next to Addy in case I need to quickly replace the scissors. Cassandra starts reading the magazine, obviously not wanting anything to do with getting caught. Gretchen holds chunks of hair out of my way as I cut one section of dry hair at a time. I hold the cut hair in my other hand and then toss it into the garbage after each snip.

"Psst!" Jonny's alarm sends the scissors sliding toward Addy, and Gretchen and I pretend to be having a conversation. *A sure give away if we don't do it right.* We follow the same routine for about twenty minutes until I have cut an inch from Gretchen's shoulder length hair, bringing it closer to her chin.

"It makes me look older, don't you think?" Gretchen

comments, swinging her new do about.

I am unmoved by Jonny Love's and Gretchen's excitement in getting away with what we have just done. I was hoping to feel excited too, but the only thing I have when I leave the room is a guilty conscience. I walk toward Robert's room, hoping to stop myself from thinking about how I've deceived Daniel and Isaac. When I peek in, I see an older man, almost Santa Claus-like. I figure he is Chad's new patient, but after hearing the man talk, I consider he may be visiting Robert. I slide down the wall outside Robert's door and listen carefully. Robert does not say a word, but the man talks about some past experiences the two have had together.

"Remember our fishing trips? Do you still have the fishing pole I sent you on your tenth birthday?" the man says.

Talk, Robert. Talk to this man. I plead with Robert through telepathy. *Please, say something, anything.*

"There you are. Are you ready?" Chad's voice takes me by complete surprise. I jump up more from shock than readiness.

We walk around the corner to the dining area instead of the conference room where we typically meet. *Why here?* I wonder. It's empty, but still I'm uneasy being here where I just cut Gretchen's hair. I will myself to stay calm.

"Chad," I ask, "who is that man in Robert's room?"

"His grandfather."

"Is this his first visit?"

"He's made several attempts to visit, but yes, this is his first time actually seeing Robert."

"He's been here before?" I ask, searching my memory

"Yes, but Robert refused to see him until today. Enough about Robert, let's talk about you."

We sit down across from each other at one of the tables. I look out the window to the darkening sky.

"How are you feeling, it being your first full day away from the back room?"

"A little crazy, I guess."

"A little crazy? How?"

I have been through this back and forth banter with Chad before. He expects me to elaborate and will not allow me to give one-word answers for long.

"Dr. Ellison wasn't too happy with me today."

"Why do you think that?"

I tell him about my meeting with Dr. Ellison and what happened at the dinner table with Addy. Chad listens intently, asking me questions here and there. I look at the clock hanging on the wall, hoping the hour is nearing an end, but only twenty minutes have passed. I feel my insides tighten as I think about telling Chad about Gretchen. My chest strains, but oddly my throat feels open and I'm breathing just fine.

I look directly at him. "I cut Gretchen's hair."

"When?"

I am glad his eyes don't change from the compassionate look of a moment ago.

"Tonight, while Addy was sewing."

"I know, Anna," he says after a dreadfully long pause.

I'm not really surprised he knows. I don't ask him how he had found out because I'm well aware of Gretchen's immature ways. I figure she lasted maybe five minutes tops before bragging about her haircut and thrill-seeking experience. I had known all along she would spill her guts, and that is why I had taken her up on her offer.

"I would like to know why, though."

I don't fumble for words or think about what might sound pleasing. Instead, I tell the truth. Chad listens as I tell him about my empty feelings and how I thought having any feeling, even if it meant doing wrong, had to be better than feeling nothing at all.

"What does your emptiness feel like?"

"I don't know," I say honestly. "It's like I should be crying or sad or angry or something, anything after the last few days, but I feel nothing. When I was locked up in the back room, I cried myself to sleep a couple of times, but now I can't remember why. I don't understand. And..." I continue lowering my voice, not wanting to hurt Chad's feelings. "Dr. Ellison and Carol and you want me to spill my guts about my sister and things that don't matter anymore; things that happened a long time ago. The constant badgering from everyone is pointless. I don't need to talk about it like everyone thinks."

Chad is not fazed like I thought he might be. His eyes remain unchanged, and he smiles, letting me know it's okay to voice my opinion. "Let's just say that you'll need to trust that we know what's best for you. You may not like it, but a sign of maturity is the ability to trust and believe that people are trying to help you."

I slump in my chair crossing my arms in front of my chest. "Yeah, right. Like most of my teachers." My sarcastic whisper escapes just loud enough for Chad to detect my resentment.

"Nobody, neither your teachers nor your parents, understood how sick you were. Your parents didn't recognize your distress in the mass confusion of an already tragic situation, much like Liz had no choice whether to live or die."

I begin to hyperventilate, pushing my chair away from the table with my hands. Chad reaches his arms across the table and takes hold of my wrists, making it impossible for me to scoot away any farther.

"Oh, no you don't." His words demand that I look at him. "These adults were people you loved and trusted. You believed in them, and unknowingly, they let you down. If they could take back what happened, I believe they would. You lost your trust in others, but it doesn't mean it can't be earned again. It's up to you, Anna. It's going to take faith and courage on your part to trust us completely."

Chad's not going to stop until he has made his point, but neither am I.

"I told you about Gretchen. That's trust."

"Yes, but think about what happens when I mention Liz? Or your nightmares?"

I so want to save face and tell Chad he's wrong, that I can handle it all. But hearing what he has said stirs emotions inside me. I look over to the clock again, nervously anticipating what's next and wanting the hour to be up before Chad can continue. "I'm kind of tired. Are we almost done?"

"Stop right there. This is exactly what I mean. You are uncomfortable when pushed past what you think you can control." He pauses for what seems to be an eternity. "What we are asking you to do is not easy; I know that. We all know that. But we need you to completely trust us and trust in yourself to let go of whatever you're holding back."

"Chad..." I want to ask how I am supposed to do this, but I can't get the words out before I break down in tears from frustration. Pulling my arms away, I tuck my hands under my face and lower my head to the table. It's a short-lived cry, but I feel better when it's over.

"Why the tears?" Chad asks.

"I can't, Chad. I can't talk about the things you want me to."

"Is it that you can't or that you won't?"

"I can't. Why won't any of you believe me? I can't tell you."

"Because Anna, I believe you can. All of us do. You're a fighter. You have it in you to help yourself just as you help others."

"Chad, I do...trust you."

"I know you do, Anna. And I believe in you."

This time it is Chad who looks over at the clock. "All in good time," he says, motioning for me to show him my bandaged hand. He pulls up a piece of gauze to look underneath. "But in the meantime let's get your hand rebandaged."

Turns out, the patient Chad spent most of the day

checking in is my new roommate. Betsy is petite like me but taller. Her curly red hair is so frizzy her head looks doubled in size, but it's styled nicely with wisps of hair pulled back in a barrette so it doesn't overtake her face. Chad introduces us. It is awkward being forced to sleep in the same room with someone I have met less than an hour ago. I empathize with Lottie being forced to accept me as her new roommate when I first arrived. It had been Lottie's fault for acting like a lunatic, but it had been my fault for overlooking her sleeping habits. I figure it's better to ask Betsy about her habits right away, so I don't find her leaning over my bed in the middle of the night, clawing at the wall and screaming obscenities. She says she doesn't care either way, giggling when I tell her why I'm asking.

"And you two had to stay roommates?" she asks.

"Yep, even though she nearly killed me."

"Was it awful?"

"Nah, not really. It was actually sad when she left. I mean, the entire time she was here, I wanted her to leave, and then when she left, I missed her."

"How about everyone else? Nice? Cool?"

"I'd say pretty cool. The MHTs, which by the way stands for Mental Health Technicians, can really be fun, especially on walks on the exercise trail. The nurses, they're more into procedure and stuff, but they're pretty cool, too."

Betsy smiles. Her dimples match her easygoing personality. "So...what's this exercise trail like?"

Sitting cross-legged on our beds, I tell Betsy about the trail and other things she can expect while she's here, like arts and crafts and boring weekends. I can tell she is interested by the way she asks questions about the things I mention. I like this about her, the way she's not afraid to ask. She genuinely likes knowing all the little details that most people don't bother to notice. Neither of us tells our life stories, but the simplicity of our chitchat is a welcome diversion from earlier today.

By the time we settle into our beds for the night, Chad comes waltzing into our room. "Dr. Pins will be here early tomorrow morning to look at your hand."

I am not surprised Chad called someone to look at it because when he had taken the bandages off, two of my knuckles, which had gotten the worst of my wrath, looked quite nasty.

"Have a good night's sleep. I'll see you tomorrow." He switches off the bedroom lights, leaving the bathroom light on. Tonight, for the first time, having a roommate feels good.

thirty

Being twenty, Betsy attends the adult group sessions instead of my teen group, so it was during quiet time when we had really gotten to know each other. But today I find myself alone in my room. I wish Betsy were here to keep me company. Our conversation, I am sure, would keep me from mulling over the past several days since my release from the back room.

Betsy has been forthcoming about why she is here. Her younger sister was killed in a car accident a few years back. In one of her therapy sessions, she made the mistake of telling her therapist she was thankful Cook County was free of cliffs because, given the opportunity, she would consider throwing herself off one.

"Would you really jump?" he had asked, and Betsy had said, "Yes, I believe I would."

It wasn't supposed to be funny, but when she explained how it happened, we both giggled. Afterward, she quieted down, and I wondered if there was more to the story than she was telling me.

I consider peeking over into Gretchen's room, just to keep my thoughts from drifting back over the past couple days, but reconsider. Having Betsy for a roomie makes Gretchen's immaturity seem more pronounced. I sit at my desk, looking at the things I have collected during my stay here. The bottom drawer contains the kitten puzzle, a couple untouched crossword books, several packs of Dentine gum, Payday candy bars, a deck of cards still wrapped in its cellophane, and a few pens and pencils. Most of the items are the things my mother brought in the bag of necessities when I first arrived. I reorganize the drawer—first by blowing away dust and scraps that have settled in the corners and then by replacing everything neatly inside.

From inside the top drawer, I pull out a thick stack of letters and cards, many of which I had received from friends at school. I reread the one from Janet. She says she misses me and wished she could have seen me when she stopped by the other day. Other cards I reread say about the same thing. I'm ashamed thinking I had refused to see them, just like Robert refusing his grandfather. Letters from neighbors whose kids I babysat and friends of my parents I didn't even know had come in abundance. I had cards from family and relatives, all wishing me well and sending prayers and good thoughts my way.

One letter in particular catches my eye, mostly because it's written on thin, blue colored paper that stands out among the white envelopes. I pull it from the stack gathered in my hand. It's from Jim, who over the years had sent many letters home about his travels and adventures on this same kind of fine, colored paper. The letter is addressed to me and mailed from China. It's strange to think I had not remembered Jim's visit to the fifth floor when I first received this letter. Just holding it reminds me of when I was little. A letter like this brought a lot of excitement and hope that he was possibly coming home. And when the letter didn't say, Bridg and I would guess where he would go next.

I open the letter again, to remind myself of his exact whereabouts, when something jolts a faint memory. I concentrate. My mind races toward the unclear memory, trying to make sense of it. Then it hits me like an iron fist. There is another letter, from years ago, addressed to the entire family and sent from England. My mother opens the letter as Bridg and I prepare to listen to her read. She sits in her rocking chair and Bridg and I sit on the arms of it, looking over Jim's letter.

The letter I hold in my hand crinkles under the pressure of my closed fist. I want to shake my thoughts, unsure if I want to reconnect with the past, but my mind races onward, examining every detail. The words are printed in blue ink on the same kind of fine, blue paper I am holding now. The date stands out in bold, written on top and to the right, June 14, 1975. There is no flash or image or reeling film. This memory is vivid, attached to my thoughts as plain as day. My breathing becomes heavy and steady. *I must continue.* I concentrate harder, fearing my visual might fade.

Five months had passed since Liz's death; I am eight. My mother begins to read aloud. I smile with anticipation. *It's rainy there. He's traveling to Sweden soon. He paints his red car blue. He hopes everyone at home is in good health and enjoying summer vacation. Something about Meg's graduation and Marie's driving license. Jim asks about Kyle and high school, and he can't believe Timmy will be a freshman. How are the little girls? Tell Anna to write. I want to know if she's excited about third grade.* "And Bridg," he says, "must be growing like a weed." "Sincerely, Jim," my mother says, and it's over. My smile fades.

I stare at the white wall, the same sensation of years ago falls over me. Jim had forgotten Liz. He didn't write a single word about her. She no longer existed, to him or anyone else for that matter. She had been alive in my mind but nowhere else. My memory sidetracks to after Liz's death. The white wall blurs, and I am aware that my eyes are moving rapidly, scanning the house, searching for her existence. There are no pictures of her; they have disappeared from the top of the silenced piano and from the walls. They are gone from nightstands and from my room. So absent from everywhere it appears that she never lived.

Everyone had forgotten Liz.

I am grasping the bundle of cards so tightly that the forming scabs on my hand pull, causing me to lose focus. *Why? I don't understand. Why had everyone forgotten her? Had I been wrong to keep her alive in my mind?* I toss the stack of letters from my hand and into the wastebasket, hoping to rid myself of this memory. I sit back in my chair, staring at the white wall in front of me. Recovered, the memory lingers, revealing my first uncut memory of Liz fading from the minds of those I loved. I take the wastebasket from the floor, looking at the letters inside. I reach in and pull out every single one and return them to my desk drawer.

Taking *To Kill a Mockingbird* from the same drawer, I glide my hand over the cover. I immediately open to page ninety-eight and again read the passage Ben read aloud weeks ago. I have come to understand why this passage was so important to him. Where most people couldn't see any harm in hurting a fly, Ben could. I think back to what he said before he left me sitting alone outside Robert's bedroom door. Questions ramble through my thoughts. *What truth? How? When? Who needs help? Is it me?*

If this gets any more confusing, I may consider finding the cliff Betsy mentioned to her therapist. I place the book back in the drawer and take out the only remaining item— the journal Chad had given me sometime during my first days on the fifth floor. He asked me to write down my nightmares when I had been trying so hard to convince him they were only dreams, which occurred so seldom I could hardly remember them. How naive I had been to believe I could lie to him about the one thing keeping me awake at night and causing me to scream as I slept. I redden, embarrassed by my immaturity—no different really from my accusations about Gretchen.

I open the journal and fish around for a pen in the bottom drawer. I flip through empty pages, smelling their newness. I turn to the first page. I have no idea what to write. Taking the pen in my right hand, my scabs pull, causing me to cringe and giving me an idea.

Dear Journal,

Wow! Chad wasn't kidding about Dr. Pins arriving early. Carol called for me to come along quickly, so I rushed to brush my teeth before running down the hall to catch up with her. The sound of the back room's buzzer had me feeling queasy. I pretended I was wearing imaginary blinders on the sides of my eyes as I darted toward Dr. Pins' office.

Dr. Pins actually remembered me, which made me feel good. Chad had done a crappy job of wrapping my hand because when Dr. Pins unwrapped the bandages, the gauze underneath was stuck to my knuckles with dried blood. He soaked it for a few minutes to detach whatever gauze he could and removed the rest with tweezers. He placed my hand in the same kind of solution Virginia had, and it stung like crazy. After he was done torturing me, he put plain old Band-Aids on instead of gauze. When he finished he said, "I see you've put meat on your bones. Keep it up, young lady." His voice was bubbly, making it kind of funny. Boys will never learn the right things to say to girls.

I chuckle as I write the last sentence. My older sisters often said this about their boyfriends. I suppose they're right because if Dr. Pins were a girl, he would understand why having meat on my bones is not considered a compliment. I read and reread my entry before tearing it carefully from its binding, ripping it in half, and throwing it into the wastebasket. I begin again.

Dear Liz,

I miss you so much.

I close the journal and tuck it back into my desk drawer. Betsy still hasn't returned. I imagine she is stuck with Dr. Inkblot. I wish I had thought to tell her to identify each blot as an eagle. I look at my clock when I hear others beginning to move about. It's four on the dot. I walk from my room to seek out Robert. When I don't see him in the TV lounge or his bedroom where he normally sits against the wall, my heart races as it did when I first discovered Ben had left. I quickly take another glance into his room, calming down when things seem to be in place.

"Robert?" I call from the hallway, unable to see him from where I am standing.

"Yeah."

"Are you okay?"

"Yeah."

I step into his room, knowing that entering another patient's room is off-limits. Robert is sitting at his desk, looking at a photo album. He glances at me and then returns to the photos. I stand next to him, looking over his shoulder, and when he doesn't object, I pull the other chair next to his. I stay quiet as he slowly flips through the pages. His grandfather, who has visited Robert three times this week, is in a few pictures. One picture shows Robert around nine or ten ready to cast his fishing line. His grandfather is standing behind him with his hands over Robert's hands, like he's teaching Robert the right way to hold his pole.

When he flips to the next page, I see pictures of a woman holding a small boy, who I assume is Robert. Because the same woman appears in pictures alongside Robert as an adolescent and some when he's older, I assume she's Robert's mother. It's odd to see such a happy child in picture after picture when Robert looks so misplaced and abandoned now. His mother, I guess, is dead since she's never visited.

On the next page, there is a picture of a young man. He looks much like Robert does now except the man in the picture wears a wide smile and seems to be enjoying himself, waving at the camera. From the corner of my eye, I see Robert's face flush as though he is holding back tears. I continue to stare at the picture as he does for far too long.

Ben's words surface, *Use your scars; use them for good.*

"Is that your dad?" I whisper.

Robert nods.

"Did he die?"

"When I was nine."

I had forced back enough tears over the years to understand the look on Robert's face. My heart is heavy with hurt. I want to open up, to tell him I understand, that I have lost someone close to me too, but I don't.

"A drunk killed him...," he says nonchalantly, "and my mother, too."

I don't understand. Who was the woman in the pictures? I am hesitant to ask, afraid I've already asked too much.

Robert turns toward me, making eye contact for the first time since I entered his room. His face is brightly flushed. His nose almost beet red from holding back a raging river of tears. His eyes reflect a desperate solitude. I sense he wants to free himself from his past, but he doesn't know how.

I have no idea what to say, so I just begin. "I'm your friend, Robert. It's okay." Robert scans the room frantically before he reconnects with me. "You're safe. I promise." I take a deep breath. "What happened? What happened to your parents?"

One large tear streams down his cheek. "When I was nine my dad...was killed by a drunk driver," he says, struggling with his already tortured words. "One day...he was just gone. Gone from late nights...with Johnny Carson. Gone from Sunday fishing. Our family days were over."

By the time he speaks of his mother's death, his face floods with tears and so does mine. His voice is barely heard through his sobs, but I can understand through my own experience. He cries for some time, holding his photo album close to his chest, and when he has cried enough, we sit side by side in his room, against the rules that today are meant to be broken.

IT TAKES EVERYTHING I have to get through dinner, but after eating, I'm feeling better. Gabe and my sister-in-law come to visit. We make our way to the TV lounge for some coffee. It's awkward having anyone other than my parents here. While the two of us girls sit on one of the lounge couches and chat, Gabe reads the newspaper. I don't blame him. This is an awkward place to be, and if I were in his shoes, I'd be hiding behind a newspaper too. They stay for about an hour, and I can't help thinking all three of us are glad when it's over. I see them out and head for my room.

Only a few minutes pass before Chad walks in and pulls up a chair. I hadn't thought about it before, but now I'm wondering why Chad hadn't been around earlier for our scheduled one-on-one.

"How'd your visit go?"

"Good."

"Do you have it in you to talk for few minutes?"

"Sure," I say, thinking it would be nicer to relax.

"Your brother, right?"

"Yeah. Gabe."

"Good conversation, I hope?"

"It was okay."

"Fill me in." Chad leans back, crossing his legs; his ankle positioned on his other knee.

"On what, the Tribune's headlines?" I say, jokingly. I give myself time to think. I'm glad Gabe came, hiding behind a newspaper or not, he was here. "There's not much to tell," I say, "because we didn't really talk about much. I don't see him much anymore. Honestly, I remember Gabe more from when I was a kid than I do now."

"What are the things you remember?"

"Like a four shelf stand. The plastic and cardboard kind, like the ones they put in grocery stores to stock things on, like chips. Gabe brought one home for me once, when he worked for Royal Crown. It was easy to put together, but the two of us sitting on my bedroom floor connecting the pieces was like…" My voice aches to say the words hiding in my throat.

"Like…" Chad says, raising his eyebrow and encouraging me forward.

"I felt like… he didn't just bring it home *to* me, but he had thought about bringing it home *for* me. Does that make any sense?"

"I think it makes perfect sense. Seems like a pretty good guy if you ask me."

"He is, Chad," I say, thinking about the fun we used to have. "We had this thing we used to do on the stairs in our house. Gabe would stand on the bottom step, and I stood on the top step with my back toward him. When he counted to three, I fell straight back like a mummy, and he would catch me on my way down."

"Sounds frightening," Chad says, but when I see his excitement instead of the disapproving response I usually get from the typical outsider, I realize he understands the true dynamics of my family.

"You know something? I never once doubted him, and never once did he miss catching me." I contemplate my next words carefully. I not only *want to say* what I'm thinking, but I *feel a need to say* it. "He was there for me…" My chest tightens. "I was so afraid after my sister died. I heard his voice in the hallway outside the bedroom where Bridgett and I were sleeping. We were in bed for the night, and I called for him. I needed his help because…because…" I hesitantly look for words.

"Why did you call for him?"

"I was scared because I wet the bed. There was no one to help me, and then I heard his voice. I didn't realize it then, but I know now Gabe's presence was my first shred of hope."

There is something else, but I'm reluctant to ask. I think back to my talk with Robert. I had expected him to trust me.

Chad is asking the same of me. It is time. *Take a deep breath. Trust.*

I hope Chad is listening closely because I am certain I will utter this only once.

"I honestly can't remember when or where Bridget and I were taken, but I can easily relive how terrified I felt, wondering what was happening and why we had been left. I remember playing with Barbie dolls, pretending to be happy, wanting Bridgett to be happy. I remember wrapping her with blankets as she slept, and still nobody came except for Gabe. And when he left, I hated myself for not begging him to take Bridget and me with him. I can't explain why I didn't or why I had been so stupid to let him leave without us."

Chad scoots forward in his chair, sitting about a foot closer to me. His hands rest on his knees, and his eyes are on mine. As I had chosen my words hesitantly, Chad chooses his carefully.

"I can't answer your question of why, but I can tell you that nobody truly knows how they will react or what they will say when tragedy occurs. Our bodies are set up for survival, and everyone has it built into them a little bit differently. Your parents thought it would be best that you and your sister be spared the horrible reality of death. It didn't occur to them that you were prone to the same suffering and helplessness the rest of the family faced. And you, being so young and being told nothing, had to make choices based on the unknown. You were unclear on what to prepare for, so your defenses prepared you chaotically for all situations. I would guess you planned first for abandonment, being placed away from your family so suddenly without explanation. You were frightened beyond recognition, and still you did what you needed to do for yourself and Bridgett the best you could. I want you to try something for me. Are you listening?"

I nod.

"Forgive."

"I am not blaming anyone."

"You are, Anna. You're blaming yourself. You said you were frightened because you wet the bed. The way I see it, you wet the bed because you were frightened. You need to forgive yourself for this. You had no control over what happened. You need to forgive yourself for not asking Gabe to take you and Bridgett home. You need to forgive yourself for feeling powerless. Like your parents, you reacted out of survival. I don't believe most adults could bear what you endured at such a young age. And one more thing," Chad says, sitting back in his chair, "today you showed Robert extraordinary compassion. I want you to consider showing yourself some compassion."

Chad stays for a while, but neither of us has much to add. My mind is racing. Chad had come looking for me and found me, but for whatever reason, he had neither stopped me from entering Robert's room nor minded that I had broken the rules.

thirty-one

*A*gain, the film stops. Then it skips forward, but this time it's Liz who sits on the couch, pulling me into her open arms.

"I'm sorry," I cry.

"It's not your fault," she whispers. She slowly moves my ear to her chest.

My chest opens, and my breathing calms. Embraced in her hold, I stare at the back of the golden couch. It looks smaller than I remember. Even the wall behind it, holding it in place, has lost its powerful look.

Liz unwraps her arms from around me. Frantically reaching for her hands, I interlock my fingers with hers.

"Let go, Anna." I look to her, searching for reassurance. She smiles. "Let go."

Our outstretched fingers, barely touching, separate. Alone, I lay my head where Liz's head once rested when I was seven. "I'm sorry," I say, closing my eyes.

Betsy is still asleep when I wake and venture to the bathroom to shower and dress. I hurry, trying to be considerate of another person using the same bathroom. When I finish, Betsy is awake staring at the ceiling.

"It's a weird feeling being here, isn't it?"

"Yeah." She moves her hands to her eyes, covering them. *No, please don't cry.* Her face reddens under her hands.

"Betsy, are you okay?"

"Um-hm," she sniffles.

I slowly make my bed, hoping it takes me as long as

it takes Betsy to stop crying. I look at my clock every five seconds, and I swear time is moving backward because the minute hand appears to be in the exact place as minutes ago.

"Can I get you something?"

"Are there any tissues around here?" Betsy rubs her eyes, taking in big sniffs as I hurry to the bathroom for toilet paper.

"Is this okay?" I shove a long piece at her. My actions must look comical because she smiles.

"Thanks. Reminds me of home. We always use toilet paper to blow our noses because my mom refuses to spend money on tissues. She says it's a waste."

"I never thought about it, but I guess it's the same at my house."

Betsy blows so much that I grab the roll for her to keep at her bedside. This time she laughs.

"Are you okay? Really?"

"Yes, just thinking about things." She springs out of bed like she's ready to conquer the world.

"About your sister?"

"I suppose she has something to do with it. But enough of this pitiful conversation, we've got a family weekend coming up."

"You have a family visit already?"

"Yep, tomorrow, and I plan on living it up." Her eyes light up with a fun-loving glimmer. "How about you?"

"Tomorrow also, but it sounds like you're planning more fun than I am."

"Aw, c'mon. Get home and call some friends, and you'll do all right."

"Want to bet on it? Five bucks says that you have more fun."

"Sounds like a deal except I don't have a penny to my name." Betsy smiles.

"Me neither." I laugh.

As we head to breakfast, Jonny Love pulls up an extra chair, and everyone repositions so we can all fit at one table while other tables go almost completely unoccupied. I'm not surprised when Cassandra tells us she's leaving tomorrow morning. The others ask her questions as I pick at my food. I look over at Betsy. She's listening quietly to the Q and A around the table. As selfish as it sounds, I am happy she is here. She's fun and mischievous in an adult kind of way.

Carol comes over to check on me. She glances at my plate, wishing us a good morning. I appreciate that she doesn't make her reason for being here obvious. I keep eating, knowing better than to second-guess her or Chad's requirements. Strangely and unbeknownst to Betsy, her arrival has kept me eating suitable portions of food. As far as I know, she knows nothing of my food issues, and if at all possible, I plan to keep it this way.

I ask Carol when Dr. Ellison will be here.

"Soon. Why? What's on your mind?"

"Do you think she'll let me finish my mom's hotplate today instead of therapy? I want to give it to her this weekend."

"Being Friday, I doubt it, but it doesn't hurt to ask."

TURNS OUT MY day continued its upswing. Dr. Ellison shows up right before nine.

"Carol says you want to finish a project you're making for you mother."

"Um-hm." I nod my head yes. "It's almost done." I was not expecting Carol to mention it, but I am glad she had because otherwise I would have chickened out.

"I'll tell you what, you can finish your project, and I will come back at one."

I guess Dr. Ellison and Carol discussed the details beforehand since I usually meet with Carol at one. Of the two, I would rather meet with Carol than Dr. Ellison because

Dr. Ellison believes in pushing me past my limits.

Jonny Love, Addy, Betsy, and I all push into the art room at nine o'clock. My sessions with Dr. Ellison every day have kept me from the progress on everyone's projects. Addy is making a dog collar similar to the one I made for Oreo. Jonny Love works on the obvious peace poster, and Betsy is finishing a leather belt that looks as good as one bought from a store, better actually. She must have stamped designs into the leather all week by the looks of it. Today she's hammering buckle holes through the leather.

My hot plate is on the back window ledge. It seems like an eternity since I glued the tiles onto the wood. Blowing away the dust, the tiles glisten, showing their real beauty. I mix water and powder and stir it to make grout.

"Is that for your dog?" I ask Addy. She holds the collar up to the window to get a better view of the stamping.

"Yep. I hope he'll wear it. He's a pretty picky brute."

"What kind of dog is he?"

"A mutt, but the best mutt anyone will ever have. He's a mix between German shepherd, Rottweiler, and I think he's got some wolf in him the way he howls."

I can't help thinking he sounds like the perfect dog for her. If asked to describe Addy, I suppose I would say she too is a mix between good and badass—a good person with a shell of armor.

"What's his name?" I ask.

"Pinky." She diligently works on the collar without an ounce of recognition that what she has said is quite comical.

The others stop working on their projects. Betsy looks at me, I look at Jonny Love, and we all look at Addy, who doesn't notice our stares or that it has gotten quieter in the room.

"You mean to tell me you've got a German shepherd, Rottweiler, wolf mix, and his name is Pinky?" Robert asks. The four of us turn toward the doorway. Robert has a big smile on his face. Our smiles could light up Chicago the way our faces brighten.

"Really? His name is Pinky?" he repeats.

"Yeah, what's wrong with Pinky?" And before she can finish her remark, we are all hysterically laughing, Addy included.

Robert sits down, and we treat him as though he has been making conversation since the day he got here. I finally have the grout the right consistency. I spread it over the tiles, making sure each tiny crevice is filled, leaving no air holes as the art teacher advised. Once it's spread, I wipe away the streaks of white left on the tiles with a wet cloth. I look at it carefully, admiring my hard work. I hand it to Robert.

"What do you think?" I ask.

He holds it up to the window, angling it in different ways, admiring the changing colors of the tiles. "Who's it for?"

"My mom. So, what do you think?" I ask again, craving conversation more than his opinion.

"I think your mother will be honored to have such a keepsake."

Robert's manner changes over the short time between laughing about Addy's dog to admiring my mother's gift. I sense he is thinking about his mother and father by the way he holds the piece, admiring something that isn't there. I want to turn away to escape his hurt, my hurt, but I don't. How alone he must feel to have his parents taken away because some idiot decided to drive drunk.

WHEN WE HEAD into the dining area for group, Jonny Love is placing a small, wrapped gift on each chair in the circle.

"Come in my fellow friends," he says. "You'll find a gift from me to you, wrapped in friendship. Please take a seat and enjoy the day."

Jonny Love's manner is so genuine that everyone is happy to go along with his request. Each package is wrapped the same, in old Christmas paper secured by mounds of Scotch tape. We take our seats and unwrap the small presents. Inside each is a five-stick package of Wrigley's Juicy Fruit gum. A bunch of thanks echo around the room in one form or another.

"What's the occasion?" Holly asks.

"No occasion, just wanted to do something nice."

"Most of us chew one or two pieces right away.

"Since most of you are on family visits tomorrow, let's talk about your plans," Carol says, swallowing down a mouthful of gum juice.

At first, we are more interested in getting the few seconds of flavor from our gum than talking about the upcoming weekend.

"Cassandra, how are you feeling about leaving us tomorrow?"

"Great. My dad and brother are coming at nine."

"Are you doing anything fun?" Jonny Love asks.

"Don't laugh, but the Lincoln Park Zoo...it was my brother's idea."

"I wish I were going with you," Gretchen whines.

"That would be nice," Cassandra says.

"Am I the only one not going home tomorrow?" Gretchen asks. We all look at each other. I do feel bad she'll be alone.

Addy speaks up, "Sorry Gretchen, but I'm out of here. My parents promised me a night with my friends. We're seeing Indiana Jones and then later back to my house for pizza. No parents allowed."

"Oh, that sounds better. I'd rather go home with you than to the zoo."

Ethan quickly changes the subject. I think he feels just as bad for Cassandra as I do after Gretchen's remark. "I need a couple of suggestions," he says. "Usually on weekends, my family and I eat out for just about every meal because we love burger joints. In here I'm fine, but at home I can't resist."

"What about the gym? Are you planning on working

out?" Holly asks.

I wish Holly had mentioned friends instead of the gym. Ethan spent most of the week talking about the gym membership he and his father signed up for. He keeps us updated on his weight loss too, but I rarely, if ever, hear him talk about friends.

On the other hand, when Jonny Love mentions friends, I imagine he has thousands of them. I picture a large group of his friends sitting in a circle swaying and singing. "I'm going to Michigan," he says, "to my father's lake house with a couple of my buddies. My dad's taking us out on his boat."

I'm surprised, not by the fact that Jonny Love wants to sit on a boat all day mingling with friends, but because of the chilly weather. Jonny Love seems like a guy who would fare better in the warmer weather of California.

"How about you, Robert?" Holly asks.

"I'll be visiting my grandparents on Sunday."

Grandparents? Robert's response surprises me more than Jonny Love's. It's the first mention of a grandmother. Robert says nothing more, obviously satisfied with his group contribution, but I am disappointed. I want to hear more. I want to hear his voice. I want to know he is going to be okay.

"It's your turn, Anna," Gretchen says. I want to be annoyed she has narrowed in on me, but because she actually thought of me instead of herself, I'm not.

"Nothing much. Just going to do family stuff, I guess. I'm not really sure."

It's bothersome that everyone but me has plans for the weekend. Even Gretchen, I suppose, is dreaming up a way to persuade Isaac into taking her on the exercise trail. I hadn't anticipated anything besides giving my mother a homemade hotplate.

AT ONE I head to the conference room to meet with Dr. Ellison, feeling confident. I consider Betsy's arrival and Robert's willingness to share as making a difference in the way I feel, or possibly because I had already screamed my guts out leaving nothing left inside me. Exactly a week has gone by, and still I can't recall a single memory of what occurred last Friday in the back room. It's obvious Dr. Ellison avoids it too, and it gnaws at me when I'm alone.

Every day this week she hounded me about memories and nightmares and events leading up to the time I woke screaming. She insisted on talking about Liz, my childhood, and family but questioned me little about my days in the back. Sometimes I refused her access to my thoughts, and other times I was adamant that everything was fine. Neither tactic deterred her. On Wednesday, she kept me an hour longer until I caved, which infuriated me. I figure she won't stop until I work through whatever has gotten me right here, right now. And I will, as long as I can keep my deepest secret from her.

I enter the small room where Dr. Ellison is waiting. The room holds a round table and two chairs. Usually I squeeze in between the far wall and table, but today Dr. Ellison is sitting in my spot, so I sit in her usual spot—the chair next to the door. Facing the wall instead of the door feels weird. Once I'm seated, we get down to business. How nice it would be to just shoot the breeze about my home visit tomorrow, but since Dr. Ellison has never been about unnecessary chitchat, I quickly ignore the idea.

"Did you get your mother's project done?" *OK, not bad. Maybe there's a chance.*

"It's finished and wrapped with love." I've heard Jonny Love use this line, so I take a stab at it, hoping to keep the mood light. I'm self-conscious once I say it, realizing it's so not me, but nonetheless, Dr. Ellison smiles. She has not opened my binder to look at yesterday's notes like she normally does. I begin to think she has our agenda already set. Sitting across from her at this angle has me uptight. She doesn't do anything without a purpose. She has me in this chair for a reason.

"Any nightmares?" *Here we go again.*

"Nope," I fib. I did have one last night, but it wasn't terrorizing, so I keep it from her, not wanting to get into the details of it.

Instead of digging further, Dr. Ellison is quiet. She leans back in her chair, looking at me as though she is contemplating if I am ready to hear whatever it is she plans to say next. Feeling uneasy, I look at the wall behind her, then at the table, and then at my hands.

"Anna," she pauses, waiting for me to look at her, "who is Sissy?"

I couldn't have acted undisturbed if my life depended on it. Frozen, I sit staring at the same exact place from a millisecond ago. A chill runs up my spine to my brain, encasing time. My body goes numb. I feel nothing in my legs, my arms, my anything. Cold air fills the room. I let go of my breath after the pressure of unreleased air builds to an unbearable intensity. My thoughts narrow in on a memory, much like a train heading toward a dark tunnel is pulled into its blackness by a one-way track. I blink and darkness surrounds me completely as my mind binds me to one tiny fraction of my childhood. In the distance, just a small dot at first, but emerging brighter as my mind races onward, the first image emerges. My mind grabs at it, forcing it over a tiny severed link in my brain. I want to lie, tell her I don't know who she is, but I can't.

Dr. Ellison's voice is a fading echo. She has moved herself closer to me. The door has been opened, but I don't know when or by whom. She is giving me a choice. I know she won't stop me if I get up and walk out, but I don't. There is no way around it—no other path to lead me elsewhere—and only now do I truly understand, I never had the choice.

My thoughts are engulfed in a tunnel of darkness before

they are released into the open. The image is beautifully brought forward. We are giggling, Sissy and I, and holding hands. Our curls wafting in the breeze; a breeze that seems to carry us to a magnificent swing set. We climb it and hang from the top bar that stretches from side to side. It appears to glisten with happiness as two small girls enjoy its purpose.

"Catch me." Sissy laughs. Hanging from her knees, she holds out her hands as she swings back and forth, slowly at first, then faster as she gains momentum.

"Three." Her hands come toward me as I reach out and miss. She releases her knees from their hold. I jerk, hearing a thud as she hits the ground.

"Sissy, Sissy." I hear her name being called. I don't know if it has come from Dr. Ellison or my thoughts. I grab the armrest of the chair.

"Stay focused, Anna." Dr. Ellison has somehow positioned our chairs closer. The door is open wider, giving me the option to bail at any time.

"I cannot read your thoughts. Talk to me. Who is Sissy?"

The tightness of my grip to the arms of the chair has given lift to my body before I realize I am barely on the seat. I can't hold it any longer.

Before releasing my grasp, I cry out, "Sissy is what I used to call Lizzy." I hear the thud again as I release my grip and fall into my chair.

"She can't move." I look to Dr. Ellison for help.

"Who can't move?"

The pain of repeating it is just too much, but there is no stopping.

"Sissy!" I yell. "Sissy, Sissy, please get up."

"Is she hurt?" Dr. Ellison pulls at one of my arms, hoping to turn my eyes in her direction. "Is Lizzy hurt?"

"Don't call her that!" My eyes plead with hers. "Please, I'm begging you, don't call her Lizzy. Her name is Liz."

"Is Liz hurt?"

Deciding I have had enough, I look to the open door. Dr. Ellison adjusts herself in her chair, distracting me from thinking about my escape.

"Anna, what happened when Liz fell from the swing set?"

My pulse races as I look to Dr. Ellison and then away, shifting my eyes, trying to recall how she could know about the swing set.

"I couldn't catch her," I cry, shaking my head in disbelief that I have said this much. "I tried, but I couldn't. I missed her hands, and she fell on her head. I called for her to get up, but she just lay on the ground and the..."

I stop, chills running down my spine. A vivid memory enters my thoughts. I think about Sissy and me walking quietly into the house after she fell. Things changed after that day. Sissy was different.

"The what? Anna, tell me...and the what?"

"Couch." I barely get the word past my lips.

Dr. Ellison intervenes. "You were very frightened when you found Liz crying on the couch."

I don't bat an eyelash at what Dr. Ellison has said. I never told her or anyone about Liz's fall from the swing set or the night I covered her with an afghan as she lay on the couch crying. It doesn't take a rocket scientist to figure out how she knows. There is no reason to hide the truth or keep it bottled inside me any longer. My crying fades to almost nothing. I look to Dr. Ellison, knowing I will get answers to my question.

"What else did I mention last Friday?" I ask.

thirty-two

"Here you go," I say, handing my mother her gift as soon as she comes for me on Saturday morning.

"Oh, Anna, it's beautiful." She goes a little over the top, but she genuinely cherishes anything her kids make, crap or not. Displayed on the bookcase in our dining room are vases and ashtrays from years of high school ceramics classes.

When we arrive home, my dad is pulling out of the garage on his way to Saturday morning grocery shopping. We wave at each other as my mom pulls up the driveway. Once inside, things don't seem as different as my first visit. Oreo looks the same, and she's still wearing her new collar. Bridg exits her room, obviously just waking, and greets me in the hallway before she makes her way into the bathroom. "Hey, Anna," she says, slightly lifting her hand, giving a small wave. It's not much, but it's a better feeling than last time because today feels like I never left.

Making my way down the hallway to my room, I stop in the doorway of Bridgett's bedroom. I laugh at the mess inside. I think back to the years when it was only Bridg and I who shared this room after Liz's death. I needed the beds made and the floor swept and the furniture dusted, and she hadn't cared one way or another. I spent Saturdays cleaning, moving furniture around, and hauling everything from the closet to be rearranged in perfect order, and within a day or two, Bridg had things pulled out and messed up again.

I think of Bridg reading her books and magazines, going

gaga over Simon Le Bon of Duran Duran as she lie flat on her back on her messy bed with her feet propped up on the wall and her knee socks dangling from the ends of her feet. I complained of the black streaks that had become semipermanent from her dirty feet. After Marie moved out a year ago, I claimed her room, happy to be away from dirty feet on walls and disorganized closets. And now, I would give anything to share this room again.

My room is in the same condition as when I saw it last. I stare at its perfection. Four shelves full of collectible horses dusted and perfectly placed. A brand-new matching dresser and headboard neat and tidy, and the bed made with Marie's old bedspread and pillow shams. Everything just the way I liked it. I know now it was Liz's death that changed things for me in this way. I separated from playful and fun-loving Anna, to neat and clean, perfect Anna. I went from playing hard and taking risks to suddenly becoming a serious girl with no room for fun, trying to make everyone's life perfect. All I ever really wanted was to be accepted by my siblings. Only now do I understand they wanted the same thing. Liz's death had killed us all.

I head over to my bed, rip off the bedspread and rumple up the blankets and sheets in defiance of the last nine years. I lie back on my pillows and place Jingles on my chest. I put my hands behind my head and stare up at the ceiling. I think about the wager between Betsy and me. My gut tells me she's a sure win.

I can't stop thinking about yesterday's session with Dr. Ellison. It had gone on for almost two hours before I left the tiny conference room. She hadn't held back on anything that happened that Friday. She said my subconscious had taken hold of me most of the day as I fell in and out of sleep. She was able to put together most of what happened on the days leading to my sister's death and those afterward. Beyond my control, my secrets made their way past my lips, and though

I intended to never discuss them with anyone, I was actually relieved that my darkest days had come to light.

"My main concern now," Dr. Ellison had said, "is convincing you that Liz's death was not your fault."

"But she died after she fell," I sobbed.

"Liz falling from the swing set and dying of a brain tumor are two separate incidents," she told me. "I can understand how you connected what happened, but you must trust that you had nothing to do with Liz's death."

"I get it. I didn't kill her, but do you think she forgives me?"

"I think you ought to stay here tomorrow," Dr. Ellison had said, so I halfheartedly agreed with her explanation just to get what I wanted. I didn't think for a minute I had convinced her I was on board, but for whatever reason, she gave me permission to come home for the day. I imagine she warned my mother to watch for any reactions that might occur, but I know better. There's no reason for any reaction.

"Hey, you want to take me to McDonald's?"

I am startled to see Bridg standing over me. "What time is it?" I ask, more out of surprise that I had fallen asleep than wanting to know the time.

"Almost two. What about McDonald's?"

"Yeah, sure."

Bridg and I drive to Micky D's to pick up lunch for my parents and us. She orders her usual cheeseburger, fries, and orange drink, and without a second thought, I order my usual quarter pounder with cheese and a cherry pie. We steal several fries from the bag before we make it home.

"Thanks," I say, pulling a couple bills and coins from my shorts pocket and handing it over to my father as soon as Bridg and I are up the steps and into the living room.

"Sure," he says, placing the bills neatly in his wallet and the coins in his pocket.

The four of us sit at the kitchen table—something we

haven't done together in the last two years. Bridg and I pull the food from the bags and hand my mom a hamburger and small fries and my dad two cheeseburgers, fries, and a chocolate shake before we take our own. My mom holds most of the conversation. We both keep to one-word answers to her questions while we're around my father. Anything more and we'll likely be reminded he's uninterested in what we have to say.

I look around at the four of us sitting at the table, eating our food, with our eyes scanning the kitchen walls instead of each other. I can't figure out if the scene before me belongs in a TV show drama or the newspaper funnies. At just the right moment, I see my dad pick up his chocolate shake, bringing the straw to his lips. I kick Bridg under the table and then look at my mom, moving my eyes from hers to my dad, so that she looks at him. The three of us bust out laughing. My father looks up, giving us a better view of the vein bulging in the middle of his forehead from his attempt at sucking the thick milkshake through the straw. We laugh louder, and my father laughs the loudest.

After lunch, Bridg and I listen to music—something I rarely do—and just hang out. We clean her room and rearrange posters hanging on her bedroom walls. Later, when her friend Jenny comes to spend the night, I find myself lying on the edge of my mother's bed talking about nothing in particular while my father watches TV downstairs. My mom gets off her bed, goes to her dresser drawer, and digs around in the back, pulling out a half empty bag of fun-size Snickers. She reaches in and pulls out several, placing a few in front of me and keeping the bag for herself. She unwraps one and pops it into her mouth. I don't ask why she has candy bars hidden in her dresser drawer, but I guess this is her weight gain culprit.

"Mom," I say, second-guessing what I'm about to ask. "What happened?"

Her look tells me that she knows I am talking about Liz's death. She focuses on the hot plate, running two fingers over the tiles. She looks at me and then lowers her eyes. She begins, not because she wants to, but because she knows I must hear it.

"Ten days before Lizzy died, she went to the nurse's office at school feeling sick. I picked her up from school and took her to the doctor. He didn't seem to think anything was wrong, but I thought it odd when he gave me a name of a specialist he wanted Lizzy to see. I called early the next morning to make the appointment, too early I guess, because the doctor was annoyed by my morning call.

"When the doctor looked into her nose and throat he had a funny look—one that told me something wasn't right. But he could not find anything wrong either. Maybe he hadn't wanted to commit himself to something he didn't understand. Within a day or two Lizzy started complaining of headaches, and I noticed her face had broken out in a rash. I knew then something was terribly wrong. Your dad and I took her to the hospital early the next morning. I remember you watching us, Anna, dressing Lizzy. I wish so badly I could go back and give you the attention you needed. I never thought about it. It was plain stupid."

The abandoned look in my mother's eyes and the distress on her face show a decade of regret.

"Mom," I say, my words labored, "you didn't mean to hurt me. I don't blame you for what happened." Although I could cry at this very moment, my mother's composure stays unmoved.

"The doctors ran tests, and there it was staring us right in the face, a tumor on her brain. The doctors told us it had to be removed because it was growing near the part of her brain that would affect her breathing."

My mother lingers, giving me a chance to cautiously interject. "Was she scared...about the operation?"

"If she was, she never acted like it. 'Mom, you have two heads,' she would say, and then she laughed and laughed. She thought it was so funny, so I said, 'Lizzy, really, it must look so funny,' and then we would laugh together."

"Why did she say you have two heads?"

"Because her brain tumor was causing her to see double."

Liz's voice echoes through my mind. Hearing the way she would have said it and the way she would have giggled rips at my insides. I want to burst with tears.

"She didn't know why she was seeing double, so both of us enjoyed the silliness of it. You remember, don't you, how much Lizzy loved to be silly? She giggled up until the time..." She pauses, her eyes distant. A faint smile appears. "Anna, I'm going to tell you something I have never told anyone. One day while sitting near Lizzy's hospital bed, she quieted. I thought she sensed my concern; she told me not to worry because Mary and Jesus were going to take care of her. I swore she could see them both by the way she kept looking to the corner of her room. I looked from Lizzy to the corner and back again, trying to understand what she was doing. And then it hit me.

"Nine months before Lizzy died, a strange feeling came over me. I feared someone close to me was going to die. Then two days before Lizzy passed away, I was in church praying for the Lord to make her well. As I walked up the aisle to Communion I saw an image of Jesus with Lizzy standing behind Him. I didn't know what to think of it. The next day, it happened again. I saw the same image of Jesus, but this time to His right, and with a great big smile across her face, stood Lizzy. I knew immediately I would not be bringing her home. Lizzy's words and selfless acts confirmed she knew too."

I can't keep my tears away any longer. "Was she scared knowing she was going to die?"

"I don't believe so, Anna. She was at peace. I don't think

she recognized death like we do as adults. Children have a different way of accepting whatever they must do, much like you did after losing her. She felt safe and cared for. I believe this is all that mattered to her."

"How did she die?"

"Near me. I had been with her all day, holding her hand and talking. One of her nurses came in to check on her. She said she would come back when Lizzy wasn't sleeping. 'Lizzy isn't sleeping,' I said to the nurse. She left and another nurse came in, took one look at Lizzy, and ran out of the room to call Code Blue. They immediately took her to surgery, but she was already gone. She never suffered, Anna. I prayed that she not suffer, and she didn't."

When I look to my mother, I believe she's been slightly liberated. In her attempt to bring back the events of years ago in order to help me, my mother has freed herself from her own bondage—one she hadn't known existed.

"Do you feel like sitting on the back patio? I'll make us some iced tea," my mother asks.

My heart aches for more, but I know my mother cannot bear it, and I don't have the heart to make her try.

"Sounds good," I say. "I'll unfold the patio chairs. Meet you out back." And we both walk down the hallway. My mother turns into the kitchen, and I make my way down the stairs to the sliding glass door in the foyer that leads to the back patio.

Once outside, a warm breeze touches my face. I am compelled to look to a familiar spot. I stare to where the swing set used to be. Swings swaying in the wind and creaks of the glider used more for a trapeze than a two-person glider and the laughter of children playing fill my mind. Another warm breeze blows a few strands of hair in front of my eyes. An image of Jim, home from one of his world travels, occupies my thoughts as the laughter fades. He contemplates the job my mother has asked him to do.

"It hasn't been used in years," she said. And by the time I was twelve, the swing set had been rusted over, making it easy for my brother to crush with his bare hands. Echoes of its weak frame crumbling remind me of its past purpose. I wonder if it was glad to be taken away instead of sitting alone in the backyard where once two little girls played happily. Tears swell in my eyes. I turn away and unfold two chairs.

My mom and I sit quietly, drinking our iced tea and enjoying each other's company.

"Anna," my mother says, looking out into the yard. "When you were a little girl, you asked me if I thought you were good. Do you remember?" she says, turning toward me.

Nodding, I smile, reassuring her I remember.

"You are good, Anna. I want you to know that."

Sitting on the back patio, drinking iced tea, talking with my mom, had not been what I expected on my visit home, but I am happy it turned out just as it did.

As the hours pass so does my time at home. I run downstairs and into the basement to dig out a hammer and nails. I stop momentarily, noticing the spot where a large bag of Liz's Christmas gifts sat for more than a year before they were given away. "You can each choose one gift," my mother had said to Bridg and me. I chose a small doll dressed in clothes from Holland—the kind of doll to be admired. I remember exactly where I hid it away—in a small box tucked in the back corner of my closet. I used to peek at it from time to time and then quickly put it back in its place. I look to the corner of the basement again and smile.

In the kitchen, my mother is carefully watching a pizza bake, making sure she doesn't burn Bridg and Jenny's dinner.

"Where should I hang the hot plate?" I ask

Looking around for every possible spot, my mom points to the narrow wall between the spice cabinet and the stove. "I think this will be perfect," she says.

"So do I." I hammer a nail into the wall and hang the hot

plate. My mother and I stand back to make sure it's straight. The tiles glisten as they catch the last bit of sunlight coming through the kitchen window. They appear to be dancing.

thirty-three

Returning to the fifth floor on Saturday evening is not comforting like it had been the last time I returned from a home visit. Then I had been glad to be back to my secure bed and room, but tonight I can no longer place myself here. My room, my bed, the layout of the unit seem foreign to me. Betsy arrives around the same time.

"Hey, you two up for a walk?" Isaac says.

"You're kidding me, right?

"Of course not, I trust you. Are you up for it?"

"No way," I say, shaking my head and raising my eyebrows.

"Count me in," Betsy says, grabbing her Chicago Bears pullover sweatshirt.

"I thought we could talk about our fantasy wager," I say, disappointed she's accepted the invitation.

"There'll be time for that when I get back."

Once she's gone, it actually feels good to be alone. I walk down the hall to be with Robert, but he and his grandparents are visiting. His grandma looks a lot younger than his grandfather, provoking a second look to make sure his mother hasn't come back from the dead.

"Anna, I want you to meet my grandparents."

We make our introductions, and then I leave so they can continue their visit. I am truly happy for Robert. I suppose it won't be long before he's on his way, just like Ben. I wonder about myself as I walk toward my room.

When you are ready. I had asked myself many times what Dr. Ellison's meant. *What does ready look like? How will I know?* The answer is near. It's coming. I can feel its presence.

On Sunday, Betsy, Gretchen, Ethan, and I are stuck here, bored, while the others are out. We are watching Sunday morning cartoons by request of Gretchen, but I am enjoying them too. I believe we all are.

Betsy announces, "Today can be entertaining if we do things right."

"Like what?" I say.

"I dare you to pull the plug." Betsy points to the vacuum cord plugged into the outlet. I hear the vacuum somewhere down the hall, thinking Agnes is probably pushing it back and forth with a slight swing of her hips to her every push. Agnes is about thirty-five and takes her job seriously, pushing away furniture to suck every single crumb from the carpet. She's here only on the weekends, but by the way she interacts with everyone, laughing and holding lengthy conversations, it's like she works on the fifth floor seven days a week. I walk over, look around, pull out the plug, and then quickly walk toward the back of the couch where the others have already ducked out of sight. We watch it play out. Agnes plugs the cord back in without much thought. I pretend to read her thoughts, *Maybe I tugged too hard*, was probably her thinking.

I turn to Betsy. "You're next."

Betsy repeats my same strategy, acting casual while she's up to no good. We quietly laugh as Agnes looks at the plug then the outlet, trying to figure out if one of the two is faulty.

"You go, Gretchen," Betsy says.

We don't peek from behind the couch because we assume Agnes might be looking for the culprit. We know a fourth time will really overdo it, but we can't help ourselves.

"I can't believe you guys are making me do this," Ethan says.

"C'mon, Ethan. You've got to. It's your turn." Gretchen can barely contain her laughter. She's squirming, rocking side to side on her ankles. Ethan moves like a detective, looking over his shoulder with every step, making the scene hilarious. He pulls the plug. Agnes comes from around the corner ready for him. He jumps behind the couch trying to lose her, but we are no match for Agnes. "Gotcha," she says, laughing. Gretchen shrieks and then runs down the hall to the bathroom.

"Ah, we're just kidding you, Agnes," Betsy says.

"Well, keep it up," Agnes says, "because that's the most fun I've had all morning."

Isaac comes from the nurse's station and gives us a look of something between *okay, have your fun*, and *stay out of trouble*. Ethan takes the cord from Agnes and plugs it into the wall. "How about I give you a break?" he says, turning on the vacuum.

"If you insist." Agnes leans against the hallway wall. Her big smile indicates, without a doubt, she's enjoyed the diversion from her usual Sunday morning routine.

We pull the folded gymnastics mat from the art room to the hallway. We attempt chicken fights, but Gretchen can't hold me, so we give up. Instead, we perform death-defying rolls as one of us runs, jumps, tucks, and rolls over the other three.

During breakfast, we ordered prunes on our lunch menus and then arrive first to lunch to sneak them onto other patients' trays. Some adults eat them happily while others look quizzical, trying to remember if they had ordered them. After dinner, Isaac has had enough.

"Daniel and I are taking all of you to the exercise trail to rid you of this overabundance of energy. No exceptions—we are all going," he says.

I run to get my hooded sweatshirt and pull it on over my head. I grab the Payday candy bars from my desk drawer and slip them into the front pocket. It feels good to be in the open air. I can't help wondering how Isaac and Daniel can be so trusting of me after last time. We compete brutally with each other. Eventually, Daniel joins in while Isaac keeps score. With the exception of Daniel's thirteen pull-ups, I come in second with six. Ethan is best at running through the twelve tires laid out side by side—an event Gretchen can't seem to complete without laughing hysterically.

We gather at the high bar. Betsy is first to climb up the side ladder, making her way across, sliding hand to hand to get to the other side, but instead she stops midway. She pulls her legs up, tucking them under and then over the bar, securing her bent knees around it. Letting go of her hands, she is now upside down.

"No, Betsy!" I scream in horror.

"Hey, Anna. Calm down. She's fine," Daniel insists.

I ignore him completely. "Please, Betsy. Get down."

"Anna, I'm fine." She moves her arms back and forth. "Here, grab my hands, and I'll swing down."

"No! Get down!" I scream louder. I grab at Isaac's arm. "Please tell her to get down."

Betsy looks around. "Hey Ethan, grab my hands so I can swing down."

Ethan grabs for Betsy's hands.

In complete terror, I scream, "My God, Liz, get down!"

"Betsy, get down now," Daniel commands as Isaac takes my arms, pinning them to my sides.

As soon as Betsy is on the ground, I begin to calm. Everyone is staring.

"Who's Liz?" Gretchen asks.

Had I said Liz? My chest tightens. Isaac looks at me, his eyes encouraging me to tell them. *There's no going back.*

"She was my sister."

"What do you mean was? Where is she? Did she…"

"Gretchen, hush, would you?" Ethan reprimands.

Betsy's remorse is genuine. "Hey, Anna. I'm fine. Nothing happened. I didn't mean to scare you."

"I'm good. Really." I wriggle away from Isaac's hold.

We continue to walk along the path until we get back to the hospital's front doors.

"Well, who's up for stopping at the snack bar?"

It is Gretchen who gets the most from the vending machines this time: a bag of chips, a root beer, and Twizzlers. I pull out the Paydays from my front pocket. Breaking them into small pieces, I insist we all share. Ethan and I take the smallest pieces. I am proud of Ethan for not overindulging and even prouder of myself for indulging a little in front of my friends.

Betsy and I settle into our room for the night. Sitting on our beds in our pajamas, leaning against opposite walls, talking has the feel of a slumber party but with only one friend. We decide yesterday's bet is a tie.

"With that out of the way, you don't think I'm going to let you off the hook about the bar ordeal, do you? I want to know everything about your sister Liz."

"I don't know where to start," I honestly reply.

"Younger? Older? Spill your guts."

And I do. We stay up for hours talking. Memories come with ease once I begin. I tell her about Liz's silly ways and her walk-a-bird walk. I tell her about the forts we built, the trees we climbed, the games we played, and her mischievous ways.

"She loved to laugh. Sometimes, I can still hear her giggling. Do you think that's weird?"

"I think it's cool. What about the path, though? Why did you freak out when I was hanging from the high bar?"

There is something about Betsy that makes me feel safe. I can trust she will take my secrets to her grave, but still I can't go back to that time.

"Hey, maybe another time," Betsy says, sensing my

reluctance.

"Maybe." I am grateful she doesn't continue to pry.

Isaac is on his way out for the night when he pops his head into our room. "Girls, it's eleven o'clock. Let's get these lights out," he says with his hand on the switch.

"Yes, Sire," Betsy kids.

"Your wish is our command," I add.

"I'm not kidding, queens. You need your beauty rest." Isaac smiles. "Now get to sleep."

I can't remember a night I slept so well. The next morning, Betsy and I are off to another busy weekday.

"Hope to see you around sometime," she says, leaving for breakfast.

"Yeah, right. Save me a spot, will you?"

"Yep, your tray will be waiting, Miss. Wasn't it prunes you ordered?" She giggles all the way down the hall.

BEFORE GROUP, I walk to my room, waiting long enough to make sure I am alone. I open my desk drawer and pull out my journal. Opening to the second page, I stop for a moment in thought before I write.

Dear Liz,

I am so sorry. I hope you can forgive me.

Anna

I turn toward Robert's knock.

"Group is in a few minutes. Are you coming?"

I stuff my journal back into my desk drawer. "Do I have a choice?"

"I suppose you could hide under your bed," he says, smiling.

"No thanks. I've already tried hiding and found it to be a bad idea," I say. We both laugh.

Everyone had successful family visits, for the most part. We laugh when Jonny Love tells us about his boating experience and how he and his friends didn't last more than half an hour on the boat before they pleaded with his father to take it in.

"Man, it couldn't have been more than forty degrees out there," he adds, making us laugh again.

When it's Robert's turn to tell about his weekend, I am truly interested in hearing every last detail. I think back over the weeks when he didn't talk at all. It's hard to believe only a short time ago he made his first effort to connect with me. Now because he no longer sits staring at his hands, dead to the world, everyone expects so much more. I can tell Robert is deep in thought by the way his eyes seem to be looking deep into his soul. He sits tall and confident, so different from when I first met him, slumped and alone. His face is relaxed along with the rest of him, and it's this that allows me to see that Robert has changed from a boy to a man. He looks at me and then to everyone around the circle.

"When I was nine, my father was killed in terrible car accident. We were okay at first, my mom and me. My father's parents took care of us, but as the months went by, my mother continued her struggle with our loss. She removed his pictures from the house, and eventually my father's name was no longer mentioned. Not even a year had gone by before my mother moved us here. She said she needed to take an important job so she could support us, but as I grew older I figured it was her way to remove every last memory that reminded her of my father."

Robert looks over at me again. I know he is coming to the most difficult part of his life. I don't know if I should encourage him to continue or beg him to stop for fear that I will cry in front of the group. *How can I be this selfish?* My anxiety rises as I barely lift my eyes, encouraging him to continue. I am moved that he has such trust after all he has been through.

"By seventh grade I was officially the man of the house; my mother became ill and needed my help to take care of things until she was able to make it back to work. She depended on me, and it gave me a sense of worth. I often prayed to my father for guidance in how to best protect my mother. Eventually, things seemed good. My mother had a job that paid the bills with a little extra for us to go to the zoo or the occasional splurge on an ice-cream sundae.

"Once I entered high school, most weekends were taken up by basketball. I loved the game, and my mom, God, I think she loved it more than I did by the way she hollered from the stands."

Robert's broad smile releases my tension for a moment. He hadn't elaborated like this when he first told me of his mother's death. This version told more than just tragedy. He somehow had been able to look beyond what had happened and remember the happy times. I take my eyes off Robert to glance around. He has everyone's attention. I look at Addy and Gretchen, Ethan, and Jonny Love. I am embarrassed to admit that I truly don't know what has brought them here to the fifth floor. Had they not shared their stories, or hadn't I listened? I'm ashamed to think that maybe I wasn't capable of considering anyone's life as important as my own.

"When I was fifteen, I came home from school more occupied with thoughts of that night's basketball game than anything else. I went about my afternoon getting my homework done; something my mom required before sports or watching TV. When she wasn't home by the time she was supposed to drive me back to school for the game, I called some buddies of mine to pick me up. I was just a dumb kid not to realize my mother had never been late before. After the game, when my mother still had not shown, I knew something was wrong. My coach drove me home, and not a single outside light was on. It's strange, I think, that my most vivid memory of that night is noticing the only lights that lit the house were the ones I had forgotten to turn off in my hurry to leave for the game. As my coach called for help, I tore into the house and flew up the stairs to my mother's bedroom."

Sobs break out around the circle. I move my focus from Robert to my lap several times, desperately trying to maintain my composure. Tears glide silently down Robert's face as he looks up toward the ceiling, searching for the right words to continue. After a long pause, we seem to disappear from his surroundings. He continues more so to himself than to us.

"She was up there all day, and I was too involved with nothing but myself to even notice." He gives himself a moment of silence before he reconnects with the rest of us.

"My mother swallowed a bottle of pills. She left a note telling me she loved me and that I should be good. She wrote how sorry she was, but she couldn't go on without my father. I told myself I had failed to take care of her, and in return, she left me; she had chosen to be with my father over me. I came to despise them both. My hatred grew, and I refused to ever mention my parents again."

Robert lowers his head and cries and so do the rest of us. Except for the sobs, not another noise can be heard. "If no one minds, I need to continue," Robert says

Unable to speak through tears, Holly gives a quick nod.

"There are people in this world who are predestined to help others, angels I presume, and my grandparents are two of these people. But too angry and filled with hatred to recognize their efforts, I refused their help, so they sent me here. Then another appeared, one who kept watch over me for endless hours, giving of herself to help me. It made me think of the nights I prayed to my father for guidance. Maybe my prayers were being answered. I didn't know what to do or how to act any differently, so I just sat and listened. I listened for answers, many of which came from outside my bedroom door."

It is only now that I realize Robert is speaking of Ben and me keeping watch while we talked outside his door night after night. I am glad to know we kept him company, but it was Ben who had all the good things to say, not me.

"No, Robert..." I can barely get my lips to move. "It was Ben who..."

"Yes, Anna..." Robert positions himself in his chair facing more toward me. I look at him, shaking my head no.

"Anna, do you remember what you told me about the mockingbird; the mockingbird that reminded you of me because you believed I could bring good to others, like the mockingbird does with his song? You were right, and because of you, I believe I can find good from my past. But you also said that I had been hurt by people's cruelty. You were wrong. Others didn't throw sticks and stones at me; I threw them at myself. I lost both of my parents—my father to a drunk and my mother because of it—and..."

Tears flood Robert's eyes, but I don't say a word. I understand he needs to finish for himself, much like I did that night I had spoken to him. "And because of you, I choose good. It's time to put my past behind me and do what I can for others. I am asking you with all my heart to accept my gratitude."

Although my voice strains, I manage to whisper, "You're welcome."

IN THE DAYS that follow, things change drastically for us both. Robert and his grandpa talk about fishing trips with so much enthusiasm, I get excited overhearing their conversations. His grandma comments more than once on how exactly they plan to fit her into their adventures, and I smile when they laugh together. I no longer keep watch over Robert; there is no need. During group, Robert and I often catch sight of each other, and when nobody is watching, he winks at me.

Betsy and I had formed a closer bond. We talked a lot and laughed a great deal more and when time allowed, just had fun. I shared with her the many events in my life that I had tried so hard to forget, and she too told stories of her sister and how much she missed her. Listening to Betsy tell of her struggles after her sister's death made it more possible for me to explain why I had been so frightened the night she had decided to hang upside down from the high bar. Betsy listened without saying a word. Her facial expression was agonized with empathy, as was mine when she finally admitted she had been driving the car that had killed her sister.

ROBERT'S ROLE HAD changed. He was a man now with a different agenda. Although he didn't speak of any changes, I could tell his thoughts were on his future. And that's how it came to pass that ten short days after Robert's first home visit, he said his good-byes. It was not as difficult as I thought it would be. Robert had helped me embrace the separation. As he followed his grandparents out the door, I called to him, and when he turned, I winked.

His broad smile lit up his face. "You're welcome," he said, then turned and was gone.

thirty-four

If it had not been for Betsy standing at a distance, waiting for the right moment to help me embrace Robert's departure, I would have gone back to our room and cried. Instead, she was there.

Tonight, Betsy and I and Jonny Love are without visitors, so we ask Chad if we can go on a walk. The weather is nice for a change. Finally, spring has let go of its insistent chill, and I can smell the sweet aroma of freshly cut grass. The path seems more crowded than in the past. Maybe because of the nice weather or maybe because we are here on a weeknight, but whatever the reason, I enjoy being around normalcy. It seems as though people are springing with happiness as they jog by or simply give a nice hello as they pass. Some stroll, looking content with this very moment. I wonder if their lives have taken them in different directions than what they imagined when they were my age.

As we pass the different apparatuses, we continue walking without the usual eagerness to compete or the slightest interest in walking a beam or crawling through tires. The weather is pacifying, absorbing us in our own thoughts. An older couple strolls by holding hands. They each send a nice smile but focus more on their steps so as not to trip on the flattened mulch. I don't know why I notice them more than anyone else, but I do. I wonder where they have been and how they have lived. Had they reached their goals and dreams, or had they gone along being satisfied by the unexpected turns life had dealt them? Had they looked at me and wondered where time had gone?

I'm thinking about things that never entered my mind before. My wrinkle free skin and shiny hair and healthy lungs and a strong beating heart are expected gifts of youth taken for granted. Every physical aspect I need, to be whatever or whomever I want, lies within, ready at my beck and call, but never before had I given it one single thought. I am ashamed for my ungratefulness. My thoughts bring forth awkwardness at first. I know most kids my age never give much thought to this kind of reasoning; the kind that I suppose Jonny Love has stowed in his mind.

I look around noticing the sun's rays cascading to the earth; its beauty inspiring me. The oak tree just a few feet away with its branches stretching toward the sky illustrates strength beyond what I can imagine. I look over at Jonny Love. His eyes sparkle with the beauty surrounding him. His face glimmers with hope. How foolish I have been to believe Jonny Love didn't get it—to think he was only living in the past or was a boy with strange ideas. *How had I misled myself?* Jonny Love had found the importance in every day living, something I had never explored before this moment.

In no more than a couple hundred steps, we will reach the high bar. I give way to my thoughts as I veer off the path and head toward it, well aware Betsy and the others are staring at my back. I climb the side ladder and make my way to the middle and hang for just a moment. I don't need to gather much momentum to get my feet above my head and lock my knees to the bar before dropping my hands. It feels good to hang upside down. I haven't done this since I was seven, and the memories of pure fun and utter joy broaden my smile.

"Give me your hands," Betsy says.

"Oh no. I'm on my own for this one." I swing back and forth, gaining just enough speed. I know the time is right. I had done this a hundred times as a child, and it feels much like riding a bike. I am reminded of my past; Liz encouraging me to go faster, giggling with excitement. The memory fades, and it's Betsy who cheers me on. One last swing upward and I unhook my knees, letting go. I land perfectly on my feet, sticking my landing and throwing my hands above my head. Betsy runs overs and hugs the breath out of me, and I hug her back. We resume our place on the path and continue on.

"So...how do you feel?" Betsy asks, smiling.

I want to tell her, but I'm not sure how to say it.

"Spill," she says. *I swear she can read my thoughts.*

"It's strange. When I was swinging back and forth, I swore I saw Liz standing off to the side smiling, but when I looked again, it wasn't Liz; it was you. You remind me of her, Betsy. You have her contagious giggle and her mischievous ways. When I took my final swing, I no longer reached out for a figment of my imagination. I reached for something other than my past. I reached for now. And when I landed...I felt free."

"There's something I haven't told you."

"What is it?" I ask inquisitively.

"You know when you begged me to get down from the bar the last time we were here?"

"How could I forget?" I frown.

"When you screamed for Liz, I thought you meant me. It hadn't struck me that you were referring to anyone other than me until Gretchen asked you who she was."

I look to Betsy in confusion.

"Don't you see, Anna? My name is Elizabeth. Betsy is just a shortened version."

Chad and Jonny Love are following so closely behind that when I stop dead in my tracks, Chad nearly stumbles over me.

"What's wrong?" He takes hold of my arm as though he thinks I might pass out. "What just happened?" Chad looks to Betsy for answers as he instructs me to lie down across the bench sitting alongside the path.

"I'm fine," I mumble, giving Betsy a hint not to say a word. If she mentions it, I will be forced into every detail of why I feel this way. I take my only way out. "I'm light-headed from swinging upside down, that's all. Really, it's no big deal."

I would rather not bear Chad's reaction to my explanation, but I figure it's better than undergoing an hour-long session on the real issue of why I am in a total state of eeriness.

I don't even have a moment to tell Betsy I'm okay with Chad hovering over me the entire walk back.

"Lie down," Chad says, when we reach my bedroom. "I'll be back." He doesn't need to tell me it's food he is ordering from the kitchen. When he leaves, Jonny Love sneaks in with Betsy.

"Are you all right?" Betsy asks.

"Yeah, I'm fine. Just a bit of a shock at first."

"I hope you don't mind, but I told Jonny what happened."

"Very cool. There's no such thing as coincidences in my book. I mean look at what you got here...same name, same..."

"Curly hair." Betsy's remark is meant to sidetrack Jonny.

"What?" I ask, eyeing first Betsy and then Jonny Love. "You better tell me before Chad gets back with a crap load of food. He thinks I'm faint from famine, and I don't put it past him to sit with me until I shovel a four course meal down my throat."

"I'm just saying things happen for a reason. We're all in the world together trying to find answers, trying to live in harmony..."

"Jonny!" I insist. "Same what?"

"Same age," Betsy spews. "Look. I just think it's kind of strange, don't you..."

"Not strange, more like awesome," Jonny chimes in.

Betsy gives him a look that makes him hush.

"Betsy, stop. I know. We both have known for a while,

but neither of us had the courage to say it aloud. I'll be honest, I didn't realize the name thing, that came as a total shock, clearly putting the icing on the cake, but for everything else, well, I suppose I just didn't want to think about it."

"Jonny, you are not supposed to be in here," Chad says.

"I was just leaving." Jonny walks toward the door. "Remember, there are no coincidences."

"Betsy, you too. Anna needs her rest."

"I'm going."

"Feeling better?" Chad asks, handing me a vanilla Ensure.

"You're kidding, right? You know, you could have surprised me with a hamburger or pizza, but instead you bring me an Ensure?" I say jokingly.

Chad smiles. "I don't know what I was thinking."

I open the can. It actually tastes pretty good.

"What was Jonny referring to about coincidences?"

"You know Jonny. He was just being himself. Chad," I say, "can I ask you something without you questioning why I'm asking?"

"Sure."

"Do you believe in angels?"

"Yes."

"Do you think they're here on Earth? You know, like watching over us?"

"I can't say for sure, Anna, but I trust that it's possible."

It had been a long day, and by the time I finish my Ensure and Chad leaves, I am exhausted. I take a long shower, knowing Betsy will roam around the unit trying to coerce one of the nurses into letting her stay up later than normal since Chad told her I needed rest, which I had to admit, I did.

My bed looks inviting. I lift my pillow slightly and turn down my quilt and climb into bed. I lie on my back, staring at the ceiling for quite some time before I pull myself from my warm sheets and head for my desk. Taking my journal from the drawer, I open it and turn to my second entry. I tear it from the binding and throw it away and begin again.

Dear Liz,

I imagine in Heaven you are surrounded by glorious parks, and in those parks are glorious swing sets, and on those sets I imagine there are swings that reach up to the rainbows. I imagine the eagles are glorious, too, and as you swing higher than the impossible, I imagine they soar alongside you into the heavenly skies.

I imagine in Heaven you are surrounded by castles, and in those castles are glorious angels. I imagine you walking the walk-a-bird walk among them, and when you giggle, they giggle, and then I imagine that all of Heaven sings with laughter.

I imagine in Heaven there are many children, and in the gathering of children is one child in particular who reaches out for you. That child needs you, loves you, and adores you. Build forts with her, and when those forts are built, take her secretly into hiding and tell her stories. Tell her stories of a sister you had when you lived on Earth. Tell her how much you loved her and how much she loved you back. Tell her that someday she will get to meet her, but for now the two of you will have to wait.

I imagine in Heaven you sleep upon a glorious bed made from the puffiest of clouds, sleeping securely in our Creator's palms. As you sleep, sleep peacefully knowing that your sister and all your sisters and your brothers and your parents too, love you forever, and until the end of time, you will always live in our hearts.

I CLOSE MY journal and hop back into bed. The sheets have gone cold. I snuggle in once again, this time turning to my stomach and tucking my hands underneath my pillow, hoping the sheets will warm sooner than later. My hand touches something. An envelope is tucked under my pillow. I lean up on my forearms and take it into my hands. It is sealed, but written on the upper right hand corner is a scratched note.

Anna, I was asked to give this to you when I thought the time was right. That time is now. Your friend, Robert.

I turn it over and open the envelope carefully as if its contents are fragile. Inside is one sheet of loose-leaf paper folded into three parts. I unfold it, unsure if I want to read it or find out who it is from. My eyes immediately scan the page. Halfway down is Ben's signature. My insides stir from anxiety and excitement, so much so that I read the first sentence three times before I can grasp what I have read.

Dear Anna,

I have no doubt you have learned a great deal since we last spoke. As I write to you I think back to the morning we met. You didn't say more than a few words, but your eyes spoke volumes. You held within you secrets of great loss and sorrow, but as you sat and listened I saw something erupt inside of you that I hadn't seen in a long time. You looked to Robert and you changed. You saw something in him the others could not see. You saw more than a tormented boy hidden within a tormented soul. You saw more than a scarred body as you had seen in me. You saw more than a mockingbird whose purpose in life is to bring good to others. You saw a Boo Radley. You saw a boy who had been touched by sorrow, abandoned, and left to face life alone, and yet you knew that his only crime was innocence. I see in you the same innocence you wholeheartedly see in others. You have a special gift in understanding those who have suffered great loss, and with heart you bring great hope.

Someday we shall meet again.

Until then,

Ben

PLACING THE LETTER back in the envelope and returning it to underneath my pillow, I feel happy. I consider Jonny Love's observation. Betsy being twenty and me seventeen makes us three years apart; the same three years separating Liz and me. The same number of years separating Betsy and her younger sister. I wonder if it is a coincidence. *Nope. Jonny Love is right. Coincidences don't exist.* I flip to my side and place my hands in a prayer-like fashion under my cheek. I close my eyes and sleep.

thirty-five

The night of my death-defying dismount from the high bar was the beginning of the end. Instead of the typical chaos on the fifth floor, everything seems to be coming together. Conversations are more distinctive. Addy, thumbing through one of her designer magazines during lunch, surprises us when she closes it and proclaims to the rest of us her future.

"Do me a favor?" she says, looking around the table at us. "If you ever see my designer clothing dangling from a rack, be it at a thrift store or a Lord and Taylor, buy something would ya'? 'Cuz God knows I'm gonna need the cash."

We all agree, and before opening her magazine again, she adds, "Thanks, I'll be sure to remember you all in my will."

Jonny Love's affection for people continues like always. He enjoys conversing with visitors who come to the fifth floor. One afternoon, I overhear him enlightening a gentleman twice his age about living life to the fullest and the importance of giving to others in need as a way to say thank you for our lives. I smile. *Yep, Jonny's got it together.*

I sense my therapy sessions with Dr. Ellison and my one-on-one meetings with Chad and Carol are coming to an end.

During a session, when I know the time is right, I ask Dr. Ellison, "When will you know I'm ready?" I don't wait for an answer, just hearing my question spoken aloud has me answering it for myself.

I reflect on my time thus far on the fifth floor. Over the

past weeks, reliving my past had become fond memories of growing up the ninth child of ten. I had shared stories of celebrating Christmas and birthdays in a house full of kids. I talked about Liz's entertaining personality and how I followed her wherever she went. I smiled telling Chad about all the fun I had when I was little, either being swung by my ankles or swinging from the swing in the backyard or climbing an old oak tree overlooking my small world. These memories, buried deep within my soul, had been the ones to eventually resurface.

I know it goes much deeper than this, though. It has been my realization that the same tragic memories I sealed shut within myself had been the exact ones that escaped, fragment by fragment, haunting me throughout my childhood. Nine years after Liz's death, almost to the exact day, my grief had been immobile, until one evening sitting on the couch, waiting for her to come home, I decided my wait was over.

As I grieved my loss, I better understood how others felt. I understood Carol's grief with the loss of her husband, Robert's loss, and Betsy's too. These losses were easily detected by death, but beyond death I came to understand Ethan's loss of friendship, Gretchen's loss of attention, Addy's loss of direction, and Jonny's fortunate loss of what others perceived as reality. Cassandra had lost the will to live, and Ben too had suffered loss as he and his mother escaped from the safety of their country. In one way or another, the very same thing connected us all. I think back to when I first arrived on the fifth floor. Over time I changed. I had looked to these people as possible allies to use for my own purposes, but instead, they became my friends.

No longer am I confused by Ben's departing words. Tightly wrapped within my soul, my wounds had never been given the chance to bleed. Many times I wanted to take flight, but instead I chose to fight, and in doing so I have learned the true meaning of happiness.

I look to Dr. Ellison after my moments of silence. She has not disrupted my thinking.

"No need to answer," I say. "Jonny is right; we are all connected, trying to live our lives in harmony."

Dr. Ellison smiles and then closes my chart.

WALKING FROM MY living room into the bedroom a decade later, I pull my journal from the top shelf of my desk and open it to the second to last page where I left off yesterday evening. Reaching for a pen, it's hard not to notice the faded scars on two of my knuckles. I pause for a couple seconds, considering how best to end. Reuniting pen and paper, my beautiful cursive sweeps across the line.

I know it is not everyone's good fortune to get a second chance. I did, and for this I am truly grateful.

acknowledgements

G. B. Stern once said, "Silent gratitude isn't much use to anyone." With that in mind, I will do my best to express my thoughts into words so all members of my family and friends, and my readers whom I have not yet met, sense how thankful I am.

It wouldn't be right if I didn't start with my husband Mike, who is not only my go-to PR guy and biggest fan but also my best friend. Your patience and understanding throughout this new journey of ours was more than I ever expected. Thank you from the bottom of my heart for constantly reminding me: "I can."

And for keeping the "I can" alive, I am forever indebted to Daphne Tantalo, Candy Tumidalsky, Linda Peaslee, and Elizabeth Meagher who spent countless hours reading numerous drafts, paragraph-by-paragraph, cover-to-cover. You understood where this story was coming from and helped bring it to light.

In addition, I had an amazing assemblage of first readers, Jean Hailmann, Rene Welch, Chris Craine, Jim Mahar, Jennifer Ross, Jan Fling, Marcia Flaherty, and Tracey Beidelman, who all graciously ignored my innocence when I handed over what I thought to be a finished masterpiece two years before this book ever saw the light of day. Thank you for your suggestions, many of which later become powerful additions in future drafts.

Thank you, with gratitude, to my editor Joni Holderman. Without you this book would have found only one home, mine. I cannot thank you enough for your guidance, support, and encouragement with every draft, edit, and revision. Your undivided attention to detail is impeccable. And Heather Ruffalo, who completed the copyediting and proofreading process before The Fifth Floor went to print. Thank you for sharing your expertise in catching every last little detail.

Many thanks go to my graphic designer Elizabeth Watters who read my novel in order to create the perfect book cover. Your ability to capture an entire story through a single piece of artwork is brilliant. Thank you for going above and beyond. Your work ethic and diligence is among the best.

To Kevin Moriarity, an amazing tech person, who researched many different avenues to find the best answers to my hundreds of questions and guided me through the publishing world one keystroke at a time. Thank you.

I offer a special thank you to the teachers and staff, students and parents at Beebe School, who often flagged me down to inquire about the progress of my book. I am humbled to have so many readers awaiting my first novel.

And to my first, second, and third grade students – you're incredible! Not a day goes by that you don't inspire me.

Thank you to the nurses, mental health technicians, doctors, and volunteers, who because of their outstanding teamwork and perseverance, have helped so many teens discover a new beginning.

I think it best to end, as I did to begin, by using a quote. "Kindness is the language which the deaf can hear and the blind can see." To use Mark Twain's words here are most understood by those who know my parents intimately. Mom, thank you for opening shielded memories to help me write this book, and Dad, thank you for showing me what a fair deal really means.

Made in the USA
Lexington, KY
07 October 2015